THE
Icecutter's
DAUGHTER

Books by Tracie Peterson

www.traciepeterson.com

*with Judith Miller   **with Judith Pella

THE

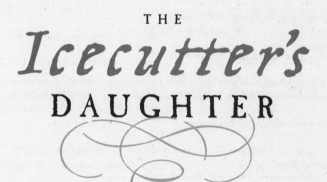

Icecutter's
DAUGHTER

TRACIE
PETERSON

BETHANYHOUSE
a division of Baker Publishing Group
Minneapolis, Minnesota

© 2013 by Tracie Peterson

Published by Bethany House Publishers
11400 Hampshire Avenue South
Bloomington, Minnesota 55438
www.bethanyhouse.com

Bethany House Publishers is a division of
Baker Publishing Group, Grand Rapids, Michigan

Printed in the United States of America

Library of Congress Cataloging-in-Publication Data

Peterson, Tracie.
    The Icecutter's Daughter / Tracie Peterson.
        pages cm. — (Land of Shining Water)
    ISBN 978-0-7642-1076-1 (cloth : alk. paper)
    ISBN 978-0-7642-0619-1 (pbk.)
    ISBN 978-0-7642-1077-8 (large-print pbk.)
    1. Families—Minnesota—Fiction. 2. Minnesota—History—19th century—Fiction. 3. Christian fiction. 4. Love stories. I. Title.
PS3566.E7717I28 2013
813'.54—dc23   2012040440

Scripture quotations are from the King James Version of the Bible.

The internet addresses, email addresses, and phone numbers in this book are accurate at the time of publication. They are provided as a resource. Baker Publishing Group does not endorse them or vouch for their content or permanence.

Cover design by Brand Navigation

13 14 15 16 17 18 19   7 6 5 4 3 2 1

To the ladies
of our Monday morning Bible study

You are a great joy and inspiration to me.
I'm so blessed that God put us together.
Thank you for your friendship.

Chapter 1

Merrill Krause tucked an errant strand of hair under her knit cap and sighed. There were two things she knew to be completely unpredictable: one was Minnesota winter weather, the other was the foaling of a horse. Glancing into the birthing pen, Merrill noted the mare looked to be no further along than half an hour earlier.

"Poor girl." The Belgian mare whinnied softly and rolled onto her side. Merrill entered the pen and knelt by the horse's head. "You can do it, Addie girl." She stroked the mare's neck, then stood to check the progress of the foal. Merrill could clearly see the first showing of a hoof as the mare contracted. "You're such a good girl. Keep pushing, and soon your little one will be here."

But Merrill knew that might not necessarily be the case. Just last year when Molly, their nine-year-old Belgian, gave birth for the fourth time, the process stretched for hours after the hooves appeared. Addie had already been in the pen for over two hours, with minimal progress.

Merrill made a face—she knew that just like watched pots hesitated to boil, watched mares seemed to be just as stubborn to deliver. Most mares preferred to give birth without an audience or assistance of humans, but because this impressive stock was an important part of their income, the Krauses tended to keep a close eye on their broodmares.

After one more glance at Addie, Merrill continued with her other chores. Despite it being the last day of December, she couldn't help but whistle a Christmas carol. All morning long she'd had the tune in her head, and when she reached the chorus she began to sing, "Come and worship, come and worship, worship Christ the newborn king." They were the only words she was certain of, so she went back to whistling another stanza. After a mild fall, the winter weather had turned bitter cold, and Merrill found whistling helped her to forget about it.

"Addie doing all right?" Her brother's voice carried across the length of the barn.

Merrill turned toward the sound and leaned on the pitchfork she'd just taken up. "She's taking her time. How about Molly and Pat?" All three of their Belgian broodmares were due to foal right around the first of the month. Addie had just decided to beat them to it.

"They seem to be fine," Tobe said, coming into sight. "I've got them in the pen closest to the barn, though. No sense havin' them give birth out in the field. Especially not with these temperatures. Pa said it could snow tonight. Said he feels it in his bones."

"I feel it in mine, as well," Merrill muttered. Despite having worn a red flannel union suit under two pairs of trousers, a camisole, blouse, flannel shirt, and coat, the cold still penetrated her body.

He nodded, picked up a couple of metal files, and headed for the door. "We're getting the cutting blades sharpened. Pa said to tell you we'll be in for dinner around one."

Merrill had already gone back to mucking the empty stall but called over her shoulder, "I'll have a nice hot meal waiting for you."

With four older brothers, Merrill had been responsible for the house and kitchen since their mother died some ten years earlier. Even so, Merrill had plenty of other responsibilities that tended to rob her of the chance to show her feminine side. Folks spoke highly of Merrill's baked goods and cooking, but she was also highly regarded for being able to handle a team of draft horses better than most men. She knew horseflesh from the tip of their tails to their velvety muzzles—something her father took great pride in. He loved having his family at work all around him.

The Belgians were her father's pride and joy. They were some of the best stock in the country, and with three good broodmares, he earned a nice bit of money on the side selling the offspring. Merrill spent a sizeable portion of her time with the animals, especially during the winter months. Foaling was something she generally oversaw. She also made sure the geldings were in top-notch shape for the ice harvest and other work they did. Numbering more than twenty, the animals definitely kept the family busy.

Merrill was pushing a full wheelbarrow to the manure pile when she caught the sound of a team approaching. She shielded her eyes and saw it was Granny Lassiter's buggy. No doubt she and Corabeth were coming for a visit.

Frowning at her soiled and frumpy attire, Merrill knew there was no time to change. She hurriedly dumped the manure and returned the wheelbarrow to the barn. With one more quick check on Addie, Merrill felt all right about spending a few moments with her visitors. It was always nice to see Granny and Corabeth. With no other women in her family, Merrill often longed for female companionship.

She closed the barn door and hurried across the yard as Granny brought the team to a halt at the back of the house. Merrill took hold of the team and waited for Granny to set the brake.

"You sure picked a cold day for a visit," Merrill quipped, and the three women chuckled.

With the team secured, Merrill quickly helped Granny and Corabeth from the buggy. Corabeth was all petite delicacy and femininity, even in the cold of winter. Her maroon wool coat was stylishly trimmed in black velvet, and the matching bonnet had been carefully placed so as to do minimal damage to her nicely arranged hair.

"We had to come see you," Corabeth announced. "Granny made you a new hat."

Merrill nodded her head and smiled. "Well, let's get inside and warm up. I've been mucking stalls and waiting for Addie to foal. I could use a cup of coffee."

She led the way in through the back porch, pausing only long enough to cast aside her outer coat and knit cap. Her wild curly hair shot out around her shoulders.

"Mercy child, you should at least braid that mess." Granny sounded dismayed.

"I usually do, and I will now. This morning I was in a bit of a hurry." She knew she sounded defensive, even though she didn't feel it. Life on the farm was different from living in town. Granny and Corabeth were used to being ready to receive visitors or go out where they would be seen. Here, Merrill was far more likely to see her brothers and father than any other woman, so her appearance never concerned her that much.

"I do wish you wouldn't wear those trousers," Granny continued. "You're never going to catch a husband looking like a young man."

Merrill laughed and washed her hands in a basin of water. "I'm not trying to catch a husband. At least not today. Today I'm helping deliver a foal." She quickly dried her hands and pulled the coffeepot from the stove. "We've some coffee left over from breakfast." She took three mugs down from the cupboard and poured the coffee. After returning the pot to the stove, Merrill turned to find Granny and Corabeth still standing.

"Would you like to sit in the kitchen or in the front room? I'd prefer the kitchen myself as I'm rather muddy. But I can always throw a sheet over a chair."

"Nonsense," Granny declared. "We won't stand on ceremony. The kitchen is nice and warm, and we can have ourselves a good chat."

"Do you have other visits to make before you head back to town?" Merrill asked, setting the coffee mugs on the table.

She hurried to retrieve the cream and sugar, knowing her guests were fond of both.

"We thought we might see a few families on the way. Given that tomorrow is the first, we wanted to share some treats and good wishes for the new year. We'll finish up by seeing Carl Jorgenson. Poor man has no one but himself."

Merrill smiled. "He's got all of us. I can't imagine the man goes too long between visits. Besides, his furniture business keeps him busy."

"Still, a man his age would be better living with his children—if he had some." Granny gave a *tsk*ing sound, then put a spoonful of sugar in her coffee. "Seems to me he might at least hire a woman to come do the housework."

"Goodness, I didn't even think to take your coats," Merrill said, looking at the women apologetically.

"No matter," Granny assured. "I'm still a bit chilly. I'm just fine and so is Corabeth. Sit down here with us."

Merrill took a seat at the table and brushed her hair back with her hand. She began to braid the thick, curly mass into order, then tucked the end of the braid into itself and hoped it would hold. It did. At least for the time being.

"So don't you want to see the new hat Granny and I made you?" Corabeth asked. She took up the hat box she'd brought in from the wagon and placed it on the table. "It's a real beauty, if I do say so myself."

Not wanting to seem ungrateful, Merrill nodded, and Corabeth quickly pulled the lid from the box. Without further ado, she lifted out a nicely decorated straw bonnet.

"I found one of my old poke bonnets," Granny said as if

reading Merrill's thoughts. "You know there are some very similar bonnets being worn these days, although the brims are much narrower. I trimmed this one down a bit, and then we went to work to make it a tad warmer. I lined it with a nice bit of wool that you can remove come spring."

The bonnet was trimmed in dark green ribbon and piping. The color was one of Merrill's favorites. "It's really pretty. Thank you—"

"It'll go well with your plum wool," Granny cut in. "Be a nice bit of color, and if you trim the neck of the gown with that pretty green scarf Corabeth gave you for Christmas, you'll see that it matches quite nicely. Match your eyes, too."

Merrill nodded. Granny and Corabeth were always doing what they could to "pretty her up." She'd been a tomboy even as a young girl, but after her mother died, Merrill gave up worrying about being very girlish. Her father needed her—her brothers, too. She didn't have time for frills and flounces.

"Well, aren't you going to try it on?" Corabeth asked.

"I'm hardly dressed for putting on such a fine hat," Merrill replied.

"Nonsense," Granny said. "Give it a try."

It sounded like an order, so Merrill put down her mug and picked up the bonnet. "I'm sure it's the nicest I've ever had." She placed it atop her head and snugged it down against her braided hair.

"Here, I'll tie the ribbon, and then you can go see how nice it looks," Corabeth announced. She got to her feet before Merrill could protest and quickly fashioned the ribbon into a bow. "There. It's perfect. You look so pretty."

Pretty wasn't a compliment Merrill usually heard. She had been called a handsome woman, but never pretty. That was a word reserved for the smaller, dainty ladies who wore more fashionable gowns and carefully styled their hair.

Merrill got to her feet and went to take a glance in the only mirror they had in the house. A small, simple framed mirror had been hung next to the front door by Merrill's mother when they'd first built the house. As the story went, Mother wanted to make certain she would look her best when greeting visitors, so she would pause by the mirror, adjust her hair, and recite the words of Hebrews thirteen, verse two: "Be not forgetful to entertain strangers: for thereby some have entertained angels unawares."

Looking in the same mirror, Merrill felt a bit closer to her mother. Her father often said Merrill favored her. But where Merrill was tall like her father and brothers, Edeline Krause had been small. Her mother had always been a great beauty, or so Granny had often told her. There had been more than one man who'd hoped to marry Edeline Crowther, and the suitors had competed fiercely for a chance to court her. Bogart Krause, however, had captured her heart and won the prize. They'd married when Merrill's mother was only seventeen.

Merrill touched her hand to the bonnet and felt a strange sense of pride. She looked quite smart in the hat. Almost as feminine and stylish as any other woman might. If she didn't look down at the rest of her attire.

I'm almost pretty. She reflected on her image for only a moment longer, then hurried back to the kitchen where Corabeth anxiously awaited the verdict.

"It's very lovely," Merrill declared. "I don't think I've ever had anything so nice."

Granny and Corabeth exchanged satisfied smiles, and Merrill took her seat. "You really shouldn't have gone to so much trouble, though. I know you both worked hard to make all those gifts you handed out at Christmas. Goodness, but everyone at church is still talking about how generous you've been. Making all those scarves and hats . . . oh, and the mittens . . . for those in need. Why, that must have kept you busy most every night."

"It did consume quite a bit of time," Granny admitted, "but it was the Lord's work. We were doing it unto Him, and He always has a way of multiplying the time and reducing the effort needed."

"So you really do like the bonnet?" Corabeth asked. "You aren't just saying that to make us feel better?"

Merrill looked at her friend and shook her head. "I'll admit I seldom have time to concern myself about such things, but I will make good use of this bonnet. It's very pretty, and I feel like a different woman wearing it."

Corabeth clapped her hands, then wrapped them once again around her mug of coffee. "I'm so glad. You can wear it for the church winter party in February."

"Maybe if you wear it to services sooner, you'll have someone ask to escort you to the party," Granny suggested with a gleam in her eye.

"I think it would take more than a pretty bonnet," Merrill said. "My brothers have scared off just about any fellow who showed an interest in getting to know me."

"Well, if a man can't stand up to those brothers of yours," Granny replied, "you needn't even consider him. A man ought to be able to hold his own with his wife's family. You don't want any mealymouthed ninnies to come calling."

"No, for sure I don't," Merrill replied. *But it would be nice if* someone *came calling*, she thought.

"Well, I think Granny is right. You should wear the bonnet for church on Sunday. It makes you look quite lovely."

Merrill touched the rim of the hat. "I suppose I might," she said.

"Merrill! Merrill Jean, where are you?"

Merrill hurried to the back door just as her brother Zadoc came bounding through. She barely managed to sidestep his advancing bulk. "What's wrong?"

"It's Addie. The baby looks to be stuck. Leg's bent. You're gonna have to help me. I had just come back for a vise and . . . well . . . come see for yourself."

Merrill didn't even bother to take up her coat as she ran across the back porch. They couldn't afford to lose either mother or baby. She raced for the barn, easily keeping stride with Zadoc.

In the birthing stall, she saw the trouble immediately. Addie was lying on her side, panting in misery. One of the foal's legs appeared to be bent back. Instead of a hoof presenting, Merrill found the bend of a knee. "We'll have to push it back in and try to maneuver the leg straight. Secure Addie's head, and I'll do what I can."

Zadoc didn't hesitate. He immediately went to the panting mare and took hold of her bridle. Merrill, meanwhile, rolled up her sleeves as best she could. "Now when she rests between contractions, I'll go to work. She won't like it, but hold her fast and keep her down."

Her chance came within moments, and with a quick twist and shove, Merrill pushed the foal back into Addie with all her might. She could tell the leg was still bent, though. Merrill felt the horse contract against her, the pressure numbing her arm and hand. It was almost impossible to move her fingers.

Addie was most unhappy with the situation. "I'm sorry, girl." Merrill felt the birth canal relax a bit and hurried to do what she could to help the horse. After a few more contractions, during which she managed to twist the unborn foal into a different position, Merrill felt the leg straighten at last. "I've got it." She pulled away from the mare just as another contraction started.

"No wonder she's been at this for so long," Merrill said, rubbing her hand to get the blood flowing again.

"Things ought to go a sight faster now."

Merrill nodded and watched the progress with a practiced eye. Addie labored to expel the baby from her body. After a time, both legs appeared as well as a hint of muzzle. Addie panted and fought against the pain. Without warning she scrambled to her feet, nearly knocking Zadoc backward.

"Watch out!" Merrill said, knowing that a horse in the pains of birth could be quite unpredictable.

Zadoc didn't seem to mind, however. He took hold of Addie's bridle and spoke in a soothing manner. Meanwhile, the mare continued to contract.

Addie was progressing, but the time dragged on, and Merrill

could see that the mare was tired. Poor horse had been laboring hard for hours due to the bent leg. "I'm going to help her," Merrill declared. "You hold her tight. I'll try to pull a bit. Maybe we can get this baby born."

The little legs were slick from fluid, making it hard for her to get a good grasp. Merrill's leather gloves were in her coat pocket on the back of the porch, however, and there was no time to retrieve them. She saw the horse bear down, while at the same time trying to move away from the pain. Unfortunately for Addie, there was no way to distance herself from the labor.

Merrill pulled on the legs just enough to help ease the head from the birth canal. She pulled back the birthing sack and could see a lovely white blaze down the baby's nose. "Gonna be a beauty, Addie girl. Just keep pushing."

Zadoc continued to murmur in the mare's ear while Merrill worked to help the baby. Before Merrill knew what was happening, the mare gave one more heave, and the foal slid out quickly. Merrill took the foal in her arms but lost her balance and fell backward against the wall of the stall. The warm, wet horse lay perfectly still in her arms, and Merrill wasted no time. She ran her hand into the baby's mouth to expel the mucus and fluid, then began to rub it furiously to stimulate it to breathe. It was only a moment before the tiny animal responded.

"Looks like we got us a little girl," Zadoc said, coming to help Merrill. "Probably a good thing, too."

"Why's that?" Merrill asked, struggling to ease the foal onto the straw so that Addie could tend her. Merrill got to her feet with the help of her brother and looked at him with a frown. "Why is it such a good thing it's a girl?"

"Well, what with your pretty bonnet and all, I think a boy might take offense."

Merrill had forgotten all about the new bonnet. "Is it ruined?" she asked, not wanting to touch it with her slimy hands.

"It looks right nice," Zadoc replied. "But maybe a little fancy to wear to birth a foal."

Chapter 2

"What do you mean, you're leaving for Minnesota?"

Rurik Jorgenson looked down at the small blond-haired woman and tried to offer a sympathetic smile. "Just what I said, Svea. Uncle Carl needs my help. He's been sickly of late and asked if I could come and lend a hand. Since he and my *Farfar* Jorgenson taught me to make furniture, it seems only right that I do what I can."

"But I'm sure Grandfather Jorgenson meant for you to use those skills here, not in Minnesota. That's so far away. What about me? Everyone expects us to marry."

Svea's pout made her look rather childish, but she didn't seem to care. For Rurik, it only confirmed his decision. She was much too young to marry. He had wanted to talk to Svea about delaying their engagement for a long time, but this wasn't the place. Not here in the middle of town with her brother Nils standing beside her.

"I shouldn't be gone too long," Rurik said. "Maybe just a few months. It will give you time . . ." He let the words trail off. He'd very nearly spoken of her immaturity, suggesting she needed time to grow up. "Besides," he began again, "I need to learn all I can before Nils and I open our own furniture business. I know a great deal about making furniture, but very little about keeping the books and dealing with customers."

"I have plenty of experience in that area," Nils offered quickly. "You forget I keep the books for my father's dairy. I can teach you all you need to know. There's no need for you to go—"

"The need is Carl's." Rurik shook his head. "He hasn't been well, and he has specifically asked me to come. I don't feel I can say no."

"You just want to get away from our engagement," Svea said, folding her gloved hands together. "And after all that our fathers did to work out this arrangement."

"That's . . . partly the problem," Rurik said. "Our fathers decided it would be good for us to marry. You and I have had very little to say about it. I think the time apart will do us good."

"See?" Svea said, her eyes tearing up. She turned to Nils. "He wants to put an end to our engagement."

"That's not what I said," Rurik protested. He looked at Nils. "I don't think this is the best time and place to discuss the matter."

"Why not?" Svea said, her voice rising. She waved her hands in both directions. "Why not let all of Lindsborg, Kansas, know that you no longer care for me."

"Because that isn't true," Rurik countered. "I didn't say I was breaking our betrothal. I only think it would do us good to have some time apart to think on it."

21

"But I don't want time apart." This time she truly did sound like a little girl.

Rurik looked to his best friend, hoping for support. "Nils, would you please help her to understand I'm not deserting her? I'm merely going to help my uncle, and in turn it will help us."

Nils fixed Rurik with a hard gaze. "I think she's right. You two should marry, and we should start up our own business—just like we've always planned. Svea's a woman full grown, and there doesn't need to be any delay in you two marrying. Your uncle can hire someone to help him. Doesn't he already have a group of men who work for him?"

"He does, but—"

"But nothing. There's the answer. Those men know what he needs—after all, they've been working with him all this time. He and your grandfather might have taught you to build furniture, but you don't know anything about the business he's running now. Besides, Minnesota is a really cold place to go."

"What does the cold have to do with it?" Rurik asked. "It's cold in Kansas, too." He was starting to think that neither of the Olsson siblings had any sense at all. If they did, they certainly weren't allowing it to guide their reasoning.

Nils shook his head. "You wouldn't be doing this if your father were still alive."

"Look, why don't I come out to the farm, and we can sit and talk about this away from all these folks." He motioned toward a number of the local gossips coming their way. The last thing he wanted to do was create a scene. "I'll even explain it to your mother and father."

"This shouldn't be that big of a problem," Nils argued. "You know as well as I do that the betrothal should be honored. Our plans should be honored, as well. I've been counting on it."

"Rurik doesn't care about honoring promises," Svea said with a toss of her head. "I'm going to the dressmaker. You try to talk sense into him." She turned on her heel and headed off down the boardwalk, plowing right through the gaggle of women. Several gasped their astonishment, but Svea didn't appear to care. She scowled at the women, causing them to hurry on their way. Without another word or look, she disappeared into the dressmaker's establishment.

Rurik felt utterly confused and dismayed with the encounter. He hadn't thought this would be an issue when the letter arrived from his uncle two days earlier. "You are closer to her than anyone, Nils. Try to help her understand. I never meant to hurt her."

"I'll talk to her, Rurik, but you have to stay. I need to get away from the dairy," Nils said, now sounding desperate. "You know I don't fit in there. My brothers may have a passion for dairy farming, but not me. I only do the office work because it keeps me out of the milking barns. I've been looking forward to this for a long time, you know, that we'd open our furniture business."

"I have to go, Nils," Rurik said, shaking his head. "My uncle needs me. Look, I'm still planning to have my own shop. The fact of the matter is, we can't open that shop until Svea and I marry and I come into my marriage money. I've not made any plans to do that right away, so I guess I'm kind of puzzled as to why you are talking like this."

Nils shook his head. "I figured the way Svea talked, you and she would be marrying this year."

"Well, this year has barely begun. Look, your sister is a sweet young woman, but I've had misgivings about this arrangement for some time. Neither of us have ever had any say in the matter. I know my mother wasn't all that keen on arranged marriages."

"But our fathers were."

"And mine is dead now. My mother also. For me, that kind of changes things," Rurik answered.

"But it shouldn't." Nils's voice had sounded almost frantic. "It was our fathers' will that you two marry. They saw it as a good business arrangement. Your family farms, and mine has the dairy. The two can help each other greatly."

"*Ja*, I know all that," the tall Swede replied. "But we're not talking about two farms getting married, are we? There's no reason our families can't continue to help one another. That is the Christian way."

"Don't bring God and religion into this," Nils spat out.

Rurik frowned. "Why not? God is at the center of all I do. In fact, He's the reason I feel it's important to go to Minnesota."

"Oh, don't go blaming this on the Almighty. If you plan to back out of your promises, you need to take the responsibility of it yourself. I won't have you breaking your engagement to my sister and telling everyone that God made you do it."

"But I haven't broken the engagement." He looked at Nils and tried not to sound as angry as he was feeling. "I haven't broken anything. I still plan to work with you and for us to have a business. I will honor my father's desire for me to marry Svea—that is, if after this separation we can both agree it is the right thing to do. The fact is, though, I would kind of like to be in love with the woman I plan to marry."

"But you love Svea. You always have."

"I love her like a sister. I love her as I love you—like a brother." Rurik stepped closer and pulled Nils into the alley with him. "But the truth is, I'm not in love with Svea."

"But that will come. You and I both know that marriage has very little to do with love. Marriages are made for the advantage of the families."

"That might have been the old way—the Swedish way, even—but it's not my way. I will not marry anyone unless I love the woman with all my heart. I cannot in good faith allow your sweet sister to marry a man who isn't worthy of her—and that would happen if my feelings don't change. Added to that, she's still very young."

"Bah! You're just using that as an excuse," Nils shot back. "I ought to deck you for this. Folks will talk, and her reputation will be ruined."

"Her reputation will be just fine. The people of Lindsborg know we have never courted without you at our side. She has never been unescorted even in church. Frankly, I wouldn't have it any other way. I want her reputation upheld. A woman's virtue is as important as a man's name."

"Then why would you risk both by going away? She obviously loves you, and since that's so important to you, that should be enough."

For a moment Rurik considered his friend's words. "No, actually I don't think she does love me. I think she's accepted that our marriage will be, but I don't believe she loves me or really understands what love is about."

"Of course she does. Our mother has trained her to know what's expected of a wife."

Rurik shook his head. "That's not what I'm talking about. Svea is but a girl."

It was Nils's turn to shake his head. "She's seventeen. That's old enough by some folks' standards."

"She's led a very sheltered life and has never had a chance to explore whether another man might better suit her desires."

"This is ridiculous, Rurik. You and Svea have plenty in common. But more important, folks around here know what's expected of you two. You should try to remember that."

Two women passed the opening of the alley and glanced over at Rurik and Nils. The men tipped their hats to the women. Once they were out of sight, Nils took hold of Rurik's shoulders.

"You have to change your mind about this. I think you and Svea should marry right away so that you and I can get on with our business. My father is pressuring me to take a bigger part in the dairy, and I have no interest. If I have another opportunity elsewhere . . . a means to make money and support myself . . . I won't have to worry about refusing his offer and hurting him."

"Nils, you're my best friend, but I cannot lie for you. I cannot pledge myself in marriage before God and this town and not know that I truly love her—that it's God's will for my life."

"There you go again. Don't try to put all the responsibility on God and make it sound like some sort of divine assignment."

"But I feel that marriage *is* a divine assignment," Rurik said. "I'm rather surprised that you can speak with so little feeling in regard to your sister's happiness. I've never known two siblings to be more devoted to the happiness of each other. I thought you loved her."

"I do. My love for her has never been in question. It's yours that seems to be a problem."

The whistle sounding from an arriving train signaled to Rurik that he'd let too much time slip away. "I need to go. You should get back to Svea."

"I know how to take care of her. You're the one who's failing in that area."

"Nils, I care deeply for her. Look . . . I . . . I'll go help my uncle, and when I return we can decide this matter once and for all."

Rurik left Nils standing in the alley and made his way to the railroad depot. He wanted to check on the schedule and see what kind of arrangements he could make for tickets to Minnesota. The damp cold of the day made him draw his coat up closer to his neck as he trudged through the snow. He had always loved this town—especially during the holiday season. Swedes had a wonderful way of celebrating Christmas, or *Julotta*, as they called it. There were all sorts of festivities and food, parties and pageantry. The Lutheran church was always full on Advent Sundays, and Rurik had a great fondness for Christmas music. The only thing he really missed was his *mor* singing beside him during services. Nellie Jorgenson had been beloved by most of the Lindsborg residents. Rurik was certain there had never been a more generous and loving woman. His mor sewed and knit for the poor, made food baskets for the sick, and gave platters of freshly baked goodies to all of the local bachelors. When she passed on, the entire town had attended her funeral. But, he had to admit, they did that for most everyone.

The people of the town were good folks, and Lindsborg had thrived quite nicely while managing to maintain its Swedish heritage. He liked that about the place. He was proud to be of Swedish descent. His father was a second-generation American, but he could converse in Swedish as easily as English. He'd seen to it that his children could do the same.

"Hello, Rurik."

Smiling, Rurik nodded to the older man. "It's good to see you, Mr. Lindquist."

"I tink a little more snow is comin' our vay, ja? I comed to town before de snow. How is your *bror* Aron?"

"My brother is doing well. The farm kept him busy this year."

"Ja, *det var ett bra ar*," the older man said, switching to Swedish.

"Yes, it was a good year."

"So vat are you doin' in town today?" Mr. Linquist was back to English in a singsong cadence typical of the older Swedish residents.

"Checking on the train schedule. I'm going to Minnesota to help Uncle Carl. He's been sick."

"Oh, dat's too bad."

"Ja, it is, but I'm hopeful it's nothing serious." Rurik saw that the depot traffic had lessened. He didn't want to be rude, but he needed to attend to business. "If you'll excuse me now, I need to talk to the depot master."

"Ja, you go now. I tink I go buy my supplies. I vant to get home before de snow." The old man smiled and struggled from the boardwalk to cross the street.

Rurik would have offered to assist the man through the snow, but he knew Mr. Lindquist to be quite proud. It would no doubt have insulted him to suggest he was anything but capable of conducting business on his own. Nevertheless, Rurik watched until the octogenarian was safely across the street before hurrying on his way.

After a quick visit with the depot master, Rurik settled on leaving the day after tomorrow. He paid for his passage and placed the ticket securely in his coat pocket before heading back to his tethered horse.

Rurik gave the animal a quick pat on the neck, then took up the reins to mount. It was then that he spied Nils and Svea coming out of the dressmaker's shop. His hand drifted to his pocket, and he fingered the ticket within. Should he try to speak to Svea again?

Rurik paused a moment, then turned and headed for home.

Chapter 3

Rurik sat down with a cup of coffee and faced his older brother across the kitchen table. After his brother had taken over the homestead when their parents had passed away, he'd brought Rurik in as a part of his family.

At nearly forty years of age, Aron Jorgenson was fifteen years Rurik's senior. Though a bit thicker at the waist and a tad shorter, Aron was the spitting image of their father. Not only that, but his counsel was just as wise. He had always been a good source of wisdom and staid thinking for Rurik—as were his other five siblings—and now was certainly no exception.

"Ja, I think it's good for you to go and help Carl," Aron was saying. "He did a lot to help Far and Mor when times were bad. It would only be right." He stirred sugar into his own cup and nodded. "He has no one else, and it is our duty to see to his care. If he is too sickly, you might have to bring him here. Elizabeth will make a room for him."

Rurik smiled. "Your wife would make room for all the forsaken, if she thought you wouldn't mind."

"Ja, my Elizabeth is a good woman." Aron sampled the

coffee and added another spoonful of sugar. "So when will you go?"

"The day after tomorrow. I have my ticket."

Aron nodded. "And you will write to me and let me know how it goes with you?"

"Of course," Rurik replied. "You know I value your counsel." He paused and thought of his earlier encounter with Svea and Nils. "In fact, I have something more I need to discuss before I go to Minnesota."

"What's that? Something troubling you?"

Rurik pushed back his mug. "I told Svea and Nils that I was leaving to go help Carl. They were not at all pleased. Svea believes I'm running away from her and the engagement, and Nils . . . well . . . I think he believes the same thing."

"And are you?"

Shrugging, Rurik shook his head. "I don't know. I told Svea I thought we both needed time to decide if marriage was what we wanted. After all, it was a plan set in motion by our fathers when we were little children."

"That doesn't mean you should dishonor their wishes."

"Nor does it mean I should be obligated to it," Rurik countered. "Mor never liked the idea of an arranged marriage. She thought a person should marry for love and that God had a particular person in mind for each of us."

"Ja, but what if that person is Svea Olsson?"

"If she's the one, God will show me. I'm not turning away from God or the idea of marriage; rather, I'm asking for clarity on which woman it is that I should take as a wife."

"You should do as Far wished. Honoring him is as important

as anything else you can do," Aron said thoughtfully. "He didn't make the choice lightly. I remember he thought about it for a long time. Prayed about it, too."

"God knows my heart, Aron. I hold no dishonor for our parents. What of honoring our mother's wishes? Like I said, she didn't like the idea of an arranged marriage. She fought for each of you to marry for love. Have you forgotten that?"

Aron smiled. "I haven't forgotten. It just so happened that Far approved my marriage to Elizabeth. He said he had already chosen her for me. He knew she would be a good match for my temperament."

"Ja, she's the only one who can best you in an argument," Rurik said, laughing. He took a long drink from the mug and got to his feet. "I will be sorry to leave Elizabeth's good cooking. I don't imagine Carl has anyone around who can cook nearly as well."

Aron pushed back his blond hair and nodded. "No one cooks as well as my wife."

"Oh, listen to you," Elizabeth said, coming into the kitchen. "Aren't you full of compliments." She leaned down and kissed Aron on the top of his head. "So what are you boys doing just sitting around?"

"We were talking about my trip to help Uncle Carl," Rurik said. "I leave the day after tomorrow."

"I'd best get to work, then," she replied, pulling her face into a frown. "I'll need to bake you some cookies and cardamom rusks to take with you. It's a long ways, ja. I'll pack you some cheese and lutefisk, too."

"No lutefisk. They would kick me off the train for smelling

it up." Rurik didn't bother to add that he'd never been that fond of the lye-soaked fish. "I'll be happy to take the cookies and rusks. I suppose the cheese is all right, too. So long as it's not the strong-smelling variety."

Elizabeth smiled. "I'll do what I can." She looked to her husband. "Do you need more coffee?"

"No. I'm going to get back to work. Rurik and I were just finishing up."

Rurik nodded and headed to the front door. "In fact, I am going over to the Olsson farm to pick up the milk and cream you wanted."

"Oh, good," Elizabeth replied. "I'd nearly forgotten. You hurry back so I can have it for the cookies."

"Well, I kind of need to talk to Svea for a few minutes. Can it wait that long?" Rurik asked.

Elizabeth beamed him a smile. "Time with your sweetheart is always allowed."

He frowned. "Well, she's not exactly feeling sweet toward me right now. She's not happy I'm heading off to Minnesota. I told her I thought the time apart would do us good."

"Oh, Rurik. You didn't." Elizabeth shook her head as if he were a young boy caught with his hand in the cookie jar. "No woman wants to hear such a thing. You should go and tell her you were wrong. Tell her that you will think of her every day and that you will miss her. Promise to bring her home a present. Ja, she'll like that."

Rurik considered his sister-in-law's words for a moment. "I'll do what I can."

He thought of Elizabeth's suggestion while hitching a large

draft horse to the wagon. He thought even more about her words while driving to the Olsson place. There was no way around it, though. He wasn't sure he could tell Svea that he would think of her every day or that he would miss her. Truth be told, Rurik wasn't convinced he would. At least no more than he would miss Nils or Aron. He frowned. The more he considered the matter, the more certain he felt that marriage to Svea was not the right thing for either of them.

He brought the horse to a stop just outside the Olsson back door. The peddler's wagon was parked near the front of the house, so he figured Mrs. Olsson and Svea would be busy looking over his many goods. Rurik headed to the milking barn, but neither Nils nor Mr. Olsson seemed to be around. Though he didn't like the idea, he knew he would need to ask Mrs. Olsson their whereabouts, and she would no doubt want him to stay to supper. She would certainly question him about his plans, for no doubt Svea had already told her mother that Rurik was headed to Minnesota.

He sighed, walked slowly to the front door of the farmhouse, and knocked. He wiped his boots an extra time for good measure, then made sure he was smiling as the door opened. Svea looked at him with a rather silly expression.

"Oh, it's you." She giggled and stepped back. "Do come in. I was just telling Thomas . . . Mr. Samples . . . about my need for new ribbon. You know, don't you, Rurik, that a girl has to do what she can to look pretty." She cocked her head to one side, then motioned him in.

Rurik followed her into the front room and nodded at the man. Mr. Samples wasn't much older than Rurik, and the way he looked at Svea suggested he thought her more than pretty.

The man had already begun to gather up his products, but he paused to look at Rurik and extended his hand. "Thomas Samples with Samples' Samples." He grinned as if he'd just announced the cleverest of company names. Rurik briefly shook his hand before the salesman returned to packing up his goods. "I told Miss Olsson there wasn't a ribbon in my possession that could match her beauty," the man declared. "Why, she's the prettiest girl I've seen in the entire state."

Svea looked coyly at the salesman. "You are just the sweetest man to say so, Thomas." She didn't even pretend to be too forward in using his first name. She glanced back at Rurik and smiled. "I forgot to ask. Whatever are you doing here, Rurik?"

"I came for the milk and cream. Thought I'd talk to you, as well."

She gave a little shrug and all but waltzed to where Samples stood. "As you can see, I'm quite busy right now. Besides, I thought you made yourself quite clear earlier. I can't think that we have anything more to say about the matter." She reached down to pick up a pair of gloves, studying them with great interest.

Rurik didn't want to start another argument. "Very well. If you'll tell me where your mother or father is, I'll go fetch the milk."

Svea frowned. Apparently this wasn't the reaction she'd hoped for. She plopped the gloves back down. "Mother is in the kitchen, of course. Papa and Nils are gone, so you'll have to wait for them."

"I'll speak to your mother, then." He nodded to Mr. Samples. "Good day."

Rurik passed on through the house into the kitchen where he found Mrs. Olsson busy frosting a cake.

"Oh, Rurik. It's good to see you. Are you hungry?"

"No, ma'am. I came for the milk and cream. Svea said that Mr. Olsson and Nils were gone."

"Ja, but they will be back shortly. Why don't you sit and have a cup of coffee while you wait. You must be cold. It looks like snow."

"I think it will snow tonight for sure," he said. "But I'm really all right."

"And how's your family—Aron and Elizabeth . . . the children?"

"All well. Elizabeth is fretful that the youngest might be coming down with a cold, but otherwise everyone is doing fine."

"I'm glad to hear it." She went back to frosting the cake. "Can you stay for supper?"

"No. Elizabeth needs the milk and cream tonight. She's doing some baking."

"Ja, with six children that's something you have to do all the time." She grinned at Rurik. "Someday you will have children of your own, and you will see how it is. Always busy for the mother."

Rurik was growing increasingly uncomfortable. "I hope you will pardon me. I think I need to speak to Svea once more before I go."

"Of course. If you change your mind, the coffee is on the stove."

"Ja, thank you."

He made his way back through the house in time to find Svea waving from the front door. Mr. Samples was nowhere to be seen, all evidence of his traveling storefront gone from the room.

Turning around, Svea looked at Rurik for a moment, then smiled. "Thomas is just the nicest man I've ever met. He is so thoughtful, too. He seems to really understand me." She put her hand over her heart.

"I was hoping you might talk to me now," Rurik said, unfazed by her words.

"Thomas travels all over the world," she offered. "He told me such wonderful stories of his journeys. I almost felt as if I could see the places he described. I thought it all so wonderful."

Rurik could tell she wanted a reaction from him, but he wasn't inclined to give it. She watched him for a moment, then swept across the room and took a seat on the edge of the sofa.

"I think perhaps you were right, Rurik. Maybe I don't know my own heart. After all, I found it quite . . . oh, never mind."

He nodded. "I can tell that you were enjoying yourself."

She smiled. "Well, I suppose with you leaving, it only makes sense that I consider other possibilities." Again she paused as if waiting for him to react.

"That is why I wanted us to have time to think through the idea of marriage," Rurik replied. "I want only good things for you, Svea. You are like a little sister to me."

That statement put a frown on her face, which quickly

dissolved into a scowl. "Sister? I'm your *betrothed*. I'm no sister. You are such a nitwit. There are many men who would happily court me."

Rurik nodded. "I've no doubt . . . and I want you to have a chance to court, Svea. It wasn't fair of your father to force you into an engagement to me. If in time we both feel that we should marry each other, then we can consider the arrangement once again."

"I hate you, Rurik. I hate that you are ruining my life," Svea said, dropping all pretense of being amiable. "I'm glad you're leaving. I wouldn't marry you if you were the last man in the world." She scrambled to her feet, and her voice grew louder. "I wouldn't marry you if you begged me."

"What in the world is going on?" Mrs. Olsson asked, hurrying into the room.

"Our betrothal has ended. We will not marry," Svea announced, hands on her hips.

Mrs. Olsson looked to Rurik. "Is this true?"

"If that is what Svea wants."

Svea stomped her foot. "I want that and more. I want you to leave and never come back. I hope never to see you again." She stormed from the room, leaving her mother and Rurik in stunned silence.

Finally Rurik drew a deep breath. "I will wait for Mr. Olsson and Nils outside."

"I was just coming to tell you that they'd returned." Mrs. Olsson shook her head. "I suggest you get the milk and cream and leave it to me to tell Mr. Olsson about this matter. I'm sure she's just having a bad moment. You will forgive her, ja?"

"There's nothing to forgive, Mrs. Olsson. It's best this way. I am sorry," he said.

"I don't know what happened, but I've never been in favor of arranged marriages. My sisters and I had to endure such things, and while it worked out in the long run, there were many years of unhappiness." She looked toward the window as if trying to see something beyond the room. "I didn't wish such a thing for Svea. I would like for her to marry a good man like you, but I would want it to be her choice."

"Ja," Rurik replied. "That is what I want, as well. I told her as much. I'm going to Minnesota to help my uncle Carl. He's been ill. I told Svea I thought the time apart would do us good. I wanted her to have time to think about this arrangement. I've given it a great deal of thought, and in my heart I know I do not love Svea as a man should love the woman he intends to marry. I will always care for her, but she is like a little sister to me."

Mrs. Olsson looked quite sad and nodded. "It is as I have always suspected. Oh, Rurik, I wouldn't want you to marry under such circumstances."

"I know our fathers intended . . ."

He didn't know what else to say. He had clearly made a mess of things, but at least Mrs. Olsson seemed to understand.

"Their intensions were good, Rurik," she said, reaching out to pat his arm. "But they thought too much of themselves, the adjoining farms, the business side of things . . . and not enough of the heart. I will talk to Svea and help her to see the sense of this. You will come back and see us?"

"I hope so," he said, but shook his head. "I still plan to

go into business for myself." He didn't mention Nils or his desire to work with Rurik. Nils had made it clear that he wasn't telling his parents of those plans until the time came to leave his father's employment, knowing there would be hard feelings and disagreements.

Rurik had to maintain Nils's secret a little longer. "And I am praying for God to show me what is to be done with . . . Svea. I am not deserting her. I truly want to do what God would have me do. If I am to marry her, though, I must love her."

Mrs. Olsson squeezed his arm. "I agree. You must. I wouldn't want it any other way. My daughter is young, and she doesn't yet know her own heart. Give her time. Give yourself time."

"Thank you. I'm glad you understand."

"Well, I'm probably the only one who will. But don't worry. Commit this to the Lord, and He will direct your steps."

Rurik nodded. "I will."

He collected the milk and cream without seeing Mr. Olsson. Nils tried his best to pick up their earlier discussion, but Rurik put him off. He had to hurry the dairy products back to Elizabeth, he said, but he offered to meet Nils the following day if he wanted to talk more, and that seemed to satisfy his friend.

Snow began to fall and grew heavier as Rurik neared home. The wind picked up and chilled him to the bone. With a little more than a mile to go, Rurik lowered his hat to ward off the cold. He could barely see for the dimming light and blowing snow, but finally he spied lights in the window of the Jorgenson farmhouse.

But it doesn't feel like home, he thought, guiding the wagon into the barn. He shook the snow off his coat and climbed down to take care of the horse. The gelding seemed impatient to be let out of the harness.

"Easy, boy," Rurik said, brushing snow from the horse's mane. He worked quickly in the silence of the barn. Walking the draft horse to the far end of the barn, Rurik opened a pen and released the horse. "You can wait here until the storm dies down."

"Uncle Rurik?" A boy of thirteen was forcing open a small side door of the barn. "Are you in here?"

"Ja, I'm here, Michael. What is it?"

The boy struggled to close the door behind him. "Mama said to see if you needed help."

"That was good of you." Rurik smiled. "I have the milk and cream for her. You can help me carry it into the house."

The boy hesitated for a moment. "Mama said you're going away to Minnesota."

"I am," Rurik said. "Your papa isn't the only one who needs help. My uncle Carl needs my help, too."

"To make furniture?"

"Ja. To make furniture."

"I want to come, too," Michael said. "I want to help make furniture."

Rurik smiled. "Since when?"

The boy shrugged. "Since you taught me how to build that little table for my room. I like the wood. I told Father that I wanted to be like you and make furniture. I don't want to farm."

"And what did he say?" Rurik asked.

Michael frowned. "He told me I had to go to school first, and that while I went to school I had to help with the farm."

"Ja, that is right. You have to help your family. But when you are older, I would be proud to have you work with me."

"Really?"

The boy's enthusiasm caused Rurik to laugh. "Really. But you will need to finish school. Even your farfar believed we should get our education. You go to school and study hard. When summer comes and your chores are done, you can help me with building the furniture. Then when I have my own shop, maybe your father will let you come and help there."

"Will you ask him?"

"I will. But for now, we need to get this milk and cream inside. I don't think the storm is getting any better out there."

Michael went to the back of the wagon and hoisted down two large cloth-covered pails. "I'm going to miss you, Uncle Rurik."

Rurik took up the larger milk cans and smiled. "I'm going to miss you, too. But you'll see. I won't be gone long." But even as he said the words, something deep inside told Rurik that might not be the case. He frowned, but hid his face so Michael wouldn't see his expression. What was going on? Was God trying to tell him something?

Chapter 4

Merrill barely managed to remember to put on her skirt before she reached Waseca. She was so used to working around the farm in her brothers' hand-me-downs that it seemed unnecessary to don more feminine attire unless it was Sunday. Hurrying, she grabbed the rolled-up woolen skirt, shook it out, and pulled it on over her trousers. She took off her mittens to fumble awkwardly with the buttons at the waistband. The temperatures had dropped considerably. The cold air stung her fingers, making them stiff and slow.

As soon as the task was accomplished, Merrill straightened her coat and pulled the mittens back on. She blew warm breath into the heavy knit wool to bring life back into her frozen digits. The team of Belgians blew out their own puffs of air and stomped slightly against the snowy road. Taking hold of the reins, Merrill released the brake and urged them on.

As they came closer to town, the additional traffic on the road packed down the snow, making passage easier. Merrill directed the team to a blacksmith shop and had barely brought them to a stop when Jacob Anderson hurried out to take hold of the horses.

"Your pa told me yesterday that you'd be bringin' these boys in for new shoes."

Merrill picked up the bundle beside her and jumped to the ground. "Mike and Mack need to be ready for the ice harvest. I'll be back this afternoon."

"Good. I can have them shod by then."

"How's Anona and the boys?" Merrill asked the stout farrier.

"They're doin' good. The boys are comin' over later to help me. Maybe you'll see them when you pick up the team."

"Are they going to enter the family business and take over for you?" she asked with a smile.

"They take over, all right." He laughed. "Not always in the best way, but they can be good help." He began to unhitch the animals.

"I'll be visiting Granny Lassiter if you need me." Merrill didn't wait for a response, and headed off down the street. She was desperate to get out of the cold.

Waseca was a bustling little town less than one hundred miles from the twin metropolises of Minneapolis and St. Paul. Merrill had lived in the area all of her life, though never in town proper. She supposed that had a lot to do with why she lacked many of the same feminine interests and hobbies that other women had. It didn't help that she spent all of her time with five men, either. It was only at times like this or on Sundays at church that Merrill had much time to share the company of other women.

The skies overhead were a brilliant blue, and the air, although biting, was crisp and now smelled of baked goods. Merrill glanced at the small café and bakery. Granny often furnished them with pies and cinnamon rolls. It allowed her a means of making a little money now that Grandpa Lassiter had retired from working at the apothecary. Hopefully Granny would have a pot of coffee or tea brewing, and they could sit and talk in the warmth of the kitchen. Merrill picked up her pace.

The Lassiters had a small clapboard house some four blocks from the railroad on the west side of town. It was a dainty creation, if a building could be considered such. Merrill always thought it could be likened to a doll's house with its steeply pitched gabled roof and decorative verge boards. Painted a buttery yellow and trimmed in white, the two-story house was a testament of love. Grandpa Lassiter had arranged for it to be built some twenty years earlier, using a small inheritance he'd received when his father passed on. Merrill remembered stories Granny had told of how the only intention Grandpa had for the money was to make a beautiful home for his wife. Merrill couldn't imagine what it must be like to be loved in such a fashion.

"Knock, knock!" she called, opening the back door.

"Come in, child. Come in and get warm." Granny bustled across the kitchen to greet her.

Merrill stopped just inside the door. "If you'll take this bundle, I'll get rid of my boots. I'm afraid they're a mess."

Granny took the offering. "Have you brought me a new treat?"

Smiling, Merrill pulled off her mittens and stuffed them in the pockets of her coat before discarding the heavy boots. "I have. I've been experimenting with carrots."

"Carrots?" Granny shook her head and frowned. "What in the world are you doing with carrots?"

Merrill left her boots by the door and hung her coat on a peg. She padded in thick wool socks across the wooden floor of the kitchen. "I have some delicious cookies."

Granny shook her head. "Carrot cookies? Doesn't sound too appetizing to me. 'Course, I've never been overly fond of 'em. But if you're the one doing the baking, I'm glad to try." She placed the bundle on the table.

"I thought I heard your voice." Corabeth crossed the room to give Merrill a hug. "Ooooh, your cheeks are like ice. How about some warm milk or tea?"

"Thanks, I'd like tea," Merrill replied. She opened the bundle and unwrapped a smaller package inside. "I've brought something for you to try, and they are quite good with tea."

Corabeth brought a cup and the tea canister. "Granny and I were already set to have tea, so it won't take long. See, the kettle is already on." She smiled at the plate Merrill had set out. "Hmmm, what are these?"

"Try them first, and then I'll tell you," Merrill said, grinning.

Granny and Corabeth each picked up one of the frosted cookies and sampled it. Merrill waited as the women considered the offering. Their smiles were her answer.

"You say these are made with carrots?" Granny asked.

"Carrots?" Corabeth looked at the partially eaten cookie. "I can't taste any carrot. I taste orange."

Merrill nodded. "Remember the oranges we got at church for Christmas? I saved them and used the juice and zest for the frosting."

"They're wonderful," Granny said, reaching for another. "I can't believe they're made with carrots. Merrill, you have a real prize here. Although getting oranges for the frosting could be a bit of an expense."

"I'm glad you like them." The warm kitchen was heady with the scent of cinnamon. "Are you making cinnamon rolls or snickerdoodles?"

Granny laughed and shuffled off across the room to the stove. She opened the oven door to reveal pans of rolls. She closed it and straightened. "Should be ready before you leave. You will stay a spell, won't you? After driving in all that way in the cold, you should at least stay through lunch."

"I planned a nice long visit. I told Father I'd pick up a few baking supplies and get the team winter shod, so he's not expecting me back until much later."

"Good. We can talk about all the news in town." The teapot began to whistle, and Granny retrieved it before coming back to the table.

"Surely there hasn't been that much going on since Sunday."

Corabeth helped herself to another cookie and waited for the tea to steep. "Well, the dairy farmers met, and the Waseca Creamery is finally formed. John Diedrich has fifty percent of the shares, but over forty-three other farmers are involved. It's quite exciting."

Merrill nodded. "I'm glad to hear it. It's been in the works for a long while. When will they be up and running?"

Granny eased into her chair and took up a cookie. For a moment she examined it. "Can't say. They'll meet again on the ninth. I'll bet you could win first prize at the fair with these."

"I think so, too," Corabeth encouraged. "Oh, I found the prettiest material at Finsters. I think you'd look beautiful in a new dress made from it. We should go over and look at it before you head home."

"I don't need a new dress. I only wear the ones I have for church and the occasional social function." Merrill stood and reached for the teapot, hoping they'd forget the entire matter. "Should I pour?"

"No, I can," Corabeth said, taking charge. She poured tea for all three of them, then sat back with a wistful smile. "May I ask how Zadoc is doing?"

Merrill had long known that Corabeth was sweet on her brother. "He's been busy. They're gearing up to harvest ice, and you know how hard that work can be."

"Dangerous too," Corabeth said, frowning. "I wish he had a nice easy job. Like working at the mercantile or in the bank."

Merrill had to fight to keep from spitting her tea out in laughter. The thought of her brother—any of her brothers—sitting behind a desk or wearing a suit and tie in order to make a living was far too amusing. "He'd never like that. You know my brothers. If they're inside the house more than a few hours, they start to get ugly. The biggest fights I've ever seen were during blizzards."

"Zadoc could never be ugly," Corabeth said, sounding slightly reproving.

Granny laughed. "You won't ever get her to say anything bad about your brother. She's lost her senses when it comes to him."

Corabeth blushed, and Merrill picked at a cookie rather

than comment. She knew Corabeth fervently hoped that Zadoc would ask to court her.

Granny took that moment to reach for Merrill's hand. "Goodness, child, your hands are horribly chapped. Let me get you some cream for them. I have a good supply since we made a new batch just last week. I'll send a few jars home with you." Granny got up and waddled from the room.

Corabeth leaned forward. "Have you been talking to Zadoc?"

"You mean encouraging him to consider being your suitor?"

The young woman nodded. "I want so much for him to take me to the church party next month."

"Right now all he can think about is work. Father has the boys completely occupied. I'll do what I can, but it is never easy to get a private moment with him."

Corabeth's disappointment was etched on her face. Granny returned just then, however, so nothing more was said on the subject.

"You use this, and those hands will soften right up," Granny said, putting three small jars in front of Merrill. She opened one and began slathering Merrill's hands in lotion.

"You might as well put it on a pig's hooves." Merrill laughed and shook her head.

"Nonsense. This is one of my best batches."

"And how will that help me get all of my work done, pray tell? I still have two mares due to foal, and then I'll be helping with the ice harvest. You know that will consume most of my time. We go without clean clothes for weeks."

"I'll come wash clothes for you," Corabeth said. "That way maybe we can . . . talk from time to time."

49

Merrill knew her friend would use whatever excuse she could to get near Zadoc. What she probably didn't expect, however, was Granny's support of the idea. "We could both come. I could cook for you, and we can work together on the cleaning and washing."

"And who will care for Grandpa Lassiter?" Merrill asked. "You two have more than enough to do here."

"Oh, we'll manage," Corabeth said. "Grandpa spends most of his days over at the apothecary advising Mr. Malcolm on what he's doing wrong. He won't even miss us. Besides, with all the men helping with the ice harvest, you'll need extra hands for the meals. You'll want to have a hot meal ready. We can come out first thing in the morning and stay through the afternoon."

Merrill knew they were right. Preparing the food and hot coffee had become more and more difficult as the ice-harvest production had increased. Her father had only taken to hiring extra men the last few years, but the prices paid for ice had more than compensated for the extra wages. Maybe Merrill should think about hiring help of her own.

"I don't know. Let me speak to Father about it," she finally stated.

"Your father isn't doing right by you," Granny said, waggling a finger. "You are a young woman, and you should be courting and marrying. Most girls are at least engaged by your age."

Merrill didn't need the reminder that her life wasn't anything like that of a normal young woman. Nothing about her seemed to match up with her feminine counterparts, and no one was as keenly aware of the fact.

Granny seemed to recognize her frustration. "Forgive me, Merrill Jean. I know you haven't had much to say about any of this. It's just that I know your mother would be heartbroken to see you giving your life totally over to the care of your brothers and father. She would want you to have a family of your own. They should do likewise."

"Take care of your father . . . the boys. They'll need you," a voice from the past seemed to whisper in her ear.

She clearly remembered the dying request, but Merrill said nothing. Even at the age of ten, she had known the importance of easing her mother's worried mind. She had pledged her life in service to her family in order to get one final smile from her mother.

"Father will never marry again," Merrill finally offered. "He will always need me to care for him. It's my place as the only daughter."

"That doesn't mean you can't marry. In fact, you should. You could marry and bring your father into your home."

"Father will never leave the farm, and you know it," Merrill said, shaking her head.

"If your brothers would marry, they might take on the job themselves—well, at least their wives might. Your brother Leo has been courting for a time now. Since he will inherit the bulk of the farm, you could well expect his family to care for your father."

It was true that Leo had become quite serious about the young widow Sally Myers. The childless woman had been widowed for two years and lived with her aunt in Waseca. Leo had met her at church and had been smitten ever since.

Merrill was surprised that they had not yet announced their engagement. Perhaps he was giving her a lengthy time of mourning to make certain she wanted to remarry. He was thoughtful that way. Of all her brothers, Leo seemed the most concerned with the feelings of others.

"If the time comes that Leo and Sally marry and wish to take on Father's care, I will happily step aside," Merrill said, hoping it would end the conversation.

"Now, about that dress material," Granny said, returning to an equally uncomfortable subject. "You really should take a look at it. The colors are perfect for you and with the party in just a little over a month, we'll need to get busy sewing."

Merrill fought an urge to roll her eyes. Instead she smiled and asked for another cup of tea.

Later that evening, as she sat around the supper table and listened to her brothers and father talk about the day, she couldn't help but think back on the conversation with Granny and Corabeth. Truth be told, Merrill was lonely. She had always hoped to court and marry. She wanted a large family of her own, but it seemed most of the eligible men in the area were frightened off by her big, intimidating brothers. Not only that, but the vast amount of work she was responsible for kept Merrill from having enough leisure time to concern herself with courtship.

"I'm surprised you don't have something to say about that," Father said, elbowing Merrill.

She looked up to find everyone watching her. "What?" she asked. "I must have missed something."

"I'll say," Tobe countered. "Leo just said he finally got engaged to Sally."

"I figured you'd be the first to congratulate me, Merrill Jean," Leo remarked.

Flynn helped himself to the last piece of strudel, then jabbed his fork at Zadoc's hand as he tried to help himself to a bite. "You already had two pieces," Flynn reminded him. "This is just my second."

"You can't blame me for trying," Zadoc replied. "Merrill, that was about the best cherry strudel I've ever had. Those canned cherries weren't bad at all."

"I'm glad you liked it."

"So what do you think about my news?" Leo asked.

A twinge of envy washed over her, but Merrill ignored it. "Oh, Leo, what good news. Very good news. Granny and I were just discussing it this morning. She was surprised you hadn't already proposed."

"Just been waiting for the right time," Leo said, shrugging. "Didn't know the whole town was waiting on me."

Her brothers laughed and teased Leo mercilessly as Merrill slipped back into her own thoughts. Leo would marry and Sally would no doubt move here to the farm. She liked Sally a great deal and thought it would be easy enough to live with another woman in the house. Even so, it meant changes for her family, and Merrill wasn't exactly sure why that left her feeling out of sorts.

⁂

"I thought I'd come one last time to try and talk some sense into you," Nils said, looking at Rurik's open suitcase. "I see you're packing."

"I leave in the morning for Minnesota."

"You know, I can smooth things over with Svea. She'll do whatever I say. You really should stay and see what can be done."

Rurik looked at his friend and shook his head. "And what kind of husband would I be—needing my best friend to smooth things over with the one who is to be my wife? No, I think this is the best decision."

"But you won't come into your marriage money, and you won't be able to start your business very soon. I've been counting on this as much as you have."

"I can continue making furniture and selling it. I don't need a big place to do that. With each piece I sell, I can reinvest. I'll start small."

"But that doesn't help me," Nils protested. "I thought we agreed that we would go into business together."

"You could learn to make furniture. I could teach you some simple designs to get you started."

"I can't work with my hands like that. I'm better with numbers, and you know it. I can handle the business end of things for you. I can get customers for you and arrange for larger sales. You need me."

"I will eventually, to be sure, Nils. I just can't make a position where there is none yet," Rurik replied. He reached for a stack of shirts and placed them in the suitcase. "You're just going to have to trust me on this and be patient. The time for our venture will come."

"But not in time to do me any good," Nils muttered, shaking his head. "My father has made it clear that I'm through. He wants me to get out on my own and take up for myself unless I'm willing to take on more responsibility with the dairy. I can't spend my life milking cows, Rurik."

"Nobody is asking you to. Why don't you go into town and see about a bank job? Maybe you could work for the railroad."

"You're just trying to get rid of me, like you did Svea."

Rurik frowned. "That was uncalled for. Your sister is the one who dissolved the engagement. You know that as well as anyone. I only asked for time—just like I'm asking you."

"Time isn't something we all have to spare." Nils stormed out of the room, and Rurik let him go. There was no sense in making a scene in front of Aron and Elizabeth. He really wasn't sure why Nils was so desperate or why some of the options Rurik had mentioned were so unpalatable.

"Is Nils all right?" Aron asked from the doorway.

"He doesn't want me to go. He wants me to stick around and mend fences with Svea."

Aron leaned against the doorframe. "I've been considering the things you said." He looked rather sheepish. "I talked to Elizabeth, as well. I'm of a mind that maybe I spoke too soon when we discussed your marriage to Svea."

Rurik felt a sense of relief to hear his brother admit this. "I'm glad you're able to see it from my perspective."

"Times are changing. Elizabeth reminded me of that. It's nearly the nineteen hundreds, after all, and arranged marriages have been out of fashion for a long time. I guess my mind was more on what Far thought we needed. Things have changed there, as well. The wheat prices are better than ever, and we could switch to grow that instead of corn. That is, if the Olssons want to buy their feed elsewhere."

Rurik smiled. "My guess is they'll still buy your corn." Silence fell between them, making Rurik feel rather awkward. "I appreciate you coming to tell me, Aron. You know I value your opinion."

"Thanks, Rurik. I know that you wouldn't do anything without seeking God first. I should have remembered that earlier. Talk with Him, Rurik, and do what He directs. I'm confident you'll make the right choice."

Chapter 5

"Uncle Carl!" Rurik waved and stepped down from the train. He had immediately recognized the older man, even though it had been at least six years since they had last seen each other.

Carl Jorgenson smiled and nodded. "It's good to see you." He gave Rurik an embrace, but it lacked the strength he'd once demonstrated. "Let's collect your things and get out of the cold."

"I only have this suitcase," Rurik said, holding the piece up. "I wasn't sure exactly what I'd need. I figured if I needed something more, I could send for it or maybe purchase it."

"Ja, that's good. You won't need much."

Rurik tried not to appear overly concerned about his uncle's condition. It was clear the man was thinner than the last time they'd been together; his face looked rather gaunt and gray. Perhaps Carl was much sicker than he'd let on in his letter.

"It snowed last night," Carl said, as if needing to explain the icy drifts. "More snow is due."

"Ja, it snowed along the way," Rurik replied. He slowed his steps to match his uncle's. "This seems like a nice little town."

"Ja, it's a good town. The people are the best, always

looking out for one another. They take good care of me," he said, chuckling and putting a hand to his belly. "As you can see, I do not go hungry."

Rurik forced a smile and nodded. "I'm glad to hear that." He glanced around. "I've never been to Minnesota before this."

"I think you will find it similar to Kansas. Maybe more trees. And more lakes. Definitely more trees and lakes." Carl chuckled. He pointed to a large red barn-like structure. "That's my shop. The house is just behind. And we have been electrified."

"Electricity is a wonder, to be sure," Rurik said, shaking his head. "It will make the work easier, ja?" Rurik found himself falling right in with his uncle's Scandinavian vernacular.

"Ja. We have better lighting and can work longer."

"Nice and close to the railroad, too." Rurik noted that they weren't even half a mile from the depot.

"Ja. I ship furniture all over the country."

"How have they learned about you?"

"Mostly verd of mouth," he said, his Swedish accent thick. "I always keep busy. I got ten good strong men to work for me now. I had to advertise in the Minneapolis paper."

Rurik smiled. "I'm sure you trained them well. I often think of you and Farfar teaching me to work the wood. Those are my favorite memories."

"Mine too," Carl admitted. He opened a small door and ushered Rurik inside the barn. "Just put your suitcase over there for now. I'll introduce you to my men."

Rurik did as he was instructed. He inhaled deeply, the scent of various woods filling the air. He remembered his farfar's shop in Kansas. That shop had been quite small compared to this business, but the sights and sounds were much the same.

"Fellas, come on over." Carl's call interrupted Rurik's daydreaming. "This is my nephew, Rurik Jorgenson. He's come all the way from Kansas."

Rurik nodded to the men who gathered around him. He shook hands with each one and heard their names as Carl went down the line. "This is Arne and his brother Lars. Over here is Enar, then Oscar, George, Josef, Otto, Simon, and Kent."

The strong handshakes and smiles made Rurik feel instantly welcome. "It's good to meet you, gentlemen."

"The only one missing is John. His wife had a baby this morning, so we let him stay home."

The men laughed and the one named Lars added, "Ja, so he could take care of the other eight children."

Rurik laughed, too. He liked the camaraderie between the men. No doubt his uncle aimed to hire God-fearing, strong family men who were known for their honesty and hard work.

"My father and I trained Rurik," Carl stated, "when he was just a boy. He has come to help us, since the doctor thinks I need to rest more." He frowned. "I don't think the doctor knows what he's talking about, but at least this way I look like I'm listening to him."

The men chuckled. Carl said to Rurik, "I'm sure you are familiar with most everything you see, but I'll let you spend time with each man to see how we do things here." Turning back to the men, he nodded. "You can return to work now.

We've got that big library order, remember, and it has to go out by the fifteenth." Rurik knew the latter information was for his sake.

Carl headed toward where they'd left the suitcase. "I'll show you the house and your room," he said over his shoulder.

Rurik picked up his case and followed after his uncle. He noticed the man had a bit of a limp, but otherwise he seemed to move along quite well. They crossed into another section of the barn, and it was here that Rurik's senses were assaulted with the scent of paint and lacquer.

"This is the finishing room," Carl told him. "I mostly work here with John when we can keep it warm enough."

Rurik noted five finished tables and two sideboards. "Are those a part of the order you're finishing up?"

"Ja, the tables are. We're mostly done. The boys will finish today, and then we will stain and lacquer tomorrow. John will be back, and you can help if you like."

"I'd like that very much." He noted three woodstoves. "Do you have enough fuel for the fires? I could go chop wood if you need me to."

"No. I have plenty. We laid in a large supply, as you will see." He led Rurik through another door at the far end. "And here is the holding room, where we store the pieces that are ready to be shipped. The boys will move those others in here when they are dry."

Rurik squatted down to inspect the tables and ran his hand over the cabriole leg. "This is beautiful work."

"They are for a library in New York." Carl sounded pleased at Rurik's compliment.

Rurik stood and felt the satin-like finish of the top. "Walnut?"

"Oh sure. Valnut is good and sturdy. It will stand up to the wear and tear. Last a hundred years."

"Or more," Rurik added. "Do you have orders for additional pieces after this?"

"Ja. More than I can handle. I've had to say no to some. Others are willing to wait. Come, now. I'll show you the house."

They left the holding room and exited out the side of the building. The shoveled walkway led to a small white house. The gabled two-story house was simple in its styling. The place spoke of practicality with its steep-pitched roof and straight, trim lines. A single brick chimney could be seen near the crest of the roof.

"There's a nice large room for you upstairs. It used to be my bedroom, but it's gotten hard to climb the steps, so my room is downstairs now."

"It sounds perfect," Rurik said. They entered the house and stepped into the front sitting room. It felt only slightly warmer inside the house, and Rurik couldn't help but wonder if Carl had a hard time keeping the fires going or if he was simply frugal.

"Sorry, I let it get cold in here," Carl admitted, as if answering Rurik's question. "The fireplace keeps the room pretty warm. I'll get the fire stoked up for you." Stacked beside the hearth were several appropriately cut pieces of wood. Carl bent stiffly and picked up several sticks. "I've got soup in the kitchen if you are hungry. Fresh bread, too. Mrs. Lassiter brought it yesterday, and it's a good strong rye with caraway."

Rurik put the suitcase down and went to help his uncle. "Do you need me to bring in more wood?"

"Maybe later. You'll need to take some upstairs with you." He straightened and looked rather embarrassed. "I forgot to have Arne take some up for you."

"That's not a problem, Uncle Carl. Really, I'm here to help you. Let me build the fire." He shed his coat, hat, and gloves and took the pieces of wood from Carl's hands.

"Ja, you do that," Carl said, seeming glad to be relieved of the responsibility. "When you have it set, I'll show you the rest of the house."

Rurik worked for several minutes until he had a nice fire going. He held his bare hands toward the flames and relished the warmth. "There we go. I'm sure things will warm up nicely." Rurik turned to his uncle. "Are you feeling all right?"

Carl leaned against the edge of a wing-backed chair. "I get pretty tired these days."

"Then a rest is in order." Rurik glanced around the sparsely furnished room. He couldn't help but think of the adage that spoke of the shoemaker's children going without shoes. With exception to the wing-backed chair and ottoman, a single wooden chair, and a small table, the room was unfurnished. Carl didn't even have so much as a picture on the walls.

As if reading his mind, Carl smiled and said, "I don't spend a lot of time in here. The kitchen suits me better."

"No doubt I'll feel the same."

Carl squared his thin shoulders. "Come on, then. Let me show you." He led Rurik from the front room and down a narrow hall. "Over there is my room." He pointed to an alcove that was separated from the passageway by a pulled-back curtain. "The stairs are just there."

Rurik looked past the alcove to a narrow door. Carl was already on the move, shuffling to the opposite side of his bedroom. "You can shave and bathe in here," he said, tapping another closed narrow door. "And through here is the kitchen."

They entered the surprisingly large room, and Carl went immediately to the large cast-iron stove. "I put some coffee on this morning. It's good and strong."

"Sounds perfect." Rurik smiled. The kitchen was considerably warmer and more accommodating than the rest of the house. He could see the table and chairs were most likely of Carl's making, as were the cupboards. The countertop was clean and clear of clutter except for a bread box and several jars of what looked to be jellies. An icebox stood against the far side of the room, but in weather like this, Rurik imagined it was just as easy to keep perishables on the back porch.

"I'll dish you up some soup if you like," Carl said. "You can take your suitcase upstairs and bring up some wood to get a fire going for yourself." He motioned to the back door. "The mud porch is stacked full."

Rurik nodded. "Sounds good, but I can lay a fire after we eat." He turned to retrieve his things.

Carl called after him, "You make sure you have enough quilts up there."

Smiling to himself, Rurik made his way through the narrow stair door. He had to bend slightly to keep from hitting his head on the ascent. The steps were very steep and just as narrow as the door had been. Rurik straightened when he reached the top. Here he found a large, open room with a double bed, nightstand, and wardrobe on one side of the room. A chair and additional table claimed the territory in front of a small woodstove on the opposite side.

There were two large windows at each end of the room that would allow in ample light throughout the day. "Not exactly designed for my height," Rurik said to himself with a grin as he inspected the steep angles of the attic ceiling, "but workable."

He placed his case on the chair and went to the bed to test the mattress. It was surprisingly comfortable, and the bed had been carefully made. In fact, the entire room looked spotless. No doubt Carl had brought in someone to clean and set it in order.

Before he headed back downstairs, Rurik opened the wardrobe to find two additional quilts. He smiled and closed the mahogany door. It already felt like home.

He'd no sooner made it back down when Rurik heard voices coming from the front room. He made his way there to find his uncle speaking with two women.

"Oh, good, you're able to meet Mrs. Lassiter and her granddaughter, Miss Corabeth Lassiter."

Rurik extended his hand. "It's my pleasure, Mrs. Lassiter. Miss Lassiter."

"Now, you call me Granny like everybody else. Only Carl calls me Mrs. Lassiter, and that's because he thinks I'm an old lady."

Carl laughed. "It's because I was taught to respect vomen-folk. This is my nephew, Rurik. He's the one I told you about."

The older woman smiled and nodded as she took his hand. "I'm mighty glad you came to live with Carl. He's needed someone here for a long time. Corabeth and I saw to your room upstairs. If we forgot anything, you tell us."

"It looked perfect to me," Rurik said.

"Good. We brought you some cinnamon rolls for breakfast and a slab of bacon. I wasn't sure if Carl had time to shop."

"I hadn't had time. I was pretty busy," Carl admitted. "What do I owe you?"

"Oh, a couple of chairs need repairs," Granny Lassiter declared. "When you have time, you can get to them."

"Ja, I'll do that," Carl said, smiling. "I'll come tomorrow." He frowned. "No, I will come the day after. I promised to help the Krause family tomorrow. They're checking to see if the ice is ready to cut."

"You've got no business being out there," Granny admonished.

"What's he talking about?" Rurik asked. "Uncle Carl, I thought you were busy with furniture and meeting a deadline."

"Ja, but my friends need help."

"I could go instead," Rurik offered. "I don't know much about ice harvesting, but I can learn."

"That's far more sensible," Granny encouraged. "A tall, strong man like you would lend a good hand. Carl will just get to talkin', and then no work will get done." She smiled at Rurik's uncle. "I'll come by tomorrow and make sure you behaved yourself. If you aren't here, I'll send the doctor for you."

"*Uff da*," Carl muttered. "This is why I don't have a wife."

Rurik roared with laughter and noticed that the petite Corabeth seemed to shrink away. She reminded him a bit of Svea in her size and demeanor. He flashed her a smile, but the young woman seemed only more intimidated.

"Well, you gentlemen will have to excuse us. We've got a few more stops to make," Granny announced and turned for the door. "Now, Carl, you be sure to come for supper and bring Rurik."

"Thank you," Carl replied, nodding. "We'll be there at five thirty."

Granny nodded. "Good. Now come along, Corabeth."

The young woman did as her grandmother bid, with nary a glance back.

Chapter 6

Merrill looked about her and found herself wishing she could be everywhere at once. The horses knew their jobs and handled just as well for her brothers, but Merrill couldn't help but feel rather possessive. She had helped train all of the large Belgians and knew their quirks and their strengths. Even so, there were eight horses working today—four teams of two, and she couldn't manage them all.

The dun-colored Belgians seemed anxious to be about their business. Standing beside them on the ice, Merrill tightened her grip on the harness and whispered comfort to the nearest gelding. "You'll be working soon enough, Paul. You stand fast and stop being such a bad example for Peter."

Peter and Paul were fairly new at working with each other, but Merrill found them to be a good match. Even so, they were young and still learning.

"The ice is nine inches," Merrill's father called, having drilled down into the frozen lake only a few minutes earlier. Nine inches was deep enough. Merrill also knew he preferred an even ten inches, but he'd settle for nine just to get an early start on the ice harvesting. People in the South wanted ice for their drinks and refrigeration, and who could deny them? The pay was good and the commodity rare—at least farther south. Merrill couldn't help but smile as she looked around the frozen lake and snow-covered landscape. Ice was plentiful here.

With her father's authorization to go ahead, Merrill and her brothers began scoring the ice. The work was tedious, but Merrill couldn't help but feel a little thrill of fear each time she walked the Belgians farther onto the ice. The horses weighed thousands of pounds, and while the ice was thick enough to sustain them, she couldn't help worrying about coming across an unexpected weak patch. She'd seen a horse break through the water once. Merrill shuddered at the memory and quickly turned her attention back to Peter and Paul. "We'll not be having any of those accidents today," she assured them, praying that it would be so.

"You talking to the horses again?" Flynn asked as he led one of the other teams to their place.

"Sometimes I prefer talking to them," Merrill replied. "They don't talk back or ask silly questions."

Flynn laughed and kept moving. "Just making sure you haven't lost your wits, sister dear."

Merrill shook her head. Since she was the only young woman in a houseful of men, Merrill often wondered that she had any sense left at all. Peter gave a soft snort and Merrill couldn't help but smile. "You know us all too well, don't you, boy?"

"The cold can get to you before you know it," Leo Krause told Rurik. They stood in the yard near the Krause barn. "We're always glad for the extra help, but you should be aware of the risks." He handed Rurik a pair of thick woolen mittens. "These will keep your hands warmer than gloves. The air gets trapped inside and adds extra heat." He then handed over a pair of leather mittens. "And these you wear over those, and it will give you better grip."

"My uncle advised me of the dangers," Rurik said, pulling on both pairs of mittens. "However, I've not done much of this kind of work. We harvested ice only a couple of times when I was a boy. After that my father was only too glad to buy his ice from someone else."

Leo nodded. "Well, as eldest in this family, I've helped harvest ice nearly all of my thirty years. Sometimes I think I was born on the ice. Unfortunately, with machinery and other means of making ice, I think our harvesting days are numbered. Every year the orders are fewer."

Rurik wasn't sure what to say. Losing one's livelihood was a fearful thing. "Do you do other work besides the ice harvest?"

"Oh sure. We use the horses to help with logging and freighting. We definitely keep busy. It's a good business. What of your family?"

"All farmers, except me. I never found my interests in the soil."

"So you make furniture like Carl."

"Ja, that's what I'm good for." Rurik held up his hands. "And hopefully for ice harvesting, too."

"Let's get to it, then. We'll try to break you in slow—have

you drive the ice back and forth from the lake to the icehouse. I'll show you where that is before we head down. I'm sure the others are wondering where I am." Leo led the way to the wagon where a pair of sorrel draft horses, already harnessed, stamped and snorted in the cold.

They made a brief stop by the icehouse, where Leo explained what Rurik's job would be. "The men stationed here will handle the unloading." Leo waved one of the men over. "This is Basil Adlum. Basil, this is Carl Jorgenson's nephew, Rurik Jorgenson."

"Good to meet you. Your uncle is a good man. We play checkers most every Sunday afternoon."

Rurik smiled. "I imagine he's hard to beat—at least speaking from my own experience." Basil seemed close to Carl's age, but much stronger and healthier.

Leo pointed to the other men. "Basil and his sons will handle this end of the process."

"We've been doing this since we were children," Basil offered. "Hard work, but it goes much easier when you work together."

"They've brought a couple of Belgians, and they'll take turns running the lift. They'll hook the horse up here," Leo said, pointing to a series of harnesses and ropes. "As you see, it's attached to the ice lift. When they pull the horse forward, the ice will be raised to that door up top." Rurik noted the door as Leo continued. "Then other men will take the ice and position it in the icehouse and pack sawdust to insulate. The train will arrive the first of the week and take all we can load. You're welcome to come back and help with that."

"I'll see if Uncle Carl can spare me."

Leo nodded. "You can see that the lift is slanted just a bit. The men will waste no time sliding the ice off, and the man handling the horse down below will back the animal up and the lift will lower to receive another block of ice. It goes very quickly with a well-trained team."

"And we're the best," Basil offered with a smile.

"Indeed they are. We help each other with ice harvest around here," Leo explained. "Come on. We'd best get down to the lake. We're losing the day. Basil, we'll have that first load up to you soon."

Rurik enjoyed the ride out to the lake. The countryside was frosted in snow and ice, but the brilliant morning sun made the ground and trees glitter like diamonds. There was a sense of exhilaration in the air as they made their way to join the others.

There were several people already hard at work scoring the ice. The horse teams out on the lake plodded along, pulling runners that sliced grooves into the frozen lake. "Looks like they've begun cutting without us," Rurik declared.

"They'll only cut it six inches," Leo explained. "They'll score it off and then drill in and saw blocks in sections. We'll start in one area and process across the lake, being careful to leave the surface strong enough to support the teams and people.

"That's my family," Leo announced. "My father is over there. I'll introduce you." He pulled the wagon to a stop near the ramp where they would bring the ice up out of the lake. Leo carefully positioned the back of the wagon at the edge of the ramp.

"This is how you'll have to do it," Leo told Rurik. "You want to be sure and get the bed of the wagon even with the ramp to make the loading easier. We'll slide the blocks of ice up the ramp, and you'll take a hook and help pull them into the wagon. We try to get as much on each load as possible and then take it to the icehouse where Mr. Adlum and his boys can unload it." After he was satisfied with the positioning and had set the brake, Leo nodded to Rurik. "Come, and I'll introduce you to my father."

They trudged out onto the frozen lake, and Leo pointed to one of the teams of horses. "That's Merrill over there with the duns. Then to your right is Tobe, and the farther team is Zadoc. And this," Leo said, pausing in front of two very tall men, "is my father, Bogart Krause, and my brother Flynn."

"Who have we here?" Mr. Krause asked.

"This is Carl Jorgenson's nephew, Rurik. He's come to help in Carl's stead."

Rurik extended his hand. "I hope you don't mind. Uncle Carl was not feeling up to it this time."

Krause nodded. "He's not a healthy man anymore, but still I hate to tell him no. A man doesn't like to be put out to pasture. I was glad to hear you were coming to help him with the business. Good to meet you." He shook Rurik's hand. "Do you know much about this kind of work?"

"No, but I learn fast," Rurik said, smiling.

"I figured he could drive the wagon back and forth to the icehouse."

"That would be good," Krause replied. "Are Basil and his boys ready?"

"Yes. I spoke with them first. They're back there laying sawdust and readying the lift."

"Good. Well, as you can see, Rurik, we've been scoring the ice. We'll get to work cutting blocks now. It's a lengthy process, but the pay is good."

After that, there was very little conversation. Rurik insisted on helping with the initial cuts, and by the time the blocks were loaded, he was more than willing to take a break and drive the wagon. The hard work helped stave off the cold, but Rurik found himself longing for a warm fire and maybe even a cup of something hot.

Nevertheless, he worked alongside Leo and his brothers for many hours before a break was called. They threw blankets over the backs of the horses, gave them water and oats, then sat around a nice fire to warm up a bit. There were refreshments of coffee and sandwiches, and all of the men, with exception to Merrill, ate and drank their fill. Merrill, on the other hand, showered attention on the horses.

Rurik greatly admired the Krauses, an obviously industrious bunch. They worked as one, seemingly knowing by instinct what the other would do. He supposed it came from years of practice and working together. Just like a wheat harvest in Kansas.

The brother introduced as Flynn joined Rurik by the fire. "You've been a good hand to have," he told Rurik. "Sure glad you came out to help us."

"My pleasure. I was just sitting here admiring the way you all work together. It reminded me of my family in Kansas."

"We know our responsibilities. Our father made it clear

that we were each expected to hold our own. Now it's almost become a competition." He grinned. "I for one can work circles around Leo. He's getting too old and fat."

Rurik laughed. "Well, it doesn't seem to slow him much. None of your brothers could be faulted for that."

After the break they were back to work again, and Rurik felt aches and pains in muscles he'd never known he had. He knew he'd be grateful when the workday came to an end, though he had no idea of when that might happen. He had to admit, however, that he was fascinated with the whole ice-harvest process. The Krause men maneuvered the heavy chunks as if they were a part of their own bodies. The thick slabs were sawed and pried, pulled and positioned into the wagon, then driven to the icehouse. That was where Rurik came in. He found that to be much easier than sawing. The slippery, snow-packed roads were a challenge, but the horses seemed surefooted. Even so, when the light began to fade, Rurik was glad to know the workday was ending.

He had no sooner returned to the lake with his empty wagon, however, than a commotion at the lake's edge drew his attention. Bogart Krause was trying to maneuver one of the teams, and something had caused the horse on the right to become agitated. He refused to cooperate.

Rurik wondered if he should do something to lend a hand, but then, without warning, the horse began to fight the man's hold on the reins. The gelding was trying to rear, but the constraints of his harness and mate only made him more frantic.

"Whoa, Herrman. Stand fast." But the draft horse had no interest in instruction, and by now his distress was making the other horse frantic. Before Rurik could set the brake and climb down to offer assistance, Bogart Krause was knocked to the ground.

One of his sons came running, but before he could reach his father, the horse named Herrman reared into the air and came down on top of Krause. The older man cried out in pain. In one quick motion, Rurik leaped from the wagon and ran down the ramp to the injured man. He couldn't be sure which brother was working to calm the team, but there was no time for formalities or niceties. Rurik quickly grabbed hold of Bogart Krause's arm and pulled him away from the flailing hooves.

By now the Krause brothers were gathered around, and they lifted their moaning father and pointed to the wagon Rurik had been driving.

"Let's get him in the wagon and back to the house," Leo instructed.

Again the men worked as a team, each instinctively knowing what needed to be done. The exception was the one busy with the now-calmer team, leading the two large beasts to an area away from the other horses.

Leo continued barking out orders. "Rurik, you ride in the wagon with my father. Tobe, Flynn—help Merrill get the teams in. Zadoc, you come with me. I'll probably need your help carrying Father into the house."

No one questioned the man, but went quickly to work. Bogart Krause moaned from his injuries, but attempted to protest that he was fine as they made their way back to the house.

"I'm sure it's just sore ribs and such," he said through gritted teeth. "Nothing feels broken."

"Just the same, it's best that you get back and let the doctor look you over," Rurik countered.

Inside the house, Rurik helped Leo and Zadoc make their father more comfortable. With great care he unlaced the older man's boots and pulled them from his feet while Leo checked his father for broken bones. It wasn't long before the last of the brothers joined them, the one Leo had called Merrill.

Rurik was stunned, as this one began to shed layers of protective garments, to discover that this sibling was not a man at all, but a woman. A beautiful woman with soulful eyes that held great concern for her wounded father. She gave Rurik a brief nod and pulled a knit cap from her head. Long, dark curls fell about her shoulders and down her back. Rurik had a strange urge to run his fingers down the wild mane, but of course did nothing of the kind. Merrill didn't seem to notice the effect she had on him.

"Father, how are you feeling?" she asked, bending over him.

"I'm all right, daughter. You're all making too much of a fuss."

"I'd wager your body is saying otherwise." She raised his shirt and carefully began to run her fingers over the man's chest and ribs. "Are you breathing all right? Does anything feel broken?"

"Nothing's damaged but my pride," the older man muttered. "Now stop fussing." He struggled to sit up, but gasped and laid down again. "It's . . . my back," he said, looking at Merrill with a bewildered expression.

She nodded. "You boys get Father in bed, and I'll bring him something for the pain."

After some time, Merrill determined that her father's back was only strained and that the horses had done little damage overall. Bogart Krause tried to argue with his daughter when she demanded he stay in bed, but Rurik got the distinct impression he wasn't trying all that hard to fight her.

The Krause brothers insisted Rurik stay for supper, and when the meal was finally presented, he found that his appetite wouldn't have let him leave even if he'd wanted to. He sat between Flynn and Zadoc and marveled at the thick meatballs and gravy covering mounds of mashed potatoes and sauerkraut. He'd never eaten such a combination before but found the variety of flavors to be quite complementary. Added to this were buttery rolls the likes of which Rurik had never tasted—light and just a touch sweet. It looked like Merrill had prepared much of it ahead of time and finished it up after working the ice harvest all day and taking care of her injured father to boot!

Merrill checked on her father from time to time and took him additional food, but otherwise she seemed content to let her brothers do all the talking. Rurik answered their questions about his work with furniture and his plans for the future, but all the while he kept his eyes on the young woman, hoping no one would notice. She was unlike anyone he'd ever known. Even his own sisters . . . the women in Rurik's life, with exception of Svea, had all been strong, industrious workers. But Merrill seemed to outshine them all. Rurik couldn't imagine the woman ever sat idle.

After the meal Rurik helped to pick up the dishes while Merrill's brothers excused themselves to see to chores. Following Merrill into the kitchen, Rurik immediately noticed the painted cabinetry.

"This is quite beautiful," he said, placing a stack of dishes by the sink. The cupboards were painted a powdery blue and trimmed in white. The white borders had been carefully decorated with colorful flowers and entwining green vines. "May I ask who painted the cupboards?"

"I did," Merrill answered as she poured hot water from the kettle into the basin.

"You're very talented, Miss Krause."

"Call me Merrill, and thank you," she said, placing the cutlery and plates in the water to soak. "My mother taught me. She loved to paint, and I do, too."

Rurik made his way to a pie safe. On the doors, Merrill had created pastoral scenes for each of the four seasons. "This is charming. I think it would be a wonderful thing to offer on the furniture my uncle Carl builds. I can imagine women all over the country enjoying such a piece." He looked back at Merrill for her response.

She shrugged. "It's something I do to feel close to my mother. She died when I was ten."

"I'm sorry for your loss, Merrill. It couldn't have been easy growing up without any womenfolk around."

"It's worked out well enough." She shrugged. "Would you like to see a dresser my mother painted?"

He smiled. "I'd like that very much."

She picked up a lamp and led the way into a small room

off the main hallway. "She did that green piece right under the window." She crossed the room and placed the lamp atop the dresser. "She was considerably more talented than I."

"Not from what I'm seeing here. I easily note the same remarkable traits. You're both gifted."

Merrill smiled. "Thank you."

He again was struck by her expressive face, particularly her eyes.

She seemed embarrassed by his praise, so Rurik said nothing more about her artistry. But in the back of his mind he was already making plans to speak to his uncle. It was entirely possible that Miss Krause could be a great asset to them. Painted furniture was popular, and Rurik knew there was nothing like it at the Jorgenson Furniture shops.

Smiling to himself, he followed Merrill back to the kitchen. He picked up a towel and began to dry the dishes as she washed them, and considered how he might go about convincing his uncle.

Chapter 7

Sundays were a mixed blessing to Merrill. She always worked hard the day before to prepare food for the dinner they would enjoy after services. This allowed her more freedom after church, and that afternoon, her single bit of time off for the week, could be spent in more leisurely activities. But Sunday also represented the frustration of putting on a smile and pretending she fit in with the other young women of the congregation. Merrill knew she was sometimes the talk of the town because of the manner in which she labored and dressed. Granny had once told her that church attendance wasn't about her clothes or finery; church was meant for fellowship, study, and encouragement. Even so, Merrill knew that many of the women measured one's worth by the fashions worn or one's manners or other things that were neither of interest nor importance to her.

"We'd best not dawdle," her father instructed, pulling the wagon alongside the church. "Else we'll be late again."

He helped Merrill down and smiled. "You look lovely today, Merrill Jean."

She smiled back. "Thank you, Father. The bonnet is a new one Granny Lassiter made for me."

"Well, it's a doozy," he said with a grin.

"That's the one she wears to help with foaling," her brother Zadoc added with a wink.

Merrill rolled her eyes. "It wasn't my idea. Granny made me try it on at just the wrong time."

"I think it looks mighty good," her father said. "You look like a fine lady."

"I feel like a pig dressed up for the fair," she murmured, unsure that her father would understand her words. She recalled Granny's comments about the hat and couldn't help but add, "A pig in a poke . . . bonnet."

"What was that?" her father asked.

Shaking her head, Merrill hooked her arm through his. "Nothing of importance."

They made their way into church just as the organist began to play. Merrill wasn't surprised to see Rurik and his uncle in the pew just ahead of them, where Carl Jorgenson generally sat.

Merrill took her place between her father and Zadoc and quickly shed her coat. She adjusted the green scarf at her neck and smoothed the lines of her plum wool dress, hoping that she looked better than she imagined. Her hair had been so uncooperative that morning that she had been more than glad to hide it beneath Granny's bonnet.

The congregation rose to sing a hymn, and Merrill found herself standing directly behind Rurik Jorgenson. His towering height reminded her of her own brothers. None of her family was under six foot three, with herself the only exception. Rurik was every bit that tall. His golden brown hair had been combed neatly and parted to one side, and he wore a nicely fitting blue suit that Merrill imagined drew out the color of his eyes.

They sat again while a male soloist offered a hymn of adoration. Merrill's mind, however, was not on the words about God's goodness. She tried to keep focused on the Lord, but her eyes kept drawing her attention back to Rurik.

She liked the look of his broad shoulders and remembered him helping her clear the table the day of the ice harvest. He had taken off his coat, and his muscles had strained against the white fabric of his cotton shirt while he dried the dishes for her. Though she'd seen her brothers in various states of undress, this sight had felt surprisingly intimate.

The solo ended, and Merrill bowed her head with the others as the pastor led the congregation in prayer. Yet she still found it hard to think about anything but the man sitting in front of her.

Throughout the rituals and the sermon, Merrill tried to focus on God's Word and the pastor's sermon, but thoughts of Rurik continued to steal her attention.

After the service ended, Rurik and his uncle turned her way, and Merrill feared her face might betray her thoughts. She nodded and glanced down the aisle, hoping she might simply slip out of the church without having to say anything. It was not to be.

"You certainly look different today," Rurik said with a smile. "I must say you are quite fetching, Miss Krause."

Merrill felt her face grow hot. "Ah, thank you."

"We get her in a dress from time to time," her father said with a chuckle. "And isn't that a nice new bonnet?"

Zadoc leaned over. "She's only worn it once before."

Merrill elbowed him hard, but that only made her teasing brother laugh.

Carl was the next one to speak, however. "It is indeed a lovely thing, Miss Merrill, and you are as pretty as they come."

"Thank you, Mr. Jorgenson." Hoping to steer the conversation to something other than herself, she said, "How are you set for cookies? I baked several batches yesterday and would be happy to bring you some."

"I would like that. No one bakes quite as well as you," Carl said in a lower voice. "I don't want to offend any of the other ladies, however. They might stop bringing me treats."

Merrill smiled. "No worries. It's our secret. I'll bring you some tomorrow."

"Why not have Carl and Rurik join us for lunch today," her father said, "and then they can take them home with them."

Merrill tried to hide her surprise at her father's unexpected invitation. "That would be . . . wonderful."

"How about it, Carl? Can you follow us home for dinner?"

"Ja, I think we can." He looked to Rurik. "What say you?"

"I've had Miss Merrill's cooking once before. I'd certainly enjoy another round," Rurik said, rubbing his hands together in obvious pleasure and glancing her way.

Merrill felt a tremor go through her and quickly looked away. "That sounds . . . good. I have more than enough warming for us."

"It's settled, then," Bogart Krause announced. "Now, if you'll excuse me, I need to speak with Basil."

"And I have some folks to introduce you to," Carl said to Rurik. "Miss Merrill, if you'll pardon us."

"Of course," she said, glad they were leaving before she might make an utter fool of herself. Her brothers were off speaking to friends, so Merrill began to pull on her coat.

"Did you meet him?"

Merrill turned to find Corabeth at her side. "Meet whom?"

Corabeth glanced around as if trying to keep her comments secret. "Mr. Jorgenson's nephew, of course."

"Yes, he came to help with ice harvesting the other day. He and his uncle are joining us for lunch."

"I met him when Granny and I went to take Carl some food. I found him rather . . . I don't know . . . startling. Granny had him to dinner and I thought he was very stern."

Merrill frowned. "Rurik Jorgenson?"

"Well, maybe not stern. He was friendly enough." She looked confused. "He just . . . well . . . he seems rather bold—imposing," Corabeth replied. "And he's so tall."

"No taller than my brothers," Merrill said with a laugh. "And, Corabeth, I seem to recall that the height of one brother in particular doesn't bother you in the least."

Corabeth blushed. "Zadoc is much more mild mannered. I think Mr. Jorgenson might be rather . . . well, like I said . . . bold."

Merrill laughed again. "Mr. Jorgenson is perfectly well mannered and kind. I like him very much." Corabeth gave her a raised eyebrow at this declaration, but Merrill was unconcerned. "So what do you think?" She waved her hand from the top of her bonnet and down past her gown. "Does the bonnet suit the gown as well as you hoped?"

"Oh, that and more. Granny and I were commenting on it during service. We think you look quite elegant."

"What a relief. I'm glad to have met with your approval," Merrill said in a teasing tone. "The bonnet was a blessing this morning. My hair refused to do anything I wanted it to, so I finally gave up, knotted it, and tucked it under the hat."

"Maybe you should wear more bonnets," Corabeth suggested. "You look nice, the way your hair is curled around the edges of the bonnet. It's as though you planned it that way."

Just then Zadoc walked up and nodded toward the young woman. "Miss Corabeth." He turned to Merrill. "Father said not to keep us waiting too long, since we're putting on dinner for the Jorgenson men."

"I'll be right there." She looked at Corabeth and then to Zadoc. "Don't you think Corabeth looks pretty in her new dress?"

Zadoc looked down at the gown and nodded his agreement. "Fits you like a good saddle. I always did like blue."

Corabeth seemed to glow under his admiration, and Merrill couldn't help but smile. "It matches her eyes, don't you think?"

Zadoc narrowed his gaze and leaned closer. "Yup. Looks to be the same color."

Merrill lifted her eyes to the ceiling and sighed. Her brothers could all do with some lessons when it came to courting women. If their mother had lived, they no doubt would have learned to handle themselves in a different fashion.

"So you coming?" Zadoc asked his sister.

Merrill nodded. "I will speak with you later, Corabeth." She leaned over to hug her friend. "Do come for a visit when time permits."

Once they were outside, Merrill turned to her brother. "Zadoc, you really are so clueless sometimes."

He threw her a puzzled look, his lips drawn down. "What are you talking about?"

"The same thing I've been hinting to you for months. But now I'm going to just come right out with it. You know that Corabeth is sweet on you. I happen to think you like her, too. She's hoping you'll ask her to next month's church party."

Zadoc looked at her with a blank expression for a moment. It wasn't long, however, before his face lit up with a cocky grin. "She's sweet on me, eh?"

Merrill sighed. "Forget I said anything. If my brothers are too dim-witted to know when a girl likes them, then they deserve to be bachelors."

She reached the wagon, where her father took her arm and guided her into the seat beside him. Zadoc joined his brothers in the back.

"Guess what?" Merrill heard Zadoc exclaim. "Corabeth Lassiter likes me."

Merrill rolled her gaze toward heaven as her father put the team in motion. *Lord*, she prayed, *you've got your hands full with that one. Help him to not miss out on what you have in mind for him. And maybe for Corabeth.*

Rurik had figured the Sunday meal would be a simple affair, but he was pleased to discover an overflowing smorgasbord of food. Apparently Merrill Krause had prepared the meal the day before. There were dishes he recognized and some he didn't, but he was eager to try them all.

"Merrill is the best cook in the state," Carl told him. "She wins at the fair all the time."

"Oh, you can stop that now, Mr. Jorgenson," Merrill admonished. "Otherwise your nephew will come to expect far too much." She positioned a bowl of green beans and *spaetzle* on the table and took her seat.

Mr. Krause bowed his head and spoke what Rurik presumed was a prayer. He didn't understand the German words, however.

"*Komm, Herr Jesu; sei du unser Gast, und segne, was du uns bescheret hast. Amen.*"

Merrill Krause quickly interpreted, "Come, Lord Jesus, be our guest and bless what you have bestowed. Amen."

"Amen," Rurik murmured.

"My father sometimes forgets that not everyone speaks German," she explained with a smile.

"Just like my family with Swedish," he replied.

"Ja, we sometimes still talk in the old language, don't we, Rurik?" his uncle asked in that typical Scandinavian cadence.

"We do. I like to keep the language familiar," he said. "I'm sure there are many similarities between Swedish and German."

"Ja," Merrill replied, and she smiled again.

The bowls and platters were passed around the table, and Rurik found himself enjoying a most pleasant lesson in German cuisine. There were dishes that he hoped to have again soon, and some that he was less enthusiastic about. By the time Merrill brought apple strudel and whipped cream to the table, Rurik thought it would be impossible to eat another bite.

He found himself to be wrong on that count, however. The warm apple dessert all but melted in his mouth, a buttery richness that made him long for more. When the meal concluded, he was almost embarrassed to admit he'd had two helpings and would have taken a third had the platter not been empty.

"Goodness, but I don't know when I've had such a fine meal," Carl declared. "Merrill, I don't know if I've told you this or not, but your strudel is my favorite dessert. I like it better than anything else."

"You are very kind to say so, Mr. Jorgenson. And just for that, I shall make you a strudel all your own and bring it to you later this week."

The man beamed and elbowed Rurik. "See there, by golly, that's how you get a strudel for yourself."

Rurik nodded and patted his stomach. "It was quite delicious. My sister-in-law is a fine Swedish cook, but this surpasses even her abilities."

"Maybe you should get Svea up here to learn how to make strudel," Carl suggested, then turned to the others. "She is Rurik's intended. They will no doubt marry soon."

Rurik started to contradict his uncle, then thought better of it. A public setting such as this was no place to discuss family matters. Rurik had failed to tell his uncle about Svea's decision; he could explain on the way home.

"Well, you are welcome to join us anytime," Bogart Krause announced. "Now, why don't we head into the front room and we'll play some checkers."

Carl shook his head. "I'm afraid I must decline. I know it is impolite, but I think I need to get home and rest. Please forgive me, but I will have Rurik drive me home now."

"There's nothing to forgive, Carl. You never have to worry about formalities around here," Mr. Krause said. "In fact, I think I'd like a nap myself."

Rurik got to his feet and helped his uncle up. He looked back to thank Merrill again for the delicious meal but found she was already gone. No doubt already at work putting away the food and doing the dishes.

On the drive home, Rurik decided to tell his uncle what had happened with Svea. He went into some detail about wanting to do what was honorable to his father's memory, but that he didn't love Svea as a husband should and he didn't think she loved him either—in fact, she had all but banished him after their last interaction. For several minutes Carl said nothing, and Rurik feared he had offended his uncle.

"You know, a man has to trust God first," Uncle Carl said after some time. "I told your father that such marriages were old-fashioned and even dangerous in these modern times. He wouldn't listen to my advice."

"So you aren't disappointed with me?" Rurik asked just as they reached the edge of town.

"Disappointed?" Carl laughed. "I couldn't be upset at a man for listening to God. Son, you should never marry anyone unless you feel certain it is the woman God has given you for your helpmate. You cannot undo a marriage . . . I would have you pray and seek the Lord and do His will. My brother vas good intentioned, but not so good at understanding the heart." Carl grew thoughtful and was silent a moment before he continued. "You should not marry out of a sense of obligation, but rather by the Lord's direction. Otherwise, you will be most unhappy. And so will she."

Chapter 8

January was slipping by at a rapid pace for Rurik. He found his experiences at Jorgenson Furniture fulfilling; the detail and quality of the workmanship met with his approval, and he was proud to come alongside the men and be a part of the items produced. He also began to recognize the positives and negatives of handling a large number of employees and deadlines.

"You're a quick learner," Carl commented as he motioned Rurik to sit with him in his office. "You always were."

Rurik took the seat and smiled. "You are a good teacher. I'm also happy to say you've been looking a bit stronger of late. Your color is much better."

"That's what I want to talk to you about. Your being here has given me great peace of mind. I've long wondered what I would do about this place . . . you know . . . if my illness got worse."

Nodding, Rurik leaned back in the chair. "I'm glad I've been able to lend a hand."

"Well, I've been thinking about another way you could help me out."

"Anything, Uncle Carl. You know that."

The older man nodded and folded his hands. "I've been thinking a long time about expanding the business. The orders are coming in more regularly and the requests are for larger quantities. I could easily double the size of the workshop. I can certainly afford it. However, I don't have the strength to do it alone. I need a partner."

Rurik was surprised by this announcement and didn't try to hide it. "I don't . . . I don't know what to say. Are you suggesting *I* become that partner?"

"Who else?" Carl raised his hands, emphasizing his words. "All of this should go to a family member after I'm gone. If you come in as my partner, there will be no hesitation in leaving it to you. I'd like to know that it stays with the Jorgenson name." The idea of moving to Minnesota permanently and taking over the Jorgenson Furniture business had never occurred to Rurik. He had always hoped to begin his own business, but to start with something already this well established was more than he could have dreamed.

"You've definitely caught me by surprise," Rurik said. "But what about the men who work for you? Surely there's a man among them that would make a good partner."

"The men are good, but they aren't family. I've never so much as hinted that I might take a partner. I think, however, with your coming here they all figure this is what I'm planning to do. They like you, Rurik. You're honest and hardworking, and you've got an understanding of this business and my hopes for it. There's no one better suited to take over, carry it on."

He paused and looked at Rurik, concern in his expression. "I realize you would have to leave your brothers and sisters—all your friends, as well. Coming here might not be to your liking."

"It isn't that," Rurik said, shaking his head. "It's just that I always figured I'd start my own business and bring in a good friend to run the office and sales part for me. Nils Olsson is the brother of Svea—the girl I was engaged to. Nils and I have been friends a long time. I figured even if I didn't marry Svea, I would still continue with the plans to work with Nils."

"You could invite him to join us here after we expand. I would like to have someone take on the office work. That way I'd be free to do more designing. Then after I'm gone, you could make him your partner."

The idea held more potential than Rurik could have hoped. "I suppose this might sound strange," Rurik began, "but have you prayed about this? Have you sought out counsel from others? It seems maybe a bit abrupt. . . ." His voice trailed off, and he looked carefully at his uncle.

Carl laughed. "I've been thinking about it since you were a boy. When Aron told me that you had no desire to be a farmer, I have to admit the idea began to take root. I have prayed long and hard about such an arrangement, and now it's time for you to do the same. I don't expect you to give me an answer without taking time to really think it through, pray about it along with me, and talk to your own family."

Rurik nodded and rubbed his chin. "I will. Maybe I'll write to Nils, discuss it with him, as well."

"Good. That's all I ask. I can't help but believe God brought you here for such a reason. However, like you, I want to be sure."

Later, while sanding the intricate curlicues of an étagère, Rurik found himself praying for guidance. There really was no reason to return to Kansas. His brother's family didn't need him, and Svea had made it clear she would just as soon never see him again. Thinking about that now, in fact, gave Rurik a great sense of relief. He could easily send for the remainder of his things, and Carl had more than enough room for him to stay on at the house.

To his surprise, however, it was the mental image of Merrill Krause that made the possibility even more appealing. He didn't know why, but he had found himself thinking of her more and more of late. He'd seen her several times at church, as well as when she'd come to deliver food to his uncle. He'd even gone to help with another ice harvest and, truth be told, had done so in order to see her again. The feelings he had lacked for Svea Olsson were abundantly present for this young woman he hardly knew. Of course, knowing that he'd be leaving in another month or so had kept Rurik's feelings in check. However, if he stayed on in Waseca and became his uncle's partner . . .

"So, Lord, how does Merrill Krause fit in the plans you have for me?" he prayed.

⁓

"Mr. Jorgenson?" Merrill had knocked several times on the man's front door, and now she was worried. She smiled in relief when he finally opened the door and welcomed her inside. "I thought perhaps you were at the shop." In truth, however, she feared he'd fallen too ill to hear her knocks.

"No. I was stoking the stove in the kitchen. Did I keep you waiting long?"

"Not so long," she said, holding up a basket. "I come bearing gifts."

"Oh, you take such good care of me."

Merrill followed him through the house to the kitchen and waited while he checked the fire. "Ja," he said, nodding his approval. "The fire is good."

"Are you preparing a meal?" she asked.

"Ja. Rurik will be here soon." He straightened and pointed to a cast-iron skillet. "I boiled some potato sausage earlier, and now I'm frying them up for our dinner."

"Why don't you let me do that?" she suggested, placing the basket on the table. She quickly unbuttoned her coat. "I have some extra time, and besides, some of the food I've brought will go well with the sausages."

Carl didn't argue with her, but took a seat at the kitchen table and checked the contents of the basket. "I see you made *kladdkaka*. My favorite."

"I knew it was. I thought you might enjoy some. Granny gave me the recipe at Christmas."

Carl was already pinching a piece of the cake off to sample. "Just as good as my mor used to make."

She smiled. "I had a strudel for you as well, but . . . I'm afraid Flynn got into it. He didn't realize I had made it for you. I promise, however, I will make you another and hide it from my brothers."

Chuckling, Carl took another piece of the kladdkaka. "This will do for now."

Glancing around the room, Merrill didn't see any sign of an apron, so she grabbed a dish towel. Fishing out a couple of safety pins from her pocket, Merrill quickly fastened the towel over the front of her flannel shirt and wool skirt. This would save her clothes from most of the grease splatters.

"Mr. Jorgenson—"

"Please, just call me Carl. You can even call me Uncle Carl as Rurik does."

Merrill nodded. "Since I have no living uncles, I would like that very much. But in return for that favor, I would like to ask you a question. And if you don't want to answer, that's all right."

"Ja, you go ahead."

"Why did you never marry?" With the sausages starting to sizzle in the skillet, Merrill went to the table and began lifting items out of the basket. "Like I said, if you'd rather not tell me, I understand." She searched his face to make certain she hadn't offended him.

Carl smiled. "I was married once. Not long, but long enough."

Merrill frowned. "Was it . . . well, was it that bad?"

He laughed. "No, it was that good. So good I never wanted another wife. She was a very sweet woman, but she died of typhoid not long after we were married. I had loved her for a long time, and no one else could replace her."

"I'm sorry Mr. Jor—Uncle Carl. I didn't know. You must

think me terribly nosy for asking. I apologize." She held up a jar of sauerkraut. "Would you like some with the sausages?"

"Ja, that would be good." He helped himself to a cup of coffee. "You don't need to apologize. I don't mind the question."

"Well, I didn't want to bring up bad memories."

"My memories of Mary are all good—except for her passing. She was such a wonderful woman." His accent thickened. "But she was frail and tiny. Not healthy like you, Merrill."

She smiled and turned back to the sausages. There would never be anything frail or tiny about her. Taking up a fork, Merrill gently turned the sausages to brown them evenly.

"We married after the War of the Rebellion," he continued. "In August 1865. She was just eighteen. Before the first snow, she was gone."

"I am so very sorry," Merrill said, wishing she hadn't brought up the subject.

"I'm sorry for the loss, but not sorry to have loved her," Carl said. "Mary was the best thing to happen to me."

Merrill changed the topic by going back to the table and pulling a large loaf of bread from the basket. "Would you like me to slice this up?"

"That would be good." He gave his stomach a pat. "I'm mighty hungry."

Merrill heard the front door open, and her heart gave a little leap. *No*, she told herself, *he is engaged*. . . .

Carl pulled his pocket watch out and nodded. "That's Rurik. He'll be hungry, too."

"Well, dinner is just about ready. Where do you keep your dishes?"

Carl pointed to the cupboard, and Merrill went right to work. She was taking the first of the sausages from the skillet and arranging them on a plate when she heard Rurik say, "Smells mighty good, Uncle Carl—" He stopped. "Miss Krause, I didn't know you'd come to visit."

"Ja, she brought us some good food and then stayed to cook for us," Carl announced. "Look— kladdkaka, just as good as your mor used to make."

"Have a seat," Merrill said, keeping her voice matter-of-fact. "Everything is ready, so I'll leave you two to eat in peace."

"No, you must stay and eat with us," Carl insisted. "After all, the workman is due his wage, as the Good Book says."

"Yes, the workman is indeed due his wage," Merrill agreed, pulling pins from her makeshift apron. "But my workmen at home will wonder why they have no hot supper if I don't get going. I left them a nice stew on the stove for lunch, but they'll want something more for the evening meal."

She took the last of her offerings from the basket. "Here are some more cookies. I know you brought some home on Sunday, but I figured they didn't last long." She smiled at the two men.

"And they haven't," Rurik admitted, chuckling. "I'm afraid I'm to blame."

His bold gaze warmed her to her toes. Merrill found Rurik most compelling, but she reminded herself once again that he belonged to another.

She picked up her coat and slipped it on. "I'm glad you liked them."

Taking up her basket, Merrill bid the men good-bye and

hurried from the house, feeling overcome by her emotions. For the life of her, Merrill couldn't understand what was happening. She teetered dangerously on the brink of falling for a man who'd already been spoken for!

"Such foolishness," she chided herself.

"Miss Krause!"

She turned to find Rurik running toward her. She took a breath to still her nerves and faced him with a smile. "Yes?"

"You forgot these," he said, holding up her mittens.

"Oh, goodness. Thank you. I would have missed those for sure before I got home."

He smiled. "Thank you for seeing to Uncle Carl. I suppose you know he isn't well."

Merrill nodded. "Yes. I think the entire town knows that. He's a dear man. He's been so good to folks here that all of us want to see to his needs." Not knowing what else to say, Merrill took the mittens from Rurik and pulled them on. "Thank you again."

Rurik held her gaze and nodded. "Tell your father that if he needs my help on Saturday, I should be able to come. Just send word."

"I will," Merrill agreed.

"By the way, I wonder if I might ask you about something else?"

Merrill looked at him and nodded.

"Well, after seeing your artistic ability, I'm wondering if you would consider painting a pie safe for us. I know Uncle Carl has some buyers coming later in February. I thought if we could show them what you can do with the four seasons on the doors of the safe, it might generate some interest and orders. Would you like to try it? I mean, it could require a commitment on your part if it turns out like I'm hoping, but you would be paid."

"You mean paint the pie safes on a regular basis?"

He smiled. "I have a feeling they will be very popular. You might find yourself with more than a little bit of work."

She frowned. "I don't know that I would have the time. I mostly painted ours in the evening after chores were done." She thought of Granny's suggestion that they hire a woman to help out at home. Maybe if Merrill were making a regular wage painting the cupboards, she could pay for help herself.

"Well, you wouldn't have to do as much detail," Rurik suggested. "Maybe a simpler scene for each season. Keeping it modest might also allow for doing a number of them in quick succession."

"I suppose I could try my hand at one, and see what I manage to put together. Your uncle might not like it at all."

"I have no doubt he'll love it as much as I did, Miss Krause. I'm telling you: Women across the country will be fighting over your decorations."

Merrill shook her head and smiled. "Well, I wouldn't want to stir up fights, but if you bring a safe out to the house, I'll give it a try."

"I'll get one out to you right away."

"All right, then," she said and turned to go.

"It was nice to see you again," Rurik called after her.

Merrill gave a little wave, then hurried off.

Merrill tried her best not to think of Rurik Jorgenson and his gentle smile as she began supper preparations for her own men. She focused her attention on her tasks and reminded herself that she was most likely not meant to court and marry. As she had told Granny Lassiter, it was her duty to see to her widowed father's needs.

By suppertime her father and brothers had returned from loading ice onto the train cars. They were tired and hungry, and she poured cups of hot coffee and waited for them to wash up before coming to the table. She remembered Rurik's invitation as her father came to sit beside her at the head of the table.

"I saw Mr. Jorgenson today," she began. "His nephew, Rurik, said to send word if you need him to help on Saturday."

Her father nodded and asked, "How was Carl?"

"He didn't look too bad. I think having his nephew there has been a relief." She glanced at Flynn. "He was disappointed that I failed to bring him strudel."

"Aw, you didn't tell him it was my fault, did you?" her brother asked.

"I did, but he seemed forgiving once he tasted the kladdkaka."

Her father laughed. "That will teach you, Flynn. Your sister will no doubt start hiding the desserts from now on."

"She can't hide them anywhere we can't find them," Zadoc teased.

Father shook his fork in the direction of his two youngest sons. "You'd best be on your guard and do what you know is right. Merrill isn't above teaching you both a lesson." He winked at his daughter. "A dose or two of castor oil or ipecac might do the trick."

"Don't be giving her ideas," Flynn said, his face screwed up in disgust.

Merrill rolled her eyes. "I can think up plenty on my own. Anyway, don't forget about Rurik's offer."

Her father nodded. "This Rurik is a hard worker. I know Carl hopes he'll take over the furniture business."

"In Waseca?" she asked.

"Yes. He told me he has offered to make Rurik his partner and heir."

There was no time to ask further questions as her noisy brothers joined them at the table. Merrill couldn't help but wonder if Rurik would do as his uncle wanted. Would he return to Kansas and marry his intended and then come to Waseca to live? Would Merrill like this woman Rurik planned to make his wife?

"You seem mighty deep in thought," Leo said, elbowing her. "Father is ready to pray, and you're just gawkin' around."

Merrill murmured an apology and bowed her head while her father blessed the food.

"I suppose you're thinking on Molly," Leo said around a bite. "I checked on her just before we came in. I think she'll probably foal soon. I put her in the birthing pen. She'll be just fine there."

"Thank you," Merrill said and forced a smile. "That definitely eases my worries a bit." No one seemed the wiser that her thoughts were on a certain six-foot-three-inch Swede rather than a nineteen-hands-high broodmare.

Chapter 9

It was now early February, and Merrill had to admit she was pleased with the results of the pie safe. She had taken Rurik's advice and painted four seasonal scenes, keeping them fairly simple. Autumn showed a few cornstalks and pumpkins. Winter presented a snowy pine sheltering a white rabbit, while spring was represented by a colorful grouping of flowers surrounding a water pump. Summer bore a collection of fruits and vegetables on a table. It wasn't anywhere near as detailed as her own pie safe, but it had taken very little time to create.

Without further delay, Merrill wrapped a carriage blanket around the little safe, hoisted it in her arms, and loaded it in the wagon. She went to retrieve Jack and Jill, an older team of Belgians, and led them out of the barn.

The winter air took her breath away, and Merrill quickly wrapped a knitted scarf around her face. The cold temperatures were a blessing for ice harvesting, but not for much else. It was difficult to harness horses with mittens, so Merrill worked quickly without them. By the time she had the team ready to go, her fingers were stiff and red from the cold.

She put on her mittens, climbed to the wagon seat, and

tucked a couple of thick blankets around her wool skirt. She was grateful for the trousers and long underwear she had on underneath, but the blankets were a requirement. Merrill doubted the temperatures had even reached zero that day.

Jack and Jill didn't seem to mind the cold, their thick sorrel coats keeping them warm enough. But Merrill knew that ice would no doubt collect around their eyes and nose as they journeyed into town.

On days like this, Merrill was especially careful to make one trip count for many purposes. She had a list of supplies to pick up, a long-overdue visit with Granny and Corabeth, banking to tend to, and, of course, the pie safe to deliver.

Merrill couldn't help but wonder if Rurik would like her artistic work. She had struggled with her feelings for him the entire time she'd painted the safe, and her prayers bore witness to the wrestling of her conscience. Rurik was a handsome and considerate man, and she couldn't help but be impressed by the way he was always ready to lend her father a hand. Father had mentioned that Rurik had never asked about pay but offered his work freely as a family member might. Bogart Krause still intended to pay the Swede for his work, however, and had been setting aside a portion of the earnings for him with each and every job. She smiled, however, knowing it might well prove an interesting match to see which stubborn man won that argument.

Merrill's thoughts kept her busy and the drive to town passed quickly. She reached Waseca about the same time one of the regular trains was ready to pull out. The hissing and steam of the locomotive engine upset Jack and Jill, so Merrill drew them to a halt and waited for the train to clear the area before heading toward the furniture workshop.

"See there," she chided the horses, "it's only a much bigger horse made of iron and steam." But even as she teased the team, Merrill remembered it hadn't been that long ago that an accident with another wagon and train had claimed the life of a man. Perhaps Jack and Jill were the smart ones when it came to avoiding such encounters.

Once the train was well down the track, Merrill drew the team up close to one of the large loading doors at Jorgenson Furniture and set the brake. She put aside her blankets and climbed down from the wagon. Merrill debated whether she should manage transporting the pie safe by herself. What would Rurik think of her if she came strolling into the shop carrying the safe the way a man might?

"I'm being silly," she told herself. "I can't worry about what he thinks. I'm a strong, capable woman."

Without further consideration, Merrill wrestled the piece from the back of the wagon and maneuvered toward the shop. To her surprise, the large door swung open and with no further warning the pie safe was taken from her arms.

She knew without seeing him that the man now carrying the piece was Rurik. She followed him into the shop, pulling the large wooden door closed behind her.

"You should have come to get me," he said, putting the pie safe on the floor. "I know these aren't that heavy, but I sure wouldn't want you to strain yourself."

Merrill pulled the scarf from her face and nearly pulled her wool bonnet off at the same time. She quickly attempted to readjust the hat before her unruly hair escaped, but it was no use. Brown-black curls tumbled down over her shoulders in a most improper fashion.

Rurik's gaze lingered on her hair before he said in a husky voice, "You should wear it like that more often."

Merrill shook her head and attempted to gather the wayward locks. "Granny Lassiter would have my hide. She already gets after me for wearing trousers under my skirts."

"In weather this cold, I believe you to be the wisest woman in Waseca." He reached down for the blanket covering the pie safe. "Now, let's see what you managed to come up with." He studied Merrill's work for a moment. "How long did it take you?"

"Not that long," Merrill replied. "I did a bit on each season and let the paint dry. Then I added a little more and let that dry. Keeping the scenes simple, as you suggested, I found the work went fast. Of course, though, you might think the scenes are not detailed enough."

He shook his head. "Not at all. I find them charming." He looked back at her. "I think Uncle Carl will definitely approve. Let me see where he is."

Rurik quickly headed off to get his uncle. Merrill couldn't help but smile to herself. *He likes my painting.* She recognized the admiration in his eyes and that, coupled with his comment about the scenes being charming, made Merrill quite happy.

"Ah, Merrill Jean," Carl said as he came into the finish room. "Rurik tells me you have made something special for us."

"Well, that will depend on what you consider special," she replied. "I only followed Mr. Jorgenson's instructions."

Carl looked at the pie safe and nodded. "You're right, Rurik. I believe I could sell a hundred of these overnight." He looked back to Merrill. "I have some fellas coming in from Minneapolis soon. I'll have them take the piece back with them and secure orders. That is, if you're interested in painting more of these."

"I think I would like to give it a try," Merrill said. "It will, of course, depend on how much time it takes. I'll need to speak to Father about the matter to see if he can spare me."

"Ja, you do that. I think I'll have a big demand for this." Carl returned his gaze to the painted scenes. "But I wouldn't want to show it to my buyers if you can't supply us with more."

Merrill nodded. "I understand."

Rurik smiled at her. "I told you he would like it." He turned to his uncle. "How about we put in a little workshop for her here? We can purchase whatever paints Miss Krause needs, and since we will already have the pie safes here, it will save the time and effort of transporting them to and from the Krause farm."

"Ja, that would be good," Carl said, nodding. "There's plenty of room to do that."

Merrill frowned. She hadn't really thought of driving into town every day to work on painting pie safes. How would she keep her household duties under control? She would definitely have to hire a woman to come in. And what would she do with the team? She could hardly afford to stable them each day.

"I don't know . . . I mean . . . well, that would take me

away from home." Merrill tried to think of how she might handle the situation.

"Well, you wouldn't have to come every day," Rurik suggested. "Maybe when we have a dozen or more pie safes ready, you could come and paint all of them at once. You mentioned needing to give the scenes time to dry. You could go down the line from one safe to another, and by the time you finished with the last, enough time might have passed for the paint to dry on the first one."

Merrill nodded. "I suppose that could work, but I'll still need to speak with Father on the matter. We'll need to consider hiring a woman to come help with the chores at the farm . . . then there's the team. I'll have to figure out what to do with them."

"You can put them in the pen with my horses," Carl declared. "They should be just fine."

It seemed a reasonable conclusion. Merrill couldn't help but feel excited by the possibility of using her creativity in such a productive way. "I'll talk to Father this evening."

"Good," Carl replied. "I can talk to Bogart, too, if need be. You just let me know."

Then the small side door opened, and a man and woman entered the room. To Merrill's surprise, the young woman rushed across the room and threw herself into Rurik's arms.

"There he is! Oh, Rurik! We've found you at last."

Merrill looked away rather than let anyone see how stunned she was. The woman's companion spoke up, however, drawing her attention back to the drama unfolding before her.

"Svea, you are making a spectacle of yourself."

Svea. This woman was Rurik's fiancée. Merrill felt as if the wind had been knocked from her. She forced herself to stand steady, but in her heart she wanted to run from the room. The last thing in the world she wanted was to encounter the woman who held Rurik's heart.

As if reading Merrill's thoughts, Svea let go of Rurik and turned to Merrill.

"Goodness," she said, tipping her head to one side. "We haven't been introduced, but you probably know I'm Rurik's intended, Svea Olsson. This is my brother Nils." She motioned him forward.

"What . . . what on earth are you doing here?" Rurik asked, looking less than pleased.

Carl seemed to sense this and stepped forward. "I'm Carl Jorgenson, Rurik's uncle."

"Oh yes," Svea said, nodding. "I remember you from long ago. You're the one who taught Rurik to make furniture."

"Ja, me and his farfar." Carl smiled. "And I remember you, too. Although you were much younger then."

Svea laughed in a most feminine manner. "But I'm a woman full grown now."

Merrill felt like an intruder and wondered how she might slip from the room without being noticed. She wanted nothing more to do with this reunion. But she felt transfixed—helpless to move.

"May I ask what brings you here?" Rurik said again, this time sounding calmer as he addressed Nils.

"What a silly question," Svea said, moving to take hold of his arm. "I came to be with you, Rurik. You wrote to Nils about working here, and when he thought to come, I knew I had to join him."

"But I only discussed the possibility of a job," Rurik said, narrowing his gaze at Nils.

Nils shrugged apologetically. "I suppose I did get the cart ahead of the horse, but your letter intrigued me, and I didn't want to wait. Forgive me if this is an intrusion."

Rurik seemed unsure of how to proceed. He looked toward Merrill, and for a moment she thought she saw something like regret in his eyes.

"I need to be on my way," Merrill finally was able to manage.

"Are you sure you can't stay?" Rurik's question sounded almost desperate.

She could see Svea was annoyed. "Yes, I have a great deal to accomplish while I'm in town," she answered quickly. "It was good to meet you, Miss Olsson . . . Mr. Olsson." She turned and headed quickly to the door.

Once outside, Merrill hurried to the wagon, tucking her hair under her bonnet as she went. Her only thought was to get away from the furniture shop as soon as possible. She climbed into the wagon seat, bonnet ties flying in the breeze. Her face tingled from the sharp, cold air, but Merrill ignored it and released the brake.

"Walk on, Jack. Walk on, Jill. Warmth and good feed await you," she promised. She took a deep breath to try and get her emotions under control.

Waseca's main street bustled with activity, and Merrill found it necessary to weave the team back and forth to avoid pedestrians and other wagons. The horses seemed to understand they were headed for the livery stable, however, and made their way without Merrill having to do much to guide them.

Once she had arranged for the team's care, paying for their stabling with a large container of cookies, she took up her shopping basket along with another filled with baked goods for Granny, and made her way to the mercantile. Inside the store, Merrill found her thoughts reliving the encounter at Jorgensons'. Svea Olsson was everything Merrill had imagined her to be: petite, pretty, and fashionable. Svea had blond hair peeking out from her winter bonnet—no doubt the latest style just in from back east, not a redo of someone's hand-me-down. Merrill frowned at her ungracious attitude and tried not to allow her feelings to consume her, but she had to admit she was jealous. There was no other word for it. Not only was she jealous of Svea's delicate features, lovely clothing, and appealing figure; Merrill envied her relationship with Rurik, too.

"Miss Krause," a deep voice called. "How can I help you today?" The clerk beamed.

"I have a list," Merrill said, handing it to him along with the empty basket. "I wonder if you might fill it, and after I visit with Granny Lassiter I can come back to pick it up."

"Certainly." The man looked the paper over. "I presume your pa will want the saw blades he ordered, as well. They came in yesterday."

"Yes," Merrill replied. "I know he'll be quite happy to hear that news."

"Well, you just go on about your business, and I'll have this ready for you this afternoon. Bring the wagon around back when you're ready to go, and I'll get things loaded."

"Thank you," she told the man. "I shouldn't be much past one."

Exiting the store, she caught sight of Rurik and his visitors. Svea held his arm possessively as they entered the hotel across the street.

"Put it from your mind, Merrill Jean," she muttered under her breath.

She hurried toward the residential area, where the Lassiter house welcomed her with the promise of warmth. Granny and Corabeth looked happy to see her as usual and, amidst their rapid chatter, pulled her inside.

"We wondered if you would make a visit today," Corabeth enthused. "Didn't we, Granny?"

"Looks nice enough outside, but it's awfully cold," Granny said, taking the proffered basket from Merrill. "Goodness, but why isn't your bonnet tied?"

There was no chance to answer as the older woman pushed Merrill into a seat at the kitchen table and looked through the contents of the basket. "These look most inviting, Merrill. Thank you." She nodded appreciatively, then continued. "Did you hear the sad news about Mr. Middaugh's brother, Solomon?" she asked.

Merrill shook her head and sipped at the tea Corabeth had put in front of her.

Granny's expression grew grim. "He was making his way home, driving a wagon of lumber and tin roofing," she began. "He was about a mile from his house when something happened, and the tongue broke away. The horses were spooked and ran, and of course the wagon could not hold together in all the uproar. It sent poor Solomon into the air and entangled him in one of the wagon wheels. Broke both legs just below the knee."

"Oh, how awful," Merrill said, picturing the terrible scene.

"That's not all," Granny continued. "There was no one around to help him. He had to crawl quite a distance and bled all the way. The only thing that kept him from bleeding to death was the cold. It froze the wounds."

Merrill shuddered. "And only a mile from his house?"

"Yes," Corabeth nodded, her expression sad. "But he was alone all night."

"Some children on their way to school found him the next morning—more dead than alive. He was taken home, but I'm sorry to say he didn't survive." Granny shook her head again. "The poor horses were found later. One was still pulling the front axle and one wheel."

Merrill could only imagine the fear the horses experienced. "When did this happen?"

"A couple of weeks ago. Mr. Middaugh posted a letter in the Waseca County *Herald*." Granny picked up her teacup. "A person just never knows when life will end," she went on. "Makes you mindful of eternal matters, doesn't it?"

"Life just seems so unpredictable sometimes," Corabeth said, sounding thoughtful. Merrill wondered if she was thinking about Zadoc.

Merrill's own thoughts turned to Svea and Nils Olsson's surprise visit, and she nodded slowly. "Yes, life is full of surprises, some of them rather unpleasant." But at their quizzical glances, she quickly changed the subject.

Chapter 10

Rurik led the way into the hotel lobby. "I'll arrange for the depot master to have your bags delivered. This is a nice hotel, and I think you'll find the rooms comfortable." He stepped aside as Nils reserved two rooms.

When they reached room number five, Nils opened the door. It boasted an iron bed, small sofa, and electric lamps. The adjoining room included another bed, rocking chair, and lamp. It seemed to meet with Svea's approval, and she turned to give Rurik a smile.

"It will suit us for the time being," she said, pulling her gloves off.

"Kind of nice to have electricity, ja?" Rurik said, switching on the lamp. "Uncle Carl has it in the shop, and it's a lot easier than trying to work by lantern light."

"It's cold in here," Nils commented.

"I'll make sure you have extra blankets. You should be able to get the train back to Kansas tomorrow," Rurik declared. "I'll check on the schedule for you."

Svea stopped and looked at him with a frown. "We aren't going back to Kansas tomorrow."

"We've no reason to go back," Nils confirmed. "My father has replaced me. He hired a regular office manager. He's insisting that I get out on my own, so here I am."

Rurik shook his head. "But as I told you in the letter, there isn't a job yet available for you—"

"I can't go back." Nils's statement was simple and to the point.

Svea rushed at Rurik, her face a whirlwind of emotions. "You cannot mean to send us away," she wailed. "I'm here because I decided to forgive you and reinstate our engagement." She took hold of his arm. "You were very unkind to me, but I believe I understand now. You were just concerned for your uncle. That's actually quite admirable of you."

"I wasn't being unkind to you, Svea, and there's nothing for you to forgive . . . unless it's the fact that I let the engagement go on so long. It truly wasn't fair to burden you in such a way."

She shook her head quickly. "Rurik, our engagement wasn't a burden, and I resent you suggesting it was. Goodness knows I want to please you, but I cannot acknowledge our engagement as anything but wonderful. I'm sorry I lost my temper back in Lindsborg, but when you said you were going away . . . it frightened me."

Rurik looked to Nils, but he only shrugged and walked to the window. Turning back to Svea, Rurik tried to choose his words carefully. "Svea, I'm sorry that I frightened you, but you must understand something."

"And what is that?" she asked, obviously trying to sound coy but ending up whining.

He drew a deep breath. "I do not wish to reinstate our

engagement." He wanted to emphasize each word so there was no mistaking his meaning. "After you ended it, I felt nothing but a sense of relief. I've long feared that our betrothal was wrong. We are very different, you and I, and I cannot give you the life you desire, with travel—"

"You brought me here to Waseca," she put in stubbornly.

"I didn't bring you here," he said, shaking his head. "In fact, I had no idea you were coming at all. I'm sorry if that offends or hurts you."

"You're simply surprised to see us." Svea threw her gloves onto the bed. "I can't blame you. We probably should have sent a wire to let you know we were arriving, but then that would have ruined the surprise."

Nils turned at this. "You have to understand, Rurik, Svea and I have long pinned our hopes on you."

Rurik was perplexed at this statement. "I can't imagine why." He looked between the two of them, trying to figure out what he wasn't understanding about all this.

"Can't you?" Nils crossed the room. "You and I have been best friends all of our lives. We'd always planned to work together. I've not changed my mind on that matter, and your letter to me showed that you hadn't either."

"I wrote to let you know of future possibilities, Nils, but they were *only* possibilities. My uncle wants to take me as a partner in his business. He wishes to expand and add additional workers. I told him of the plans you and I had to open a shop together, and he mentioned that it might work to hire you on to manage the office. But that was something to consider for the future. There is no job available for you at this time."

"Then I'll find something else until you can work it out," Nils said. He brushed back the dark blond hair over his left eye. "I'm sure you can convince your uncle to bring me in sooner than he planned. You've always had a way of setting things right."

Rurik took a long breath, looking from Nils to Svea and back again. "I cannot force you to leave, but you must know that I have no intention of marrying you, Svea, or of pressing my uncle to employ you, Nils. I only wrote to let you know there might one day be a position. I was concerned you might think I'd forgotten our plans if you heard from my brother that Carl wanted to make me a partner. I'm sorry if you read any other intention in my letter."

"This is ridiculous," Svea said, stamping her foot. "We've come hundreds of miles to show you our devotion, and you shun us."

"I'm not shunning anyone, Svea. I'm trying to be reasonable. You've come at a very bad time, I'm afraid. I have many responsibilities, and I cannot act as host to you and your brother." He looked back to Nils. "And, frankly, I'm surprised that you would risk your sister's well-being, bringing her north in the winter cold, on such a pointless venture."

"I made him bring me," Svea declared saucily. "And I think you know why."

"I have no clue." Rurik shook his head. "The last thing I remember from you were the words, 'I hope to never see you again.'"

Rurik didn't wait to see Svea's response but checked his watch instead. "I need to get back to work. I'm sorry that you two traveled here for nothing. Since it seems my letter unintentionally enticed you both to come, I'll help pay your passage back home."

"We're not leaving," Nils said with a stubbornness that surprised Rurik.

He waited for Nils to continue. When the man said nothing, Rurik's irritation could no longer be held in check. "Do as you like, but this is not my problem," he said as firmly as he could without hollering at them. "I've tried to explain the situation, and I've offered to help you get home. If you choose to stay and waste your time and money, I am not responsible."

"Father won't have me back," Nils mumbled. "We've had our differences, and there's no going back."

Rurik eyed his friend for a moment. He wondered what on earth had happened to cause such an irreversible rift between father and son.

Nils turned back to the window. "I have no choice but to stay."

Rurik didn't know what to say. Nils was his friend, and he hated to complicate the man's problems. He supposed he could try to find *something* for Nils to do. Maybe he could help with the ice harvest. There were numerous people in the area who were busy with that task. Maybe a good word from Carl would allow Nils to sign on with one of the harvesters— maybe Mr. Krause?

"I'll speak to Carl," Rurik finally said. "Maybe he'll have some ideas or suggestions. Nevertheless, you need to send Svea back, and she can hardly travel alone. Why don't you escort her home and then return?" Rurik hoped that maybe by the time they got to Kansas, their father would have reconsidered whatever issue had caused the separation between him and Nils. Maybe Mr. Olsson would be so relieved to have them home safe and sound that he would welcome Nils back with open arms. And if not, it would give Rurik a week or two to look into employment opportunities for his friend.

"I cannot go home either," Svea said. "You cannot take advantage of me as you have, and then just dismiss me."

"Take advantage of you? I've done nothing, Svea. *You* were the one to end our engagement. But it was the right decision," Rurik said. "Honestly, Svea, we've been over all this. There is no reason for you to chase after me now. Find a good man who will court you as I cannot. A man who will love you as you deserve."

Svea stepped closer and lowered her voice. "You know full well why I cannot do that."

Rurik looked to Nils and shook his head. Turning back to Svea, he saw tears forming in her eyes. He was astounded. She seemed genuinely distraught. "I have no idea what you're talking about," he finally said.

"It cannot be a secret any longer," Svea said, looking to Nils. "My brother knows all about it, and in a very short time, so shall everyone else. All will know, and you will have no choice but to do right by me."

"What in the world are you talking about, Svea?" But his voice sounded distant in his own ears.

She lifted her chin and fixed him with steely blue eyes. "I'm going to have a baby. Your baby."

The words whirled through Rurik's head all during the afternoon and into the evening. He knew with absolute certainty they weren't true. He'd never been intimate with Svea Olsson or any woman. But that Svea was in such a predicament, and she'd told her brother that Rurik was responsible, was more than he could fathom. Had something happened since he'd left home? But why was she laying the blame at his feet? Was the true father not willing to accept the child as his? On and on his thoughts went as he tried to focus on the work at hand.

As Rurik tightened a clamp to glue two pieces of oak in place, he felt the enormous gravity of the situation. Svea was pregnant.

Nils had jumped right in after her declaration, saying that the entire community of Lindsborg knew the couple to be intended for marriage. Such things often happened, Nils stated, and it was no use worrying about how it came about, but rather to make the situation right. He'd not even listened to Rurik's assurances that he'd never laid a hand upon Svea in such a manner—but then, Svea and Nils were very close. They were the youngest siblings in the Olsson family, and when Nils had taken a fall from a horse some years earlier, it was Svea's faithful tending that brought him through. Rurik had never known a brother and sister to be closer. But Nils was also Rurik's friend and knew his character. Why did he doubt Rurik was telling the truth?

God, you know that I never touched her, he prayed. *Why is this happening? What must I do?*

"I thought I might find you here," Carl said, joining his nephew in the otherwise empty workshop. "Why are you working so late?"

"I have a lot on my mind," Rurik replied, straightening with a sigh.

"Ja, with your friends arriving here unannounced, I can imagine." He smiled. "If you need to take some time off for them, I can spare you a day or so."

"No," Rurik said. "It isn't that at all. Nils took more from my letter than I intended. He came with the expectation of getting a job running your office."

"That I can understand, but what of his sister? She acts as though you two are still betrothed."

Rurik shrugged and put aside his tools. "She says now she would like it to be that way. But I told her I had no intention of reinstating the engagement. I'm not of a mind to marry her. I'm more convinced than ever that we are not meant to be together, and I told her so."

"I'm sorry, son. That couldn't have been easy."

"I just don't understand why she would want to marry a man she knows doesn't love her." Though as Rurik remembered her condition, he realized she was probably scared out of her wits. No doubt someone had dallied with her, and she had yielded her innocence. Perhaps Rurik had been partly to blame, since he was the one to leave and upset her so.

He shook his head. Had his rejection sent her into the arms of a less honorable man? Rurik thought about telling his uncle about her strange declaration, but he didn't get the chance. Carl was leaning hard against the sideboard Rurik was working on, his face pale. "I think I ate too much tonight." He put his hand to his stomach and then to his chest. "I should probably lie down."

"Are you all right?" Rurik asked, hurrying to put an arm around his uncle's waist. "Is it your heart?"

"I think so, but it's nothing new," Carl admitted. "I'll rest and be fine. Just help me to the house."

Rurik all but carried the man from the workshop. "I'll get you tucked in and go for the doctor."

"No. Better to not waste his time. There's nothing he can do," Carl said, though he sounded as if he was in a great deal of pain.

Rurik wondered if his uncle's condition was a lot worse than he'd let on. Perhaps Rurik would speak with the doctor himself, see what the man had to say. If Carl wasn't going to be forthcoming, maybe the doctor would level with him.

Rurik helped his uncle back to the house and then to bed. He pulled the older man's boots from his feet. "Would you like me to help you undress?"

"No . . . I'll just rest here for a . . . a few minutes, then tend to it myself. . . . Sorry to worry you," Carl said, smiling in apology but sounding rather breathless. "No worse than it's been before. Don't fret."

Kneeling by the bed, Rurik shook his head. "I want to help you in any way I can. Just tell me what is to be done."

Carl patted his nephew's hand. "You've already done it by being here. I'm sorry to be a burden."

"You aren't," Rurik argued. "You're family, and . . ." He fell silent for a moment, then added, "My partner."

Smiling, his uncle closed his eyes. "It's good to hear you say so, Rurik. I already feel much better. Tomorrow we'll go see the lawyers, draw up the papers, and then I'll be fit as a fiddle. You'll see."

Rurik nodded, even though his uncle couldn't see him. He'd just committed himself to remain in Waseca. Oddly enough, Rurik's next thought was of Merrill Krause. Would she be pleased to hear that he was going to stay? Of course, after she'd witnessed Svea declaring them to be engaged, Rurik knew he was probably the last person on Miss Krause's mind.

Getting to his feet, Rurik determined he would let her know as soon as possible that Svea was mistaken in her comments. He would explain to Merrill how they had been betrothed by their parents when they were just children, that Svea had ended the engagement before he'd come to Waseca. He'd tell Miss Krause that he had been glad to comply with the girl's edict because he didn't love Svea and felt certain they weren't to be together.

"But how do I explain the rest?" he wondered aloud.

Chapter 11

"You seem to be in a troubled mood, daughter."

Merrill continued clearing dishes from the table. "I'm just busy, I suppose."

"How are the foals?" her father asked. "I didn't have time to check in on them."

"They're all doing well. The cold doesn't seem to be bothering them too much. I put out extra straw and hay." She picked up a nearly empty platter of chicken and headed for the kitchen. The last thing she wanted to do right now was to explain to her father why she was distraught. How could she tell him that she had feelings for a man who was all but married?

She hurried back to the table and reached for the butter dish, but her father stopped her with his strong hand gripping hers. Merrill looked to her father for explanation.

He smiled and let go. "Sit with me awhile."

Merrill did as he asked, hoping he wouldn't ask her to share what was on her mind.

"You know, a young woman like you should be receiving suitors," he said, reaching into his pocket for his pipe and tipping back on the chair legs. "But you are always here attending to me and your brothers."

She tried to smile. "As I am called to do."

"God would have you marry and make a family of your own," her father said, pulling a bag of tobacco from another pocket.

Merrill had never liked the smell of pipe smoke in the house, but it was her father's home and his right. She would never have thought to dishonor him by suggesting otherwise.

He tamped down tobacco into the pipe and continued. "I've long thought a good man would step forward, but maybe some of the fellas around here worry about what your brothers will think." He gave a chuckle. "I can't say that I haven't been glad for their help when you were younger, but now I think I will speak with them."

Merrill quickly shook her head. "Father, I haven't the time for beaus and courtship. It's my job to take care of you and the household. Goodness, with the ice harvest on now, there's scarcely time to get clothes mended, much less washed and ironed. Come spring things will settle down, and then we can see about beaus and such." She was trying to make light of the matter, knowing her father obviously had some concerns.

But he didn't seem to hear her, however. "I don't want you helping with the ice anymore, Merrill. I know you have a good hand with the horses. They obey you better than they do anyone, but they will work for me and the boys just as well. The work is too hard for a young lady, and I've been wrong to have you out there."

She couldn't imagine what had caused her father to say such a thing. "Did Granny Lassiter give you a lecture like she gives me all the time?"

"No, but she would be within her rights if she did," he said, lighting a match and putting it to the pipe bowl. After a couple of puffs, her father filled the air with a heady aroma. "Your mother would not be pleased with the way things have turned out. She would have wanted you to find a mate. I want that for you as well, Merrill Jean. It's only right."

Merrill couldn't wait for the conversation to move in another direction, so she chose that moment to bring up painting the furniture for the Jorgensons. "Well, I'm not opposed to courting, as you know. However, there is something else I wished to discuss with you."

Her father lowered the pipe and nodded. "Go ahead. You'll never have a better time than now, with your brothers all out of the house at their chores."

She smiled. "Well, you know that I painted that pie safe, and Mr. Jorgenson was quite pleased with it. He has asked me to consider painting some more. He has even suggested that he would set up a little workshop for me there in Waseca. He'd have me come only when there were a dozen or so pie safes ready to paint, so it wouldn't be every day."

Her father nodded. "Sounds interesting. Go on."

"Well, Mr. Jorgenson and his nephew feel they can sell quite a few with the illustrations added to them. I would be paid, and with that money I could hire a woman to come in and help with the house and mending."

"I've been thinking for a long time now that we should

hire someone to help you," her father said. "You work much too hard."

"I'm not complaining," she said with a smile. "But, Father, I would very much like to try my hand at painting the furniture. I think it could be quite nice to have a little of my own money—it also makes me feel closer to Mama."

"So that's why you've been troubled this evening?"

"Well, I wasn't really troubled about telling you. It was more that I had a great deal on my mind." She hoped that would satisfy him.

"I think it sounds like a good idea," her father declared, to her relief. "Do you know someone we can hire to help around here?"

"Granny suggested a couple of names a few weeks back. You know she's always after me to get more help," Merrill said, trying her best to sound lighthearted. "I don't know why she frets so. I suppose it's because she can't keep a good eye on me. You know she feels it's her job, in spite of the fact that she's Corabeth's grandmother, not mine."

"She loves you just the same," her father replied. "She always loved your mother, too. I'm pretty sure she promised your mother to look out for you."

Merrill nodded and got to her feet. "I know she did. She's told me that several times. Even so, she can't expect me to be the same as Corabeth. I'm not like her. She's grown up in town with few responsibilities, and I've grown up on a farm with many. I've a much stronger constitution than Corabeth."

She began gathering the dishes once again. Merrill couldn't help but notice her father's frown. "However," she hurried to add, "since Corabeth is sweet on Zadoc, it would probably do her well to toughen up a bit. Zadoc might well surprise us all and ask to court her one day. She'll need to be firm in order to keep that one in line."

Her father's chuckle signaled he'd let go of his worries. "Ja, and isn't that the truth of it."

Sunday after church service, Merrill hurried to find Granny and ask her again for the names of women she thought might be in need of work. Making her way toward the front of the church where Granny and Grandpa Lassiter were busy talking to the pastor and his wife, Merrill stopped in surprise when someone took hold of her arm.

Turning, she found Nils Olsson. He quickly dropped his hold. "I'm sorry for my boldness, but I called to you, and you didn't hear."

Merrill smiled. "I apologize—Mr. Olsson, isn't it? I'm afraid I was a bit focused on finding my friend."

"Not a problem. I simply wanted to greet you. I regret we had very little time to talk the other day at the Jorgensons'."

Merrill wasn't sure why he should regret anything, but there was no denying the man seemed quite serious. "It was a very busy day."

"Yes. For us, as well. You see, we had just arrived by train. The travel from Kansas was quite exhausting, but my sister insisted on seeing her Rurik as soon as possible, so I had no choice but to find him for her. Svea can be most insistent at times."

Not sure what to say, Merrill only nodded and looked away for a moment to see if Granny Lassiter was still engaged. She was. There was no reason to excuse herself just yet, so Merrill did her best to think of some small talk. "So you are from Kansas."

"Yes. Have you been there?"

"No," Merrill replied. "I've never been out of Minnesota."

"And what do you do here?"

"My father raises Belgian draft horses and uses them for freighting, logging, and the ice harvest. I've been a part of that, as well."

"Working with the horses?"

"Yes. I have to say they are a favorite of mine."

"They are quite . . . tall." He grinned. "As are you, if you don't mind my saying so. I find it . . . well, refreshing."

Merrill met his gaze. They were nearly the same height. "Refreshing? Really?"

He laughed. "Well, I suppose that does sound rather silly. I prefer meeting a person eye to eye, even a young lady—but especially a beautiful young lady."

She wasn't used to men flirting with her, and it left Merrill feeling like she'd tried on a dress two sizes too small.

Nils seemed to understand her discomfort and immediately apologized. "I suppose that was again rather bold of me. You no doubt have many suitors vying for your attention."

Again, she wasn't at all sure what to say, so Merrill hurried to change the subject. "What did you do in Kansas . . . for a living?"

He frowned. "My family runs a large dairy."

"Oh, that's very nice. You might find it interesting to learn that we have a new Waseca Creamery. There are a good many dairymen in the area, and everyone believes it will be beneficial to the town."

"I'm afraid my interests have never lingered long on my father's passions. I'm more of a book man."

"A book man?"

"Numbers and such. I find I have a head for mathematics, so I prefer to keep books." He shrugged. "I kept them for my father, but Rurik and I have long planned to go into business together."

Merrill nodded. It made sense that since Rurik was to marry Nils's sister, he had come to Waseca with her in order to get involved in the furniture business. "Have you known Mr. Jorgenson long?"

"All my life. We have always been the best of friends. Our fathers were good friends, as well. In fact, it was they who arranged Rurik and Svea's marriage."

"Arranged it?" Merrill asked. "That seems a very old-fashioned notion. Here we are, approaching a new century. I thought such things had passed away."

"I suppose they have for many. Ours is an old Swedish family, and traditions are highly regarded."

"Merrill, why don't you introduce us," Granny Lassiter said, coming up alongside her.

Relieved to have someone else in the conversation, Merrill provided the introductions. Granny looked Nils up and down and nodded. "It's good to meet you. We think highly of Rurik, and if you're his friend, we're sure to think quite highly of you as well."

Nils smiled and took the opportunity to introduce Svea as she approached with Rurik. "This is my sister. Svea Olsson, meet Mrs. Lassiter."

Svea smiled, but clung to Rurik's arm as if she would drown should she let go. "Pleased to meet you, ma'am."

"Call me Granny. Everybody does," the older woman said. "Where's your uncle, Rurik?"

"He wasn't feeling well this morning. I told him he needed to stay in bed. He wasn't exactly happy about it, but I think he knew it was for the best."

"I'll send him over some soup. In fact, why don't you and your friends come for dinner, and I'll send some food back with you for Carl."

"Thank you, Mrs. Lassiter. I cannot speak for my friends, but I would be honored," Rurik said with a smile.

Granny looked to Nils and Svea. "Will you join us?"

"Of course," Nils replied. He looked toward Merrill. "Will you be there, as well?"

Merrill shook her head. "I'm afraid I have a family to see to myself."

Nils looked around. "You are married?"

Merrill laughed. "No, but my father and brothers would be quite beside themselves if I failed to have Sunday dinner on the table—and quite soon."

Granny shook her head. "I think they could spare you, and you are more than welcome. You always have a place at our table, you know."

Merrill saw Svea frown and almost wished she could accept just to see what might be going on in that pretty little head. "Thank you, Granny, but I must decline."

"Are you sure?" Rurik asked, his tone almost pleading.

Merrill caught the look in his eyes and wished with all her heart that she hadn't. "No, I'm sorry, I can't."

"Well, next time then, my dear," Granny assured her. "Rurik, you know the way to our house. Just be there at one o'clock, and we'll be ready to sit down to dinner." She started to leave, but Merrill reached out to touch her arm.

"Granny, I wonder if I could speak to you for a moment." She stopped and nodded. "What is it, Merrill Jean?"

"I wondered if you might give me the names of the women who were looking to hire out. Father has agreed to let me bring someone in on the days when I'm here in town painting furniture."

"Wonderful!" Granny declared. "Glad to see that Bogart finally has some sense. But what's this about painting furniture?"

Rurik spoke before Merrill could reply. "Carl and I have asked her to add her charming paintings to the doors on pie safes. She's very talented, and the decorations add much value to the pieces."

By now Svea was scowling, and Merrill couldn't help but feel her piercing stare. Ignoring the woman, however, Merrill nodded and smiled at Granny. "I'm going to have a little workshop all my own."

"I think that's marvelous," Granny said, clapping her hands. "And you must come and have lunch with me every day you're here, and tell me all about it."

"I think that would be great fun," Merrill agreed. "I won't be here every day of the week, however. Just a day or two now and then."

"And in time that will no doubt increase," Rurik interjected. "I would imagine once her pieces start selling and the public sees what's available, Miss Krause will find herself with more work than she can manage on merely a day or two. It's my hope that she'll eventually join us on a more permanent basis."

Merrill's eyes widened at this declaration. She found Rurik smiling at her. "I . . . well . . . I suppose we shall see."

"Goodness, Rurik, I doubt her father and brothers would stand for that," Svea said, almost as if she held great authority on the matter.

"Speaking of your father, where is he?" Granny asked. "I want to congratulate him on this great idea to hire some help. I'm quick enough to criticize and lecture the poor man. Praise should be just as quick to come when the right course is chosen."

"He went over to see my uncle." Rurik again spoke before Merrill could respond.

She had been so surprised by Svea's interjection into the discussion that she almost missed Granny's question. Merrill cast a brief glance at Svea, then returned her attention to Granny. "I'm sure Father will support anything we suggest. Why don't we leave Mr. Jorgenson and the Olssons to meet others in the congregation, and I'll take down those names?"

Granny seemed to understand and nodded. "See you at one, Rurik. I'll look forward to getting to know you better,

Miss Olsson—Mr. Olsson." She took hold of Merrill's arm and led her away. In a whisper she murmured, "I don't think that little girl liked you much, but her brother seems quite smitten."

Merrill drew back to look at Granny in shock. "Why do you say that?"

"Well, he couldn't take his eyes off you. He hung on your every word and looked really disappointed that you couldn't join us for dinner. I'd say you have a would-be suitor. If he sticks around Waseca, I'd plan to see him come calling." Once they were well away from the others, Granny stopped. "Now, let's see about the women who might help you."

Granny grasped Merrill's hands in her own and looked so delighted she thought the old woman might well do a jig. "I'm pleased as punch over this, Merrill Jean. Just pleased as punch. Not that I want you working a job for long, but with you over there—why, you'll have any number of bachelors to vie for your attention. Carl has at least ten men on his payroll, and only about half are married. This will be a great opportunity to get you fixed up with one of them."

"Granny! That's not what this is about." Merrill realized she'd been rather loud with her response and lowered her voice. "I like to draw and paint . . . you know that."

The older woman nodded. "I do, but you'll have to excuse me if I see this as an answer to my prayers for you, Merrill Jean." She laughed and patted Merrill's arm. "God's got a hand in this, mark my words."

Merrill wanted to agree and be happy that she would spend time in Rurik's company, but of course that wasn't fitting, and she felt guilty for even considering it. Rurik belonged to another, and it wasn't going to be otherwise by any interference on her part. At least that was Merrill's sincere prayer—even if it wasn't quite what her heart was telling her.

Chapter 12

Merrill took a seat on Granny's newly upholstered sofa and gave her approval of the gold-and-white fabric. "This is very pretty, Granny. I couldn't quite picture it when you first told me about it, but now that I see it . . . well, it's a perfect match for this room."

"The shop in Minneapolis said it was a very durable material," Granny declared. She took a seat in a chair across from Merrill. "The store manager was quite impressed with our little sofa. He said it was quite a nice piece of Queen Anne styling."

"Queen Anne?" Merrill asked.

Corabeth floated into the room wearing her hair up in a new style. "What do you think, Merrill Jean? Granny helped me fix it in the latest fashion. We saw pictures in one of the magazines. It's English."

"Is that a Queen Anne, too?" Merrill asked with a grin.

"No, silly." Corabeth looked a bit deflated, and Merrill immediately regretted teasing her friend.

"You know I have little knowledge of such things," she said quickly. "I think it's quite lovely." Merrill knew that such creations often seemed to appeal to the opposite gender. She studied Corabeth for a moment, wondering if she could ever imitate the fashion. "Please let me see the back also."

The burst of curls that surrounded Corabeth's forehead gave way to rolls of twists and intertwined hair that ascended ever higher upon her head. It was quite a lot of work, Merrill decided.

"You truly look beautiful, Corabeth."

Her friend turned, her expression restored to jubilation. "Do you think Zadoc would like it?"

"I'm sure he would," Merrill replied. "Don't most men like their ladies to be all frilly and full of curls?"

Corabeth took a seat in a chair beside Granny and folded her hands. "I keep hoping he'll ask me to the winter party. I could wear my hair like this if he did."

Merrill was relieved when Granny changed the subject. "So tell us, how is Mrs. Niedermeyer working out?"

"Wonderfully. The benefit of hiring an older married woman is that she already knows so much about running a household. Father seemed pleased with her cooking, too."

"Oh, I'm so glad. You know little Margaret Niedermeyer has worked so hard to keep their family from losing the house after George's accident," Granny said, smoothing the well-worn material of her work skirt.

"I remember when Father told me about George falling from the grain elevator and breaking his back," Merrill said. "Poor man. It must have been a terrible ordeal to go through."

"Well, I'm certain Margaret is excited to have some steady income by helping you out." Granny smiled and winked at

Corabeth. "Now maybe you and Corabeth can do some court-ing. I understand your brother is finally showing some inter-est." Granny reached over and patted Corabeth's folded hands.

Merrill had hoped the subject would remain on households and duties. Instead, she found herself back on uncomfortable ground. She finally said, "Zadoc was clueless until I spelled it out for him. Now he seems quite delighted to know that Corabeth might be available."

"I've been available for years now," Corabeth said, crossing her arms. "Goodness, but a girl could get old and die before she manages to get a fella's attention. If I hadn't had you helping me, Merrill, Zadoc would still be thinking about . . . about . . . well, whatever it is he was thinking about."

Laughing, Granny pointed a finger at her granddaughter. "Mark my words. By this time next year, you'll be wed— maybe even have a little one on the way."

Corabeth blushed and lowered her head. "Granny, don't say such things. You'll jinx it."

"Nonsense. This family doesn't believe in jinxes. Never have, never will. You make your own path with the Good Lord to guide you. So, now, why don't we make some plans? Merrill, I know that Nils Olsson fella is interested in you. Why don't I invite him and Zadoc to come to dinner here with you and Corabeth? It will allow the four of you to get better acquainted in a proper setting."

Merrill felt she already knew Corabeth and Zadoc well enough. As for Nils, she really had no interest in knowing him better. She'd seen him a couple of times around the Jorgensons' shop but always avoided any long conversations.

"I really don't think I would want to encourage Mr. Olsson," Merrill finally said. She looked toward the fireplace and shook her head. "I can't say that he interests me in the least."

"Well, what about one of the other men at Jorgenson Furniture?" Granny questioned. "I could extend the invitation to any one of them."

"I'd rather a fella ask me himself," Merrill said slowly. "Of course, given my appearance that isn't likely to happen anytime soon. I'll never have beautiful hair like you, Corabeth."

"But you can change how you look," Corabeth countered.

"Perhaps I shall." Merrill raised her skirt to reveal stockings instead of trousers. "I knew it would please you if I left the long pants at home. These are not nearly as warm, but I threw on an extra petticoat."

Granny laughed and clapped her hands. "Merrill Jean, we can fix you right up. I've long wanted to help you, but with the heavy workload you had, it didn't seem possible." She turned to her granddaughter. "Corabeth, run fetch that trunk I have at the end of my bed. Oh, and bring my brushes and combs."

Merrill held up her hands. "Granny, it's not so dire a situation that you need to work on me right now." They all three laughed at her quip, but Granny was already on her feet and motioning for Merrill to follow her into the dining room. "We'll have better light here and more space to spread out."

Before Merrill knew what was happening, Corabeth had returned with the requested items, and Granny was pulling numerous things from the small trunk. "Now, the winter church party will be in just a few weeks, and we need to make sure you both are ready for this adventure. Starting with someone to escort you to the party." Granny threw Corabeth a glance. "I'm sure Zadoc will ask Corabeth, but we need to figure out a man to accompany you, Merrill."

"Honestly, is all of this necessary?" Merrill shook her head as she looked at the lace fans and gloves. There were beads and baubles, feathers and ribbons enough for twenty young women.

"It's definitely necessary," Granny replied. "A man wants to know that his woman is soft and gentle. He wants her to be frilly and feminine, just like you mentioned earlier." She held up a fan to her face and waved it ever so slightly. "Try this. You can look quite enticing with a fan in your hand."

Merrill took the fan and tried to open it. She pushed the wrong direction and found the piece unyielding. Turning it around, she finally managed to open it, but not with any kind of grace.

"Now put it to your face," Granny instructed. "Cover your mouth and nose and just peek over the top." Merrill did as she was told while Granny inspected the result.

She nodded encouragingly. "We need to figure out what to do with your hair," she said. "You look like you've been running wild in the forest." Granny selected a brush and several combs. "We need to figure a way to make your hair look soft and alluring. Corabeth, go heat the curling iron."

"Really, Granny, you don't need to go to so much trouble—"

"Bah, we're gonna have you gussied up so that every fella in town will be vying for your attention."

Merrill knew in her heart there was really only one man

she wanted to impress. A wave of guilt washed over her at the thought, however. Rurik Jorgenson made her feel things she'd never felt before. She longed to know him better—to be with him.

He belongs to Svea Olsson, she reminded herself sternly. Granny pulled hard on an errant strand of hair, and Merrill couldn't help but give a yelp.

"Sorry, Merrill Jean. Sometimes these things come at a price. Even so, you're quite blessed to have naturally curly hair. A few snips here and there and some turns of the curling iron, and you'll be the height of fashion."

She continued to pull and brush at Merrill's hair for some time. Instead of protesting, Merrill decided to yield to the attention and say nothing more. Corabeth returned with a curling iron and carefully handed it over to Granny. "It's hot, and I put two more on the stove," she told her grandmother.

"Good thing. We've got our work with this one. Never did see hair so unmanageable. You ought to try egg whites on your hair, Merrill Jean. Take about four eggs, separate out the yolks, then whip it into a froth and massage it all over your head down close to the roots. Let it dry and then wash it out. It'll do wonders to soften your hair."

"And what will I use for my sponge cake?"

Granny ignored her and continued to work.

"You know, Merrill," Corabeth said, sounding quite excited, "that material is still available at Finsters. I think after we finish here we should go buy it. Granny and I can work on a new dress for you—can't we, Granny?"

"Of course we can. We've enough time before the party.

I've already finished putting the trims on Corabeth's gown, so it won't be any problem to put something together for you."

"I couldn't ask you to do that," Merrill protested. "A new gown is a lot of work . . . and money. I'm already helping to pay for Mrs. Niedermeyer."

"Pshaw. You haven't had a new dress in years. Your father would be happy for you to have it. I remember when you were in town buying material to make the boys some new shirts—he suggested then that you pick something out."

It was true. Her father was always generous and had encouraged her to even buy one of the ready-made dresses at Finsters. Not that any of them would have fit. Merrill would have had to add several inches to the length of any store-bought gown.

"Oh, look, Granny," Corabeth exclaimed. "These blue feathers would go perfect with that material, don't you think? We could weave them into Merrill's hair and use silver ribbon to set it off." She turned thoughtful. "Do we have any silver ribbon?"

"I'm sure we can find some," Granny replied.

Neither woman seemed at all interested in what Merrill might have to say about the matter. Granny and Corabeth rambled on about what type of gown they would create and whether or not they had Merrill's most recent measurements. Finally Granny stepped back and put down her brush. Walking slowly around Merrill, she nodded. "What do you think, Corabeth?"

"She looks like an angel."

Merrill snorted a laugh. "An angel, indeed." She took the mirror Granny offered and looked at the fashionable coiffure.

"Well, how is it? Do you like it?"

She put a hand to one of the ringed curls, surprised at the reflection of a stylish young woman. "I think it is lovely, Granny, and your hard work is definitely appreciated." Merrill lowered the mirror. "But it took over an hour to do this. I haven't got that kind of time to give to arranging and decorating my hair. What sensible woman would?"

Corabeth frowned. "I spend a good amount of time dressing mine, and I'm sensible."

Merrill gave her friend an apologetic smile. "Of course. I'm sorry. That came out all wrong. I just meant that my life on the farm would hardly allow for such a thing. If I were to spend more than ten minutes getting ready in the morning, Father would think me ill."

"Actually, Merrill Jean, your father and brothers are a big part of the problem." Granny's tone was none too gentle. "They treat you like you're one of them, and you aren't. Your mother would be appalled, and it's time you started thinking of what she would want for you."

A frown knitted Merrill's brows together. She knew Granny meant well, but she couldn't help but feel overwhelmed by the moment. "My mother wanted me to be kind and helpful to my brothers and father," she murmured.

"Of course she did," Granny said, bobbing a nod. "I didn't mean to sound grouchy. It's just that you are a beautiful young woman, but you don't allow yourself to see it. I see you with your emerald eyes and dark hair and know that your beauty is unmatched. You look into the mirror and see a laborer who must work every second of the day to benefit someone else."

"But isn't that how Christ would have us be?" Merrill looked at Granny and then to Corabeth. "I think God puts us all in different situations for different reasons. If I am to fall in love and marry a man, should that man not love me no matter my appearance? Surely I won't be able to fashion my hair like this every day."

"Of course not every day, dear—this style is for special occasions. But you can learn to accent your beauty," Granny said. "You can wear more feminine attire. Add some lace to your collar, trim your blouse with some ribbon. Wear a pretty broach or a necklace."

"And gloves," Corabeth said, holding up a pair of white kid gloves. "Instead of mittens."

"But mittens are warmer," Merrill said in her practical way.

"Then wear them over the gloves and lay the mittens aside when you go into church or a gathering."

"And use the fan," Corabeth added.

Merrill sighed. They meant well; she knew that much. But she wished they could understand that their fussing only served to make her feel like more of an outsider.

The clock chimed one, and Merrill jumped to her feet. "Oh, I must go. I promised to stop over at the furniture shop before I head home. Thank you so much for your kind words and . . . and of course the help with my hair." She noted the look of expectancy on their faces. Taking up her reticule, Merrill paused. "I suppose, if you truly wish to make a gown for me, I won't object. Charge the material to Father's account, and I'll see that it's taken care of."

Granny clapped her hands. "We'll go right away." She motioned to Corabeth. "Please go tell your grandfather we're going out, and bring me my coat."

Corabeth nodded and hurried off to see to her grandmother's request. Merrill pulled on her long wool coat, then took up her bonnet. She hesitated for fear of making a mess of her new hairstyle. "Thank you again, Granny. I'm sure my hair has never looked nicer. I won't even put my bonnet on just yet."

"That's good. Let the fellas see how pretty you can be."

Merrill nodded, smiled her gratitude, and hurried outside. She knew it was silly, but the new hairstyle gave her a sense of confidence she'd not expected. She hurried through the snowy streets, carefully making her way through town and wondering what people might be thinking when they saw her. Would they assume she was putting on airs? Would they find the new style a vast improvement?

"Why should I care?" Merrill murmured to herself. But she did.

At the Jorgenson Furniture shop, Merrill found herself the center of attention. Several of the men stopped what they were doing to hurry over and show her the area Carl had set aside for her to work in.

"Your hair is different, Miss Krause," one of the men noted, sounding tentative but also approving.

She nodded uncomfortably and held up her bonnet. "I was worried my hat would destroy all of Granny Lassiter's work." The man just smiled.

"See, there's a nice long table for your paints and other supplies," Lars pointed out.

"We'll bring the finished pie safes into this room, and you'll be able to arrange them any way you like. Then you can work on them at your leisure," another of the men commented.

"Not that there will be much in the way of leisure," Rurik declared from the door.

Merrill started at the sound of his voice and turned to face him. He crossed the room and motioned to one of the nearby cupboards. "Carl has purchased some paints for you. Why don't you check them out and see what you think?"

He opened the door before she could protest. Inside were a dozen or more bottles, the colors clearly showing through the glass. He drew up behind her, and Merrill felt a shiver of delight run through her from head to toe.

"He has more ordered, and if you have a particular color you need that isn't here, you only have to ask."

The supply seemed more than enough. Merrill drew closer to the cabinet, trying to put distance between her and Rurik. "Thank you. Sometimes it's the simple things that are most needed—white and black for instance."

"You'll see that there are additional bottles of both down below."

She inspected the bottom shelf and found it just as he said. She straightened and took a deep breath before turning to face him. Smiling, Merrill wanted only to lose herself in his gaze. Instead, she looked back to face the other men. "This seems to be a very well-ordered workshop."

The men who had gathered smiled and offered comments about the way she might handle her work. In the doorway behind them, Nils Olsson watched her. Merrill grew uncomfortable.

"You fellas need more to do?" Carl Jorgenson asked, walking in from the opposite side of the room. "I'm beginning to have second thoughts about having a pretty girl join us here."

Merrill felt her cheeks grow hot. She ducked her head to avoid them seeing her embarrassment.

"It was nice to see you today, Miss Krause," Lars said. "Come on, you oafs," he called, "back to work."

Once they'd left the room, Merrill looked at Carl. "This is perfect. Thank you so much. How soon will you need for me to begin?"

"Tomorrow, if that's not too soon. I've had the boys putting together pie safes and blanket chests. I thought we might have you trim some of those, as well. A lot of folks like to give them for wedding gifts, so you could make them look appealing for a young lady."

"I'd be happy to try." Merrill was keenly aware of Rurik still standing just behind her and Nils watching from the door.

"When I mentioned the possibility to one of my buyers, he wanted to take immediate possession of anything we had available," Carl said with a laugh. "I told him he would have to wait." The Swedish accent sounded rather raspy, and Carl put a hand to his chest and coughed.

"I hope he'll be pleased," Merrill responded.

Carl grimaced and straightened. "So you come tomorrow to verk, ja?"

"Ja," she said, seeing an expression of pain cross his face. "Mr. Jorgenson, are you all right?"

Rurik pushed past her and rounded the workbench just

as his uncle started to fall. "Nils, get the doctor." He lifted Carl in his arms. "Merrill, please, would you help me get him to bed?"

She hurried ahead of him, opening doors. When they reached the house and Carl's bed, she pulled down the covers and stepped aside for Rurik. He placed his uncle on the mattress and immediately began to loosen his shirt and vest.

"Don't make . . . don't fuss," Carl gasped.

Merrill went to his boots and began to unlace them. "Mr. Jorgenson, you need to lie still. We can handle this. I help my father with his boots all the time."

Rurik threw her a grateful look. "Uncle Carl, it's not everyone who gets an angel to attend them." He winked at Merrill and went back to work, unbuttoning his uncle's vest.

Merrill found it difficult to make her fingers work properly after that. She had not expected such a compliment from Rurik—especially at such a serious time. She supposed he was just trying to ease his uncle's mind, but the memory of Rurik calling her angelic left her unable to think very well for some time.

Carl groaned and clutched his chest. "You will pray for me, ja?"

Merrill wasn't sure to whom he spoke, but she assured him before Rurik could respond. "I'm already praying, Mr. Jorgenson, and I'll continue to do so." She managed to pull off the other boot and placed it on the floor beside the first one. As she straightened, she heard the front door open.

"That must be the doctor," she told Carl and patted his hand. "He'll know what to do for you."

Carl forced a smile. "That would be news to me. He hasn't known how to help me before."

Merrill smiled and squeezed his hand. "That's because I wasn't here to aid him in figuring you out." The old man nodded, then the pain gripped him again and he grimaced. Merrill prayed that God would intercede quickly and ease the poor man's misery.

She glanced up to find Nils Olsson standing in the hall. The doctor went to Carl's side and left Merrill little choice but to move away. She didn't want to leave without knowing whether Carl was going to be all right, but she truly didn't want to spend any time in Mr. Olsson's company, either.

"Mr. Jorgenson, I'm going to go now." She spoke to Rurik, but it was Carl who opened his eyes and caught her attention.

"Keep praying," he murmured.

"I will," she said. "I promise. And I'll be back tomorrow and bring you some treats."

She moved quickly past Rurik and Nils. Without waiting for either man to acknowledge her departure, Merrill hurried outside and was halfway across the yard before Nils caught up to her.

"Let me escort you to where you're going."

"That isn't necessary," she said. "Mr. Jorgenson may need you to help with his uncle. It would be best for you to assist him."

"But you're the one I want to be with."

Merrill stopped in midstep. "But your friend is in need," she said firmly. "A true friend would go to his side and offer whatever aid he could." She hoped the admonition was taken to heart. "Now, if you'll excuse me."

Chapter 13

Dr. Hickum finished listening to the man's chest and straightened. "Carl, it's been only a few days since your last attack. Your heart is still weak. It's always going to be weak." The doctor took a moment to glance at Rurik, then continued. "You need to forget about going back to work. It's time for you to let other folks take care of the business and take care of you."

"I'm not much good if I can't do for myself," Carl murmured.

"Uncle Carl, you know that isn't true," Rurik declared. Standing at the foot of his uncle's bed, he met the doctor's grave expression. "I will see to it that he continues to rest."

"It's really the best thing for him. The medicines I have are limited in what they can do. If he takes it easy"—the doctor paused and looked at Carl—"he could live for some time to come."

Carl shook his head. "But I would be a burden."

"Nonsense," Rurik interjected. "You will never be a burden to those of us who love you, Uncle Carl. And you can design. You've got a great talent for creating furniture, and you know it. I think the doctor would agree that you should rest for now, and when the time comes, you can sit at a table and sketch designs for us." He looked to the doctor to see if he approved.

Dr. Hickum smiled. "Why, Carl, that is a perfect solution. The work wouldn't be taxing, but it would provide just what your business needs."

Carl looked unconvinced. "Vat about the office?"

Rurik thought quickly. "Well, as you know, my friend Nils is here," he began. "He was visiting our workshop the other day when you had your attack and was the one who fetched Dr. Hickum. He's handled his father's dairy farm office for years. I think he could surely manage this one—under your guidance, of course."

"See there, Carl. You won't be a burden at all," the doctor said as he put his equipment away. "I would limit the amount of time you give to any of these projects, however, for at least a few weeks."

"But there are a lot of orders to fill," Carl argued. "The books . . . they need someone to keep them."

"And Nils can manage that," Rurik reassured him. "You'll be right here if he has questions. And I will bring you a sketch pad and pencils so you can design to your heart's content." Carl said nothing more, and Rurik figured he needed to let the idea sink in for a time.

"I'll check in on you tomorrow," the doctor told Carl and turned to go.

Rurik touched his uncle's foot. "I'll see the doc out and be right back." Carl stared up at the ceiling.

Outside, Rurik held the doctor's horse while he mounted. "Carl's a stubborn one, but I'll do what I can to make certain he follows your orders."

"If he doesn't," the doctor said with a shake of his head, "he won't live much longer. The attacks are getting worse. My guess is that his heart will simply give out in time. I will check my medical library to see if there's anything else we might try, but for now, rest is best."

Rurik nodded. "He'll get it. I promise."

He waited until the doctor had disappeared before returning to the house. The winter air was damp and heavy with a threat of snow. Rurik made a mental note to check the supply of firewood they had for the house and the shop. He also reasoned that he should probably talk with someone like Granny Lassiter and hire a woman to help with Carl's care. Someone to cook and clean would give them both a bit of relief for their daily chores. He thought of Merrill but dismissed the idea just as quickly. He liked the idea of keeping her close by in the shop. He was hoping, in fact, to work up the nerve to ask her to the winter party at the church. Hopefully, by then Svea would be back in Kansas.

"But if that's to happen," he muttered aloud, "I'm going to have to speak with Nils."

Rurik figured there was no time like the present. He knew Carl would need some time alone to accept his future. It wasn't easy for a man who had always been hardworking and self-sustaining to learn that he could no longer carry on as he had. His Swedish tenacity alone would try to convince him that the doctor was in error.

Rurik returned to the house long enough to check on Carl and fetch his coat. "I'll only be gone a little while. I'm going to speak to Nils about working for us." Carl remained silent, but Rurik didn't take offense. "Maybe I'll bring you one of Granny's cinnamon rolls, too. She mentioned that I should stop by today and pick some up."

Carl seemed to rally just a bit at this, but then closed his eyes. Rurik smiled. His uncle was stubborn—but sensible. Together they would see this through.

At the hotel, Rurik sent word with the clerk that Nils should meet him in the lobby. It was only a few moments before his friend appeared, coat and hat in hand.

"You wanted to see me? You should have just come on up to the room."

"I wasn't sure you were here," Rurik replied. "Take a walk with me. We have much to discuss."

Nils nodded and pulled on his coat. "How's your uncle?"

"That's part of the reason I'm here." Rurik led the way outside. He didn't really want to discuss the details where they might be overheard. "I know it's cold out here, but I think it might afford us a bit more privacy if we take a walk."

"It's no bother to me."

They strolled past brick shops and put some distance between the hotel and themselves before Rurik spoke again. "The doctor says that Uncle Carl must not work. At least not as he has in the past. He needs a lot of bed rest—especially during the next few weeks."

"I see," Nils replied, looking to Rurik. "And does this mean you might have a job for me?"

"Ja. That's what I'm thinking. Uncle Carl has not said as much, but as his partner I believe it is up to me to manage the situation. He cannot handle the work of keeping the office, so I want you to come and work for us."

Nils couldn't contain his delight. "I'm not at all happy that Carl is suffering, but I do have to say this is a much-needed answer to my problems."

"I know. I thought of it as such. We will need you right away, so I'm thinking it would be best if you sent Svea home. You could stay with me at the house. My room isn't all that big, but we can squeeze in another bed. That way you won't have to spend the money to stay at the hotel."

"That would be good. My money is disappearing fast," Nils replied. "But honestly, I can't expect Svea to leave. You shouldn't either. Not in her condition."

"I had nothing to do with her condition, Nils." Rurik stopped and turned. "That child is not mine. I've *never* been intimate with your sister."

"Why would she lie about such a thing, Rurik?"

"Because she made a mistake? Because she's ashamed? Because she's scared? There are any number of reasons for lying about such a matter."

"She wouldn't lie to me," Nils countered. "There'd be no reason. She knows she'd have no condemnation from me. I think you should do the right thing and marry her. Then you'll come into your marriage money, and you can get a little house for the both of you and start a family. We can become partners—"

"I have a partner," Rurik interrupted. "Or did you forget?"

Nils shrugged. "You know what I meant." He took on a more humble appearance and bowed his head slightly. "Rurik, I need this job, and I need your help. I can't allow Svea to return to Lindsborg and ridicule. You cared about her once; I'm sure you can care about her again."

"I still care about the both of you, but I do not love Svea as a husband should love a wife. Not only that, but Svea knows I'm not the father of her baby. Our marriage would be built on lies from the very start."

Nils seemed unconcerned. "You must know that people will make life very hard for her if she is not married soon. And now you are finally in the perfect place to take a wife."

Rurik let out an exasperated sigh. "If marriage to your sister is a requirement of you coming to work for us, then I need to find another employee."

"No," Nils said quickly. "I didn't say it was a condition. I simply expect you to do the right thing."

"The right thing would be for you to find out who the real father is. There is a man out there who has wronged your sister. He is the one who should make this right. If I were Svea's brother, I wouldn't rest until I knew the truth of it. You say she wouldn't lie to you, but I'm telling you, as God is my witness, she has." Rurik eyed his friend with great intensity. "You seem rather cavalier about the matter. If a man, even my best friend, had taken liberties with my sister, I wouldn't be so calm about it. Are you sure this isn't more about the money?"

For several seconds neither man said another word. They stood in the cold quiet of the neighborhood and simply stared at each other for a moment. Rurik realized his statement was something of a challenge to Nils.

The man finally said, "I do need the money. I'm ashamed to admit it, but I have debts, and they need to be repaid." Nils stuffed his hands deep in his coat pockets. "But I also want my sister to have what she needs. It wouldn't be right to pack her off and leave her to face the folks and the future alone."

Rurik could see he wasn't going to convince Nils at this juncture. Maybe he could talk to Svea and somehow convince her to be truthful. If he could speak to her without Nils, maybe she wouldn't be so reluctant to tell Rurik what had really happened.

They began to walk again, and Rurik decided to change the subject. "Carl can do creative designs and answer some questions about the office, but otherwise he needs to take it easy. You would need to step in and handle the customers and orders. You would need to be responsible for keeping the books, making deposits, and paying the bills. These are all things you did for your father, but am I naïve in believing they would be similar in the furniture business?"

"Similar, yes. There are always differences, however. I would need to familiarize myself with the details, but I'm sure that I can manage it without needing to involve your uncle overmuch."

"So you'll do it? You can start right away. I can't give you a salary figure until I work those details out with Uncle Carl. But we will do right by you—you know that much."

"I know you will, just as I know you will do right by Svea.

You wouldn't want your own reputation ruined." The unspoken threat hung between them like a sword.

Rurik narrowed his eyes. "I won't be forced into righting a wrong that isn't mine, Nils. We've been friends a long time, but you know nothing of me if you think you can threaten me like that."

Nils shrugged again. "A man's reputation . . . his name . . . is really all he has. If you lose yours over a silly matter like this, you will take your uncle down with you. It's something worth thinking about, Rurik."

To Rurik's surprise, Nils started to walk away. "For a man who says he needs this job, it seems foolish to suggest my demise."

Nils turned and smiled. "Rurik, you're just bearing the consequences of your actions. Bear it like a man and do the right thing. There's no threat of demise in that. Just honor."

❧

"Oh, I'm positively over the moon," Corabeth professed after Sunday services, her hands clasped in front of her.

Merrill, who knew the cause of such a lovesick expression, said, "I'm glad Zadoc finally asked you to the winter party. He waited long enough."

"That's all right," her friend replied, tucking her hands under her chin. She looked like an actress on stage striking a pose. "He asked, and that's what's important."

"I know." Merrill reached out to pat her friend's shoulder. She couldn't help but be happy for Corabeth—and the notion her friend might one day marry into the family.

"Granny said we're going to come out and lend a hand this week since you'll be busy feeding the ice-harvest crew. I'm so excited I can hardly speak. I'll get to be close to Zadoc, and he can eat my cooking and see how congenial I am."

"Father is glad for the extra help. We'll have quite a few men to feed. Frankly, I won't know what to do with myself keeping only to the kitchen and the livestock. Goodness, but I think I've been helping with ice harvest all of my life. I don't remember a time when I wasn't out there with them."

"But you're a young lady now, and of marriageable age. You know what Granny says—it's important to find a husband before you're an old maid."

"Some would say I'm already an old maid, Corabeth. After all, there are plenty of dainty young women coming of age in Waseca. I doubt seriously that any of the eligible men are struggling to make their pick."

"There you are," Merrill's father said, coming up from behind. "There's someone here who has a question for you."

Merrill turned with a smile for her father and found Nils Olsson on his heel. "Mr. Olsson," she said, nodding a greeting but feeling her heart sink.

"Miss Krause," Nils said eagerly, "I just asked your father if I might be your escort to the winter party next week. He said you hadn't accepted any other invitations, so I am hoping that although this request comes quite late, you will make me the happiest man on earth and accept."

Corabeth gave a little squeal of delight. "Of course she will, won't you, Merrill?"

Merrill looked to her father, who seemed equally pleased.

"You and Zadoc could drive in from the farm and go with Corabeth and Nils to the party. A nice foursome."

She could see her options were quickly being taken from her. Merrill didn't want to create a scene so she nodded. "That would be . . . very nice, Mr. Olsson. Thank you."

"Wonderful. Where shall we plan to meet?"

Corabeth took charge. "You must all come to my house a half hour prior to the party. We'll have some cider and cookies. Granny will be so happy to see you all."

"That's sounds perfect," Nils replied.

"What sounds perfect?" Rurik asked. Svea followed him like a faithful puppy. She quickly slipped her arm through his once he stopped in front of Merrill and Corabeth. Without a word, he gently pried her fingers from his arm.

"Miss Krause just agreed to accompany me to the winter party," Nils said, giving Rurik a wink. "Now I won't be left without a beautiful woman at my side."

"Oh, and you and Miss Olsson must join us, too," Corabeth said, her own excitement spilling over on them all. "I just invited Mr. Olsson and Merrill to come to my house before the party for refreshments."

Rurik looked perplexed. "I had no plans to attend the event. With Uncle Carl still recovering, I don't think it wise. Svea, of course, is free to do whatever she wants."

Svea looked at Merrill and tilted her chin in the air. "I think we should change our plans, Rurik, and attend. We could have someone else look in on your uncle."

Merrill could see that Svea's comment didn't sit well with Rurik. There was a hardness that came over his expression and a tension to his shoulders that she longed to rub away. What was going on with this man and his intended? He certainly didn't act like a man in love.

"I think Svea is right," Nils declared. "We will make it a sixsome. Thank you so much, Miss Lassiter, for the invitation, and thank you, Miss Krause, for accepting my request. I will be anticipating the night of the party."

After a restless night, Merrill was still wondering how she might get out of attending the party with Nils Olsson. He seemed a nice enough man, but she had no interest in knowing him better. Surely there was some way she might let him know this without hurting his feelings.

Fresh snow made the walk that morning a little more strenuous, and Merrill found herself missing her trousers and heavy work boots. The more feminine women's boots she'd pulled on were not created for such mucking about. Nevertheless, she made her way to the Jorgenson house with food for Carl and Rurik. She hoped to leave the goods, say hello to Carl, and then go immediately to work on finishing the pie safes. With any luck, she could be home by two.

She knocked on the front door, but when no one answered she tried the knob. The door opened and Merrill stepped inside. The men were probably already over at the workshop. She knew Rurik had mentioned Carl was taking a few minutes each day to walk over and observe Nils Olsson's work in the office.

"Hello?" she called, but no one answered.

Making her way through the house, Merrill went into the kitchen and unloaded the things she'd brought. She was nearly finished and ready to leave when she heard the front door open. She started to call out but heard Rurik's voice, already in an intense discussion with his uncle.

"I don't know what to do about any of it, Uncle Carl. I didn't want to worry you and burden your recovery."

"You aren't a burden, nor are your problems, Rurik. It appears this is not an issue that will go away. If Svea is to have a baby, it won't be long before the entire town knows the truth of it."

"But I do not intend to be the one responsible for her problems. It isn't fair."

Merrill felt a wave of nausea. She took up her basket and moved quickly to the back porch. She'd never liked to eavesdrop, and this time was certainly no exception. With as much stealth as she could manage, she slipped out the back door and hurried to the workshop.

Svea is going to have a baby.

Any lingering wisps of hope for Rurik dissolving his betrothal with the young woman faded from Merrill's heart. Rurik wasn't an honorable man if he had taken advantage of Svea in such a way. Even if she didn't like the young woman, she could hardly fault her for coming to Waseca in order to get Rurik to do the right thing.

"Ready for another day of painting?" Nils asked as she entered the workshop finishing room. With his office just off to the side, he seemed to know when she came or went.

Merrill glanced at him and nodded. "I have a great deal

to accomplish today." She wondered if now might be a good time to back out of the party.

"You look quite lovely. I feel that I must surely be the luckiest man in the world."

"Uh . . . thank you." She wasn't sure why he felt lucky or what else to say. Her mind was still whirling with the terrible revelation she'd just heard.

"You look a little pale," he said, taking a few steps toward her. He offered his hand. "Why don't you sit in the warm office for a minute?"

Merrill shook her head. "You just said I looked lovely, and now you think I'm pale. Really, I'm fine. Goodness, look at the hour." She had no clock to reference, but stated it as if there was. "I simply must get to work." She put her empty basket on the workbench and started to unbutton her coat. Without giving him a chance to comment, she added, "I would imagine you have a lot to do, as well."

She shed her coat and bonnet and placed them on a peg near her workbench. Nils, unfortunately, followed her. He lifted her basket and frowned. After he checked the contents, his frown deepened.

"Your basket is empty."

"Yes." The simple word sounded defensive, even to her own ears. "I have some shopping to do before I head home." It hadn't been her original plan, but Merrill would see to it that it happened.

"Oh, well, that makes perfect sense. I thought perhaps you'd grown forgetful. Since you brought nothing to eat, why don't we have our noon meal together?"

She shook her head. "I'm expected at Granny's. Sorry." She picked up a bottle of paint and placed it on the bench.

Just then the door opened, and Rurik came in from the cold. He first looked troubled, but then he gave Merrill and Nils a smile. "Good morning, Miss Krause. Nils, I have Carl back to bed and can go over those orders with you now."

Nils sighed and moved back to the office. "Another time, Miss Krause."

She shook her head and focused on mixing her paints. She was afraid to so much as offer Rurik a glance—afraid she might well blurt out the questions that demanded answers regarding Svea and the baby . . . and what Rurik planned to do.

Chapter 14

Merrill found herself sitting alone at the dinner table long after she'd cleared away the meal and cleaned the kitchen. She couldn't remember the last time she'd felt so overwhelmed with grief and, yes, with anger. These weren't like the emotions she'd experienced when her mother passed away; this was like learning something you believed in was only a fairy tale.

She had thought Rurik to be an honorable man—and she'd lost her heart to him without ever meaning to. Sighing, Merrill tried to think through what she should do next. She'd never imagined that he'd mistreat Svea in such a manner.

The thought of seeing Rurik face-to-face, actually having to speak to him, was almost more than she could bear. But to complicate matters further, he had hired her and was her boss. *I thought him to be a godly person. But I suppose even godly men make mistakes.* Still, even if Rurik had made a mistake and given in to temptation, why wouldn't he now make things right?

"You've been so quiet this evening," her father said, taking a seat across from her. He folded his hands on the table. "I suppose this time of year is always hardest on you."

Merrill looked up, puzzled. "What do you mean?"

He gave a sad smile. "Well, it's near the anniversary of your mother's passing. I know you think about her all the time."

"I do think of her, though to be honest I wasn't at this moment. Still, now that you mention it, I suppose it was in the back of my mind."

He nodded. "It's always in the back of mine. I miss her a great deal. The boys do, too, but I figure you probably suffer more than all of us. I wasn't always the best of husbands. I was busy so much of the time, and I didn't give your mama the attention she deserved."

"You were working hard to keep your family fed and clothed. Mama never complained about that to me. In fact, I don't remember her ever complaining at all."

He chuckled. "Oh, she could complain all right. Edeline was a bear to deal with when she was fired up. She was the only woman besides you who could hold her own with me."

Merrill smiled. "Thanks for the reminder, Father. I do remember her standing with her hands on her hips, telling you quite firmly that purchasing a piece of land ten miles away was not a good idea." They both laughed.

"Yes, she was good to talk sense into my head when I wanted to start some fool venture," he admitted. "But she was supportive when she knew the project to be sound." He looked across the table at Merrill. "You do know she was never happier than when Doc placed you in her arms. After six boys, all she wanted was a daughter. You were, she told me, her gift from heaven."

Her father's expression turned mischievous. "I told her,"

he continued, "that you were most likely a reward for having endured all us males. She thought I was probably right. She was so pleased, though. I'll never forget the look on her face."

Merrill tried to imagine it, but most of her memories of Mama had faded over the years. The images weren't nearly as crisp now, and the memory of her voice was all but silenced.

"I'm glad she was pleased."

"She had so much fun getting you gussied up for church. She loved to show you off." He frowned. "I know she'd not be pleased with the way I've done things, though. She didn't want you to work like your brothers. Edeline always told me she wanted you to be pampered but not spoiled."

Merrill thought for a moment, then said, "But I wouldn't allow for much pampering. I wanted to be off with my brothers. I liked being one of the boys. They had much more fun and didn't have to worry about keeping their clothes clean. I don't think Mama would be disappointed in you, Father. You've done fine by all of us. Many a man would have had to farm his children off, but you kept us together as a family. You brought us to church every Sunday, you prayed with us, and most of all you were an example of a Christian father."

Her father nodded and looked down at his hands for a moment. He rarely ever got emotional, and when he spoke, Merrill was unprepared for the tears in his eyes. "She was the best woman in the world, Merrill Jean. I promised her that I would take good care of you all. But I especially promised to do right by you, and I don't feel I've done that. All these years you've worked just as hard, if not harder, than any of us. You're nigh on to twenty-one years of age. Your mama was married with three young ones by then—of course Berwyn had passed on. Poor boy. Broke our hearts to lose him to pneumonia." He fell silent for a moment.

Merrill knew the loss of her oldest brother and later another brother, Harlow, had been her mother's greatest grief. She had once said that as long as she lived, she would never know a greater pain than that of losing a child.

"Like we've talked about, you should be married and have children of your own, Merrill Jean. You shouldn't be here looking after me. I'm mighty glad that Olsson fella has asked you to the party. He seems a nice enough sort."

Merrill knew then and there that no matter what, she wouldn't attempt to get out of going with Nils. It would be a small sacrifice for her in order to make her father happy. He didn't need to know that the matter would go no further. At least not yet.

"You know," she said, "I made Mama a promise, too. I told her that I would take care of you and the boys. So, you see, you haven't disappointed her at all. Instead, you've let me fulfill my promise, too."

Her father looked at her and shook his head. "I still feel like I failed at mine. I told her I'd keep you safe, and in doing that I trained your brothers to keep an eye out for you. Unfortunately, they became rather possessive of you and have warded off would-be suitors. No one's ever good enough for you. I suppose that's the trouble when your brothers are good friends with those who might come courting. They know all about how ornery a fella could be." Her father finally smiled again. "I know it, too."

"Most of the time they were right," Merrill said with a chuckle. "But, you know, you did keep me safe, and you raised me to be a young woman who sought God's heart. Really, Father, Mama would be most pleased."

"I hope she'll look down from heaven and see what a beauty you've turned out to be. You look just like her, you know."

"Only bigger? Granny once said that, you know. She said I was like a stretched-out version of my mother."

"You did inherit my height rather than hers. Your mother always commented on how quickly the boys shot up. They were all taller than her by the time they were twelve."

"I remember coming home from church one Sunday, and it had been raining so hard the wheels got stuck in the mud. Leo jumped down, and when he helped Mama from the wagon he simply hoisted her into his arms and carried her home. She kept telling him to put her down, but he wouldn't listen. Instead he let Tobe have a go at the carrying. You brought me in right behind them. I felt like my papa could do anything."

"I remember that. We all had a good laugh, as I recall."

"We did," Merrill said, remembering it fondly.

Her father reached out to take hold of her hands and grew serious again. "I can't help but pray I haven't interfered with God's will for you. If I'd been less concerned about letting you go, losing you . . . well, things would be different."

"Papa, you could never lose me."

A silence fell over them both for a long while. "Time goes by so fast, and yet it seems like she's been gone forever," he finally murmured.

Memories of her mother were bittersweet to Merrill, and sharing them now with her father was a precious experience. She had no idea where her brothers were, but she was grateful for this time alone with her beloved papa.

Merrill finally spoke. "You mentioned God's will for me. How will I know what that is, Father?"

He let go of her hands and leaned back in the chair. "I've always believed it to start with prayer. The Good Book says that if a man wants wisdom, he just has to ask. I would imagine it works the same way for womenfolk. If you want to know what God's plan is—then I would ask Him. Couldn't hurt to search the Scriptures, too. And listen to what He is telling you inside. Even when you don't think you're hearing anything, keep listening. And know I'll be praying, as well."

The winter party at the church was everything the community had come to expect. The local matrons provided tables full of refreshments in a blend of German, Swedish, Norwegian, and even Scottish recipes. Games and activities—everything from ice-skating to cakewalks—had been set up to amuse the participants. Winter could be a dreary time in the north with its heavy snows, cold temperatures, and limited daylight, and a party was just what was needed to boost spirits and bring the community together.

Even Merrill had to admit that she was glad to be there. The dress Granny and Corabeth created for her was far above her expectations. They had purchased a beautiful blue and green plaid and created a stylish gown with large puffed sleeves and a high lacy collar. The bodice flaunted rows of fluted ruffles, as did the sleeves. Granny had purchased a fluting machine just the summer before, and it was one of her fondest tools. How she had managed to create such a gown in so little time, however, was a mystery to Merrill.

"You will outshine all the other women tonight," Nils had told her when she arrived with Zadoc at the Lassiters for Corabeth's pre-party gathering.

"You are kind to say so." Merrill tried hard not to sound bored with his attentions, but she felt like the evening was going to turn out to be awfully long. *And Father doesn't even know I'm doing this for him. . . .*

Across the room she couldn't help but notice another couple. She wasn't sure without staring, but Rurik seemed annoyed with Svea's company. He all but ignored her, and the idea of him scorning the young woman after taking liberties with her angered Merrill.

"I see you have spotted Rurik and my sister," Nils said at her elbow, where he had planted himself.

"They didn't join us at Granny's," Merrill said. "I'm glad they could at least make it to the party. Have they set a wedding date yet?"

Nils gave a chuckle. "No, but I expect it will be soon. Now, why don't we forget about them? I know there's a lively game of Similes going on across the room. I'm quite good, and I believe we should join them for the next round. Unless, of course, you'd like to go outside and skate?"

"No, I spend enough time on the ice." Merrill allowed him to lead her through several groups of attendees toward the far side of the room. As they reached the refreshment table, however, she halted. "I think I'd like some punch first. If you don't mind."

"Let me fetch it." He hurried over to where an older woman was filling cups.

"That fella treating you right?"

Merrill's youngest brother, Flynn, had taken a moment to check in with her. She couldn't help but smile at his care for her. "He's doing well enough. How in the world did you manage to slip away from your . . . well . . . that flock of young women over there?"

Flynn grinned. "I sent them on ahead to get their skates on. We're headed out to the lake."

"And you're going to skate with all of them?"

"Sure am. Why just take one gal, when you can enjoy 'em all?" He laughed and strode off through the crowd.

Merrill scanned the room to locate Rurik and Svea. He was still looking stern, and Svea seemed to be in a pout. She was trying to say something to him, but Rurik gave no indication he heard. Just then Tobe went up to him. Rurik smiled and nodded, talking in what appeared to be a most amiable manner with Merrill's brother.

Why should he be so cold and callous with his betrothed? The mother of his child?

"Ahem. Here you are." Nils stood with a cup of punch in each hand.

Merrill turned to him and reached for her cup. "I . . . I'm sorry. I was caught up people watching. I enjoy doing that when I can. . . ." Flustered, she couldn't think why she was feeling so defensive—and with Nils, of all people. She wondered if he knew where her gaze was fastened.

"I suppose I should be jealous that I cannot hold your attention in full," he said wryly as he took a sip of his punch.

"I do apologize. I have more on my mind than the party. I will try to put my other thoughts aside."

"Miss Olsson, I wonder if I might steal Rurik away from you for a moment," Tobe Krause asked.

"I hardly see why—"

"Let me get you a cup of punch," Rurik said, leading her over to a chair. "Sit here, and I'll be right back with it." Not long before he'd spied Merrill at the refreshment table, and it would be the perfect excuse to get a chance to speak with her.

"Ask Nils to come speak with me," she said in a rather commanding manner.

Rurik looked at her for a moment, then nodded. "I would be happy to." But his mood was anything but happy.

"Merriment doesn't seem to be on your mind tonight," Tobe declared, throwing Rurik a glance.

Rurik shrugged. "I suppose not," he answered. "I have a lot on my mind these days, including a great concern for my uncle's health."

"I understand," Tobe said, nodding. "Here's Merrill and Mr. Olsson."

"Well, Tobe, don't you look quite dapper," Merrill declared as the two men joined her at the refreshment table. "I had no chance to see you before Zadoc and I left for the party. I thought perhaps you would have ridden with us."

"Nah, Flynn and I rode our horses. I wasn't sure I'd be staying all that long. If I manage to catch the eye of a certain young lady, I might hang around. Otherwise, I told Father I'd check in on Carl and play a game of chess."

Rurik nodded toward Nils. "Your sister asked if you would join her for a moment."

Nils seemed hesitant. "I wouldn't wish to leave Miss Krause. I did ask her to the party, after all."

"That's quite all right, Mr. Olsson," Merrill quickly put in. "I'm sure your sister must need you or she wouldn't be of a mind to interrupt your evening."

Nils nodded. "I suppose you're right. I'll be gone only a moment." He looked to Rurik as if he might speak, then seemed to think better of it and hurried away.

"Doesn't seem like there are as many people here this year," Tobe said, looking around the room.

"Well, if you're looking for the womenfolk," Merrill said, nodding over her shoulder, "most are outside ice-skating with Flynn."

Tobe rolled his eyes. "It figures. He needs as much looking out for as you do." Merrill gave him a friendly little swat on the arm.

"Might I offer you a compliment, Miss Krause?" Rurik asked without waiting for an answer. "I have never seen you look prettier. The green in your gown really draws out the color of your eyes and the blue flatters your complexion."

Merrill flushed and lowered her gaze. "Thank you."

"I guess every other businessman here tonight will be just as green with envy that you work for Jorgenson Furniture and not for them." He could see that his compliments made her uncomfortable, but Rurik hoped she would also know he greatly appreciated her and her beauty.

"I need to talk to Rurik about helping with the ice next week," Tobe interjected. He looked toward Rurik and drew him aside slightly. "Pa was hoping you'd have some time to come out on Thursday. We need another hand."

"I'd be glad to help. After all, it's hard to pass up Miss Krause's cooking," Rurik replied with a little grin. "I'm sure I can get Granny Lassiter to look in on Uncle Carl. He's doing much better right now."

"Good. Pa got word from one of his buyers that they'd like to have double the regular order of ice. We'll have plenty of help on Wednesday, but Thursday was looking lean."

Rurik heard someone clear their voice and found Nils had rejoined them. "Svea said you were bringing her punch."

"Yes, that's right," Rurik replied. He turned back to Tobe. "I'll see you on Thursday. I must be about my duties." His tone was less than enthusiastic, he knew. Nils eyed him with a rather critical look. He said nothing, but Rurik could sense his anger.

He ignored his friend and went to the table for Svea's punch, knowing that if he stayed, he might well say something he'd regret. This evening he intended to have a long talk with Svea about her return home. It was the only reason he'd agreed to come to the party in the first place. They would sit and talk, and in public she would be less likely to make a scene. With any luck at all, Rurik would convince her that her child deserved to grow up with his or her rightful father.

❧

Merrill found herself praying for the party to end and for Zadoc to announce it was time to head home. Nils was making a nuisance of himself, refusing to allow her out of his sight for any reason. He rambled on and on about how charming she was and how he knew his mother would love her. He talked about Merrill's cooking, mentioning that he'd sampled some delicious bratwurst and spaetzle she'd made for Carl.

Merrill took up the fan Granny had insisted she carry and waved it rather furiously.

"Why don't we slip out for some air? It is rather stuffy in here," Nils declared, and before Merrill could protest he'd caught her by the arm and swept her from the room.

They stepped outside into the cold night air. Not far from the church a huge bonfire burned down by the lake where dozens of people were skating. Merrill immediately drew in a deep breath of the chill air and felt a sense of relief—like her soul was being cleansed. She decided to thank Nils for the evening and be done with him. Turning to face him, however, she found herself pulled into his arms.

Her mind froze, as well as her body. Nils lowered his mouth to hers and kissed her quite boldly. For a moment, Merrill's senses left her frozen with shock. Then her anger stirred. This was her first kiss, and she certainly had no desire for it to come from Nils Olsson. When she stiffened and pushed away, he finally let her go.

Nils stepped back with a smug look of satisfaction on his face. "I've wanted to do that all night."

Merrill doubled her fist and punched him square in the mouth. "And I've wanted to do that." She whirled away in an instant, not waiting to see how badly she'd hurt him or how he reacted. Spotting Zadoc and Corabeth, Merrill hurried to join them.

"Something wrong?" Zadoc asked.

"I have a headache." Merrill rubbed her head for emphasis. "Corabeth, do you suppose Granny would mind if I go back to your house and rest until Zadoc can take me home?"

"I'll take you home right now," Zadoc told her. "Corabeth and I were just saying the party is nearly over anyway. Come on. I'll get the coats, and we can leave."

Merrill knew Corabeth was most likely disappointed. She would have to find a way to make it up to her friend. "I'm sorry," she whispered. "I can't explain."

Corabeth seemed to understand and nodded. "It's all right. I know it must be a fierce pain or you wouldn't even bother."

Merrill nodded. "You are so right. It's perhaps the biggest pain I've ever had to deal with."

Chapter 15

The next afternoon, Rurik took some time during his lunch break to read a letter that had just arrived. His brother Aron shared news of the family as well as a bit of mystery. Apparently, there were rumors of a scandal going on around town, and it had something to do with Nils and his father. Aron stated that the two had argued publicly, and then without warning Nils and his sister had disappeared in the dead of night. No one knew what had happened to either one of them. They had simply vanished.

It made no sense to Rurik. Why would Nils and Svea leave without telling their family? He read on.

> Some have suspected that part of the problem had to do with Svea Olsson and her flirtatious behavior. After you left and it became common knowledge that the engagement had been dissolved, suitors started vying for Svea's attention. It has been said that there were several uncalled-for public displays. It is also rumored that the minister made a visit to the Olssons, who were beside themselves over the matter. They were quite concerned, and apparently there was talk of Svea going to live with

her older sister. Then, as I mentioned before, she and
Nils left Lindsborg without telling anyone. Naturally
the Olssons are very worried.

The rest of the letter reported on the family and asked
after Carl and Rurik, but all of that didn't matter much right
now. The only thing Rurik could concentrate on was the part
about Nils and Svea. He glanced at his watch. He knew Carl
was getting ready to walk over to the office, wanting to work
with Nils on one of the ledgers. Knowing he wouldn't have
much time, Rurik quickly took up a pen and paper.

Dear Aron,
I must say that your letter took me by surprise. Please
tell the Olssons not to fret. Nils and Svea are safe. They
came here to Waseca where Svea has tried to convince
me to reinstate our engagement.

He went on to explain that he had no intention of doing
so, but that Carl's condition had made it necessary to take
Nils on as an employee. He asked Aron if he would try to
find out what problems had taken place between Nils and
his father. Perhaps in doing so they could help Nils to repair
the relationship, and he and Svea could return to Lindsborg
without worry. Finding a replacement for Nils in the furniture
business didn't seem nearly so daunting as dealing with the
two siblings and their plans for him.

"I had a good rest. Are you ready to go?" Carl asked, entering the kitchen. His boots were warming by the stove, and
he went to fetch them.

Rurik nodded. "I'll help you over to the office, but first I need to finish this letter to Aron."

"Trouble?"

He didn't want to unduly worry his uncle. "I don't know for sure. Aron wrote that apparently Nils had some sort of falling-out with his father that led to him coming here. I plan to ask him about it when the time is right, so I'd rather you not say anything."

"Ja, sure." Carl nodded. "I'll put on my boots while you write."

Rurik hurriedly finished the letter, deciding at the last minute against mentioning Svea's condition. He tucked the missive in his pocket and hurried to where Carl waited by the front door.

"I'm ready."

"I feel stronger every day," Carl declared as they walked to the workshop. "Maybe that doctor knows more than I give him credit for. Taking a nap seems to help."

Rurik smiled despite his concerns. "Sometimes folks other than Swedes know a thing or two."

"Ja, I suppose so," Carl replied with a grin.

Inside the office they found Nils already hard at work. Afternoons proved best for Carl to offer assistance, and Rurik felt easing Nils into the position with half days was easier on his uncle. He'd assured Nils that in time they would need him full time, but for now the half days seemed to work out fine.

"G'afternoon," Nils said, trying to smile from behind swollen lips.

"What in the world happened?" Rurik asked.

"Ran into a door," Nils said. "I'm afraid the door got the better of me." He straightened. "Mr. Jorgenson, I tallied all those columns you asked me to take care of and have the figures ready for you."

"Good. In a minute we can go over those together, but first I'm going to go see the boys."

Rurik watched Carl shuffle from the room. "So are you managing the bookkeeping all right?" Rurik asked Nils.

"Things seem in good order from what I can tell," Nils replied. He glanced past Rurik to the open door and lowered his voice. "Svea tells me you tried to talk to her last night about going home."

"I did."

"She wasn't happy about it, you know."

Rurik shrugged. "I only told her the truth. I think it's important for her happiness and the welfare of her child to find the man who is truly responsible for her condition and make him take responsibility. She and I both know that man isn't me."

Nils folded his hands together. "I don't think she'll go back to Lindsborg, no matter what you say or do."

"Why is that, Nils?" His brother's letter was heavy on his mind, and he considered for a moment telling his friend exactly what he knew.

"Her condition, of course. She's too frail to travel now."

The outside shop door opened, and Rurik turned to find Bogart Krause filling the entryway. "Good afternoon, Rurik."

"Well, this is a surprise. What brings you into town?"

Mr. Krause grinned. "Secrets and conspiracies. Are you up for one?"

Rurik tried not to show his dismay at Krause's choice of words. "I suppose I am."

"Well, I have a project for you. A piece of furniture to order." He reached inside his coat and pulled out a folded piece of paper. Handing the drawing to Rurik, he continued. "Merrill's birthday is coming up in April, and I know you'll need time to get this put together."

Rurik studied the picture. "What is this, a wardrobe?"

"Similar. It's called a *schrank*. It's usually something I would have made for her years ago so she could save things for her own household. It's an old German custom. These are built quite large and can therefore be used for daily purpose, too. Clothes can be hung up, and the drawers and shelves are good for storage." The big man pointed to the page. "You'll see there from the instructions that each of the components are built separately but are put together as a whole. That way, despite its size, Merrill can take it with her when she weds. It'll be just a matter of disengaging the pieces."

Rurik swallowed hard. "Is . . . is she engaged?"

Krause shook his head. "No, but I hope that soon she'll find a young man and settle down. She's a good woman, and she's taken care of her brothers and me for far too long. I thought maybe a schrank would encourage her to look forward to a life of her own. Do you think you can work it into your other orders? I don't care what it costs. I'll have the ice money, and the Lord knows Merrill deserves even more than this."

Rurik knew even if he had to work on it at night in secret, he would see that Merrill had her schrank. "I'll handle it myself."

"Wonderful. Thank you. When I present it to her, that will make it all the more special. Now, where's that ornery uncle of yours? He owes me a game or two."

"I think you'll find him in the workshop."

Rurik continued to inspect the drawing after Mr. Krause had gone from the room. He already imagined the time he would spend working on the piece. Crafting it for Merrill.

"What do you think you're doing?" Nils demanded.

The question took Rurik by surprise. "What are you talking about?" He stared at Nils over the paper.

"That." Nils motioned to the drawing. "You're acting rather strange."

"Not at all." Rurik tried his best to sound unconcerned. No matter what Nils suspected, Rurik wasn't about to confess his feelings for Merrill. "I am quite fascinated with this piece of furniture. I've never made anything like it. I think it's a marvelous wardrobe. Here, look at it yourself."

Nils took the paper and studied it for a moment. Then with a wicked grin he handed it back to Rurik. "I'd like to help you build it. If I have my way, that piece will one day be in my house."

"And why would it end up in your house?"

"Because I intend to ask her father if I can court Miss Krause. If all goes accordingly—we might one day be married."

Rurik couldn't shake the sense of unease he felt at the idea of Nils marrying Merrill. He realized he was probably jealous, but he also felt hounded by the problem between Nils and his father. It wouldn't be good to mix Merrill up in it all. But to be completely honest, Rurik knew beyond any doubt that he'd fallen in love with Merrill Krause.

Trying his best to keep his thoughts at bay, Rurik went to work on the schrank, and for the next few days he accomplished a great deal. He worked during his evenings after Carl had gone to bed. The hours spent on the piece of furniture, using a beautiful walnut wood, only made Rurik's heart ache more for what might be. He simply couldn't allow Nils to steal her away.

When Tobe came to pick him up before dawn on Thursday, Rurik had decided he would ask Mr. Krause himself for the right to court Merrill. He would have to deal with the situation of Svea and dispel the lies she was spreading about their impending wedding. He hadn't wanted to shame her. She would deal with enough of that because of the baby. Instead, he had hoped and prayed that she would take up his offer of train passage and head back to Kansas.

"You awake over there?" Tobe asked him after several minutes of silence.

"Ja. Just thinking."

"Good time for it."

Rurik nodded. "So, how's your family?"

"Doing pretty well. We worked until dark yesterday, and I expect we'll do the same today. My father's never missed a deadline, and I don't imagine he'll start with this delivery."

"No, I don't imagine he will." Rurik could see a ribbon of color against the horizon as the sun started to lighten the sky. Low clouds, definite harbingers of snow, seemed to soak up the light and immediately diminish the glow.

"Today will go faster. We have the ice cleared of snow and scored. It shouldn't take nearly as long to cut and load. Oh, and I hope you haven't had breakfast. Merrill Jean made her famous *quark-tasche*."

"What is that?"

"Oh, it's a delicious cheese pastry. Our mother used to make it for special occasions, and it's one of my favorites. You'll be glad you came to work today. Yesterday we had plain old pancakes and sausage. There will still be sausages and other things on the table, but the quark-tasche is what I'll be eating."

Rurik laughed. "I can hardly wait to try it."

For a short time there was silence once again, and then Tobe spoke up. "I hope you don't mind my asking, but I wondered if you would tell me what kind of man your friend Nils Olsson is. I mean . . . he seems quite interested in Merrill, and we Krauses tend to look out for our own. I figure with you getting set to marry his sister, you might be the best one to know."

"I'm not marrying Svea Olsson," Rurik said, trying his best not to let his anger show.

Tobe looked at him oddly for a moment, then turned his attention back to the team. "I thought you were betrothed."

"We were, but she broke that off before I came to Minnesota. If she hadn't, I would have. Our betrothal was an arrangement put together by our fathers and certainly had little to do with anything else."

"But she was telling people at the party that you were planning to marry quite soon."

"I'm not surprised. But it isn't true. She's . . . well . . . I suppose she's just trying to save herself embarrassment. I'm hoping she'll return to Kansas soon."

"Her brother, too?"

"I don't know. I don't want to speak against my friend, but Nils is probably not the best choice of suitor for your sister."

"Why do you say that?"

Rurik wanted to shout to the skies that it was because he was in love with Merrill and was far better suited to court her. But he didn't. "My brother recently wrote to suggest there were some problems between Nils and his father," he said carefully. "I don't know what it involves, but Nils left without saying anything to his family."

"Except his sister."

"Ja. The family has been very worried about them. He brought her here hoping I might change my mind about the engagement. I think he figures I could marry her, and then we could all live happily together."

"So do you think he's dangerous?"

"No, not that. At least I have no reason to think so. Nils is more . . . more . . ." Rurik sighed and tried to think of how to express that his best friend had always found ways to use the people around him to his best advantage. There didn't seem to be a kind way, however.

"As children, Nils and I were always good friends. That friendship carried on into our adult years. However, it has not been without its problems. Nils has always been a person who sought to advance himself in whatever manner required as little effort as possible on his part. First through his family, and later with me. I've never yet seen him strike out for himself. Even his coming here was prompted because he knew I would take pity on him."

"Doesn't sound very honorable."

"I think Nils lacks the kind of ambition that causes a man to do for himself."

"I suppose if you're right, we won't have much to worry about."

Rurik shook his head. "What do you mean?"

"Well, Merrill Jean would never find herself coupled with a man like you've described. She's too driven—too hardworking. She would expect her mate to be the same. She's a good discerner of people."

Rurik felt himself relaxing. Tobe was right. Merrill was a woman who knew her own mind. He could tell she wasn't that enthralled with Nils at the party. She never showed him more than a moment's attention at work. Perhaps he was worrying for nothing.

"So your father would take into consideration what your sister desires in a husband?"

Tobe laughed. "He wouldn't dare do otherwise."

Merrill washed and dried the last of the supper dishes, pausing long enough to put her hand to the small of her aching back. Despite having stayed home to cook and feed the workers, she was every bit as tired as if she'd been out cutting ice. Her only thought was to make her way to bed.

She gave the kitchen one last check. Seeing that everything was in order, she made her way to the front room in order to tell her father good night. She stopped short, however, when she heard her name mentioned and then Nils Olsson.

"He asked me if he could court her," Merrill's father said. "I told him I wasn't opposed, but that the decision lay with Merrill."

"Well, Rurik said he's not necessarily a good choice for her," Tobe replied.

"Why is that?" Flynn asked. "They seemed to be having a good enough time at the party."

"Rurik told me Nils lacks direction. He doesn't seem to want to do for himself, but instead counts on others to make things good for him. Said Olsson has been that way since they were boys."

Merrill heard the conversation continue, but her mind whirled with indignant thoughts. How dare Rurik Jorgenson, a man of questionable character himself, besmirch the reputation of his lifelong friend?

Had she not been so tired, Merrill might well have stormed into the room and given her brothers and father a piece of her mind. But the fight could wait until the morning, and then perhaps she should take the matter directly to the one who had caused her grief. She had no desire to court Nils Olsson, and she could not deny that she at least previously had feelings for Rurik Jorgenson. But she was no man's fool. Neither man was going to take advantage of her good nature.

Chapter 16

Merrill got her opportunity to speak to Rurik the very next day. She had already completed the pie safes and blanket chests, but she had baked fresh bread and strudel and wanted to bring some for Carl. Yet she was disturbed by the fact that Rurik would also benefit from her generosity. Right now she felt anything but generous toward the man.

Most of the men at the shop were busy in the main work area when Merrill arrived. Since it was morning, Nils had not yet showed up for work—exactly as Merrill had planned. She had thought it might be difficult to get Rurik away from the others, but when she made her presence known, Rurik rather naturally followed her from the busy work area.

"I didn't expect to see you here today," Rurik said.

Merrill walked from the staining room and stopped close to the office. Rurik halted a short distance from where she stood and gave her a smile. "I see you have a basket on your arm. Am I correct in supposing you've brought us something good to eat?"

"I thought Carl might like some fresh bread and strudel."

Her tone was clipped. She gave him a hard look. "But I had hoped to have words with you first."

"Words?" He chuckled. "Sounds rather ominous."

Merrill didn't appreciate his good humor. "I know all about you, Rurik Jorgenson. I know that Svea is with child, and that you are refusing to honor your betrothal. I overheard you tell your uncle that you didn't intend to do anything about it. That it was her problem."

She paused a moment. A black cloud seemed to settle over his features. She went on. "I find such behavior appalling and certainly uncalled for—especially by a man who calls himself a Christian.

"Furthermore, you have no right to be suggesting to my brother that Nils Olsson is unworthy of my attention. I overheard my brothers and father discussing it last night, and I was dumbfounded that you would dare to say anything against Mr. Olsson—a man who so obviously esteems you. He has been your lifelong friend, but I suppose if you would do such an abominable thing to his sister, you would have no compunction about betraying him."

Rurik watched her silently. Merrill felt a bit unnerved by his steady stare, but continued anyway. "I want you to stay out of my affairs, nevertheless. It's none of your business if Nils Olsson wants to court me. I don't know why you took it upon yourself to say anything, but I won't tolerate it again."

She fell silent and realized she was panting for breath. For several long moments Rurik said nothing. His expression and the look in his eyes continued to make her uneasy.

"Well?" Merrill finally spoke. "Have you nothing to say for yourself?"

"It seems to me that you've said it all. You don't care about the truth, obviously. You've come here with your mind made up. You've judged me and condemned me, all without benefit of hearing my side of the matter."

His comment caused Merrill to stammer for words. "Why . . . you . . . I mean . . ."

He held up his hand. Merrill shook her head and felt her anger mount. He said, "I can't abide women who eavesdrop and gossip. I thought better of you, but apparently you make a habit of it. You referenced such action two times just in this conversation—or shall I say, tirade?"

Merrill pulled back as if he'd slapped her. Before she could speak, however, Rurik continued. "I might add—not that I expect you to care—that it was your brother Tobe who asked me about Nils and his character. I neither brought up the matter nor elaborated on my concerns. Furthermore . . ." He turned and stalked across the room, pausing only long enough to look back at her and shake his head. "Svea's condition is not of my doing." He walked through the open door and slammed it behind him.

Shocked, Merrill stood silent for several minutes. She stared at the closed door as if expecting Rurik to come back and apologize for his outburst. When he didn't, Merrill wasn't sure whether to be relieved or further enraged.

Remembering the basket for Carl, Merrill decided to forget about Rurik's comments and deliver the food. If what he said was true, then she'd just done him a great injustice—at least so far as the accusation regarding Svea was concerned. If he was lying to cover his sin, it wasn't likely she was going to get him to admit it anytime soon. Especially not after his response just now.

Shifting the basket to her left arm, Merrill trod across the yard between the shop and house. A terrible feeling of guilt washed over her. What had she just done? She'd thought herself perfectly justified to call Rurik out on his behavior, but he was right about one thing.

I've judged him without hearing his side of the matter.

Merrill bit her lower lip. It wasn't like her to do such a thing. Why had she allowed her emotions to get the best of her?

She knocked on the door of the house and forced a smile when Carl appeared.

"Oh, Merrill Jean, it's good to see you. Come in."

"I thought . . . well . . . I brought you some bread and strudel."

"What a treat. Would you like me to carry it for you?" He motioned to the basket.

She shook her head. "I can manage just fine. Shall I put it in the kitchen for you?"

"Please. Would you like a cup of coffee to warm up?"

"No, that's all right. I only stopped by to bring this. I'm actually going to spend some time with Corabeth and Granny. One of the horses needed some attention at the farrier, so I'm biding my time until he's ready to go."

"Well, it's good to see you. I looked over all the pieces you painted. I am impressed with the way you've brought added value to the furniture. I know the buyers are going to be very pleased. We should sit down and discuss what other pieces might benefit from your skills."

Merrill took out two loaves of bread and placed them on the counter. "Thank you, Mr. Jorgenson. I'm so glad they meet your approval. I must admit I've enjoyed the work, and the extra money."

"Rurik told me he'd never seen such quality work. He's been most impressed by your ability. Of course, I remember that your mother had quite an artistic flare."

"She's the only reason I know how to paint."

"Well, she taught you well. I know Rurik would join me in saying that your work is of the highest quality."

Merrill doubted seriously that Rurik would even allow her to return to work after what she'd just said and done. She thought to mention the incident to Carl, but she didn't want to tax his health.

I don't know what to do, Lord.

She felt just as Rurik did about eavesdropping. Why had she allowed herself to get caught up in that most dangerous activity? Even so, she told herself, it wasn't his place to interfere in the matter of Nils. She didn't need anyone looking out for her in such a manner. Her brothers had spent a lifetime doing that, and it had gotten her nothing but loneliness and spinsterhood.

Carl was saying something about painting customized window shutters, and Merrill realized she hadn't been listening.

"I'm sorry. I let my mind wander," she apologized. "I'm glad you both like the work, and I will look forward to seeing what else you have in mind," she said. "Now tell me, how are you feeling these days?"

Carl Jorgenson straightened a bit. "Better. A little stronger all the time. Rurik coming here was a gift from God."

"I'm sure you feel that way."

He nodded and sat down to the kitchen table where he'd been drinking coffee. "I know your father has benefitted, too. He told me the other day that he had never seen anyone take to the ice as well as my nephew."

"Yes, Father said he works very hard."

"Ja, that's for sure."

"What do you know about Nils Olsson?" Merrill asked, trying her best to sound casual.

"Nils? Oh, I don't know him so much. You'd do better to ask Rurik. They've been friends for a long time. I met Nils long ago back in Kansas, but never had many dealings with him or his family. Why do you ask?"

She shrugged and placed the strudel on the counter before she picked up the empty basket. "No reason. I just wondered how things were working out for you . . . with him, I mean."

"He seems to know what he's doing. He's learning fast enough."

"I'm glad. I'm glad, too, that you have the extra help. I'm sure it's been a great concern to you."

"Having Rurik here puts my mind at ease. I signed papers to make him a full partner, you know."

She nodded and forced a smile. "Well, I need to go. I promised Granny Lassiter that I would spend some time with her and Corabeth today."

"Could you do something for me?" Carl asked, heading over to the cabinet. "I have a couple of her dishes. Would you mind taking them back?"

"Not at all."

He brought her two plates. "Tell her she can refill them anytime she likes."

Merrill took the plates and headed to the door. Carl followed after her. "Thank you for the food. God has definitely provided for my every need through the hands of the townswomen. You ladies are definitely serving His purpose."

A frown edged her lips, but Merrill didn't turn. "I hope so," she murmured. But after her earlier encounter, she wasn't at all sure.

Rurik let his anger settle down while he focused on sanding the top of a sideboard. He didn't want his rage to ruin the piece, nor did he want to dwell on his earlier encounter with Merrill. He wasn't at all sure why things had gone as they had. It was obvious that Merrill had been thinking about the matter for some time. At least where the issue of Svea was concerned.

He knew without a doubt exactly when it was she'd overheard him speaking to Carl. It was that day that they'd come back to the house and found food in the kitchen. Carl had mentioned it was Merrill's doing, but he hadn't thought her to be in the house when they'd returned. No doubt when she heard their discussion, she'd exited by way of the back door so as not to be seen or to cause them discomfort. He supposed, given the conversation, she had a right to assume him to be at fault. Even so, she could have just confronted him about it rather than hurl accusations.

"Of course, I might not have handled her assumptions and questions any better," he muttered.

When lunchtime came, he put aside his work apron and decided to go to the post office and pick up the mail. Maybe there'd be a letter from Aron, although he doubted his brother would have had time to get back with an answer already.

At the post office, Rurik waited behind two other customers before asking for his mail. The postmaster nodded and went to retrieve it.

"Looks to be all business today," he said, handing three letters over.

Rurik looked at the addresses and nodded. "It does at that."

"So have you set your wedding day?" the man asked in a casually friendly manner. There was no one else in the store, so he'd already gone back to sorting through a stack of mail. "I'm sure you and that pretty little Olsson girl are going to make a nice couple. Will you live here in Waseca?"

Rurik forced his anger back. "I'm not getting married. I'm not even engaged."

The man looked up from his work. "Do tell? I was sure I heard that little gal tell someone that you two were to be married."

"We were once in an arranged betrothal, but that was ended before I came to Waseca. If anything else is being said . . . well, it's not true."

"I see. I'm sorry if I raised some unpleasantness," the man said, seeming to watch Rurik for his reaction.

"Gossips will say what they will. I hope you'll do what you can to dispel such rumors."

The man nodded and scratched his chin. "I reckon if anyone else comments on it, I will set the record straight."

Rurik tucked the letters in his pocket. "Thank you."

He left the post office and tried to figure out what he should do. He needed to make it clear to everyone that he had no intention of marrying Svea Olsson. The thought of standing up in church to make a declaration came to mind. Maybe that would settle things once and for all. Of course, it would be very embarrassing for Svea, and it wasn't his desire to draw attention to her and her condition.

Then without warning, there she was, standing in front of him. Rurik felt like he was seeing a ghost. He frowned down at her.

"You look terribly unhappy, Rurik. Whatever is wrong?" She smiled sweetly and reached out to take hold of his arm. "Why don't you come with me? Nils and I were just going to have some lunch."

Rurik pulled away brusquely. "Don't touch me."

She looked at him oddly. "What is it?"

"You know full well. You are spreading rumors about us being engaged. I want it to stop. I am not going to marry you, Svea. Not now. Not ever. I do not love you."

She looked around rather nervously. "Rurik," she said in a hushed voice, "this is hardly the place."

"Maybe it's exactly the place. After all, I've asked you in private to return to Kansas. I've asked you to stop lying about me. You've done neither. If privacy hasn't worked, perhaps a public setting will."

"You are being cruel."

"I'm being honest—something you refuse to be." Rurik shook his head and took a breath to calm himself. "I have always cared about you and Nils. You know that. But I am not going to marry you. I'm sorry. Sorry for your condition and the shame that is upon you, but I can't pretend to love you. You need to go home."

Svea stared at him, her eyes wide and lips pursed. She looked as if she might start to cry, but Rurik refused to allow her emotions to sway him.

"I intend to make certain everyone knows that our engagement has long been broken," he said firmly. "If need be, I'll declare it in church on Sunday. You would save yourself a lot of embarrassment by leaving as soon as possible. If you need my assistance in purchasing train passage, have Nils let me know."

He left her standing there and made his way across the street. A handful of people watched him, no doubt having overheard at least some of the conversation. Rurik felt guilty for having made such a public spectacle, but at the same time, he was so weary of dealing with the deception. He had tried to be kind and gentle. He'd tried to leave the matter in Svea's hands so she could save face in whatever manner she chose. Nothing had worked.

"I didn't have to be so mean about it," he muttered, feeling that perhaps he should turn back and apologize. He drew a deep breath and paused to glance over his shoulder.

She was gone.

Chapter 17

Merrill sat at the kitchen table with Granny and sipped at a cup of hot tea. She had just explained what had happened with Rurik and now waited for the older woman to comment.

"I wonder why you are so willing to believe the words of a stranger over a young man you've come to know over the last few months."

Her comment left Merrill speechless. Searching for the right words she finally said, "I suppose . . . well . . . given the fact that Rurik himself has done nothing to deny his engagement to her is one of my biggest reasons. The first time he came to dinner after church the comment was made by his uncle that he was betrothed. Rurik never denied it or corrected him."

"Perhaps he thought it too personal a matter for public discussion—after all, he'd just arrived in the area," Granny suggested. She pushed a plate of sugar cookies toward Merrill. "My guess is he wanted to tell his uncle in private and hadn't yet had a chance."

"I suppose that is possible," Merrill replied, "but he's had plenty of time since then."

"Have you ever asked him outright if he was engaged?"

"Of course not. I didn't see that it was necessary. When the Olssons first got here, they came immediately to the furniture shop. I was there. Svea made a grand display of telling everyone that she was engaged to Rurik. He didn't correct her."

"He was probably shocked by her unexpected appearance. Didn't you say that he hadn't expected either of them to show up in Waseca? Then again, he might have felt sorry for her and wanted to save her from embarrassment. If he was sparing her feelings, that's certainly no reason to hold a grudge against him."

Merrill nibbled on a cookie and tried to figure out what disturbed her so much about his not correcting things prior to her outburst. "I'm just so confused."

"Is that maybe because you have feelings for Mr. Jorgenson?"

Merrill's head snapped up. "What?" She felt her cheeks grow hot. "Why would you ask that?"

Granny chuckled. "Corabeth herself asked me if I'd seen the way you look at him. She said you were watching him whenever you could at the winter party. So is it true?"

She didn't know what to say. She hadn't acknowledged her feelings for Rurik to anyone. She'd even tried to convince herself that her misguided belief in his good character negated any feelings she might have had for him. But of course it wasn't true. The reason his character mattered so much was because she had fallen in love with him.

"I do have feelings for him," she finally admitted. "But I

beg you to keep my secret. I cannot bear the thought of others thinking me a mooning schoolgirl."

"Your confidences are always safe with me, Merrill Jean. You know that." Granny leaned forward and patted Merrill's arm with her wrinkled hands. "I think it's quite possible Mr. Jorgenson has feelings for you, Merrill Jean. Corabeth said he positively lights up when he sees you at church. He was telling everyone about the magnificent work you'd done on the furniture and how wonderful it was to have you in the workshop."

"But that doesn't mean he has feelings for me. I'm benefitting the business, so naturally he's pleased."

Granny smiled. "Child, you have a lot to learn about young men. Did it ever occur to you that maybe Rurik spoke against Nils to Tobe because he truly feels Nils is unworthy of you? And further, that maybe he wants to court you himself?"

Merrill shook her head. "I have no reason to believe that. Just because I have feelings for him doesn't mean the man has to return them. In fact, given Svea is here trying to win him back suggests to me that their engagement is far from over."

"She came here to convince him—not the other way around. Miss Olsson's behavior is quite bold, but if she is with child, as you say, it makes sense. She's probably feeling most desperate. Poor woman knows the kind of condemnation that will come down on her for such a thing."

"Obviously there's a man somewhere who participated in that matter. He also should face justice for his actions."

"While that's true," Granny replied, "it's often not the way things work out. The woman cannot deny her condition or hide the fact for long. A man can refuse to acknowledge his part in the matter, and no one is the wiser. There's no way to prove a man's fatherhood. Even if a child grew up to look somewhat like the man in question, folks could say what they like about coincidence and happenstance.

"Now don't misunderstand me," Granny continued. "The sin is upon both parties in most cases. But what if the situation isn't what we think? What if Miss Olsson was accosted?"

"You mean forced?" Merrill asked. "I'd never thought of that possibility."

"We can judge her, or we can extend a hand in Christian love."

Merrill felt shame wrap around her guilt. "I never once considered that she might be a victim in all of this. I haven't acted in a very Christian manner, have I?"

Granny shrugged. "You took the road most folks would travel, but now that you have an idea that her situation could be something else, maybe you can make it right."

"What do you suggest?"

"I'd start with apologizing to Mr. Jorgenson. You can find a way to let Rurik know your feelings for him. The matter is in part his responsibility, just as you said. He should have made the truth known. But you can apologize for rushing to judgment. You can let him know that you care about him, and that you take responsibility for acting poorly."

Merrill nodded. "You're right, of course. I don't know whatever possessed me to act in such a manner. I know better. I suppose I was just concerned with what people would think." She shook her head and got to her feet. "Granny, as always you are the voice of truth and reason."

Shortly after Sunday service, Merrill swallowed her pride and made her way to where Rurik stood not far from his uncle. Seeing her father step forward to speak to Carl, Merrill took the opportunity to motion Rurik aside.

"I know you probably hate me, but I want to apologize."

Rurik appeared apprehensive and weary. He studied her in silence, and Merrill grew uncomfortable.

"I was wrong to judge you and wrong to act as I did."

Still Rurik said nothing, but his expression told Merrill that he was listening. She continued. "I don't usually just jump to conclusions like that. You were right to chide me for eavesdropping. It was wrong, and I should have made my presence known in both situations."

"True." His single-word statement was almost more frustrating to Merrill than had he given her a long tirade.

She drew a deep breath and glanced around, hoping no one else was overhearing her confession. "I'm afraid my emotions got the better of me." She thought about telling him how she had come to care for him, but decided against it. "I hope you'll forgive me."

Rurik opened his mouth to speak, but just then Merrill's father moved closer and drew him into the conversation with Carl.

"I was just telling your uncle what a natural you have been with the ice. It's almost like you were born to it."

Rurik looked back at Merrill for just a moment before smiling at the men. "I can't say I would want to spend a lifetime in such work. It's more physically demanding than furniture building. I honestly don't think I could expend that kind of energy day in and day out."

"Well, that's probably for the best," Merrill's father declared. "They already have electrical machines that can make ice, and as I hear tell they are becoming more and more popular. It won't be long before the ice will remain on the lake." Bogart Krause shook his head. "What I'd like to know is how a man is supposed to make a living if his very livelihood is taken from him."

Merrill took hold of his arm. "Father, you have a great many skills. Just look at the Belgians. Folks will need horses for a long, long time. Especially ones that can pull."

"For now that might be true, but the horseless carriage is sure to gain popularity. They formed that Duryea Motor Car Company just last year. Not only that, but the railroads crisscross the country and make transport easier and easier. Mark my word, they won't need horses for that much longer." He shook his head. "I guess when that happens, it'll be time for me to retire anyway."

Carl patted him on the shoulder. "Won't happen in our lifetime, Bogart. We'll leave it to the children to worry over."

Merrill smiled at her father. "Maybe if it does come sooner, you can spend more time fishing. After all, people will still need to eat, and fish will need to be caught."

Her father smiled. "So if the lake can't provide one way, we'll let it provide in another, eh?"

"Exactly. Besides, you know as well as anyone that horseless carriages aren't going to be able to traverse the snows around here. If a person doesn't have a sleigh and a strong team, they won't be able to get far at all. So for now, I seriously doubt we have much to worry about."

"The turn of the century seems rather daunting," Rurik declared, his first comment in the discussion. "I've heard more than one person comment on it. Back in Kansas, preachers have been talking up a storm about the end of all time coming with the nineteen hundreds. Personally, I don't figure it will be that bad, but you know how folks worry."

Merrill nodded. "Sometimes people get all worked up over nothing but rumors." She didn't bother to look at Rurik, but Merrill could feel his gaze on her. Hopefully he would accept her apology and realize how sincere she was. She had pondered Granny's comments ever since their talk. Why was she so quick to believe the worst about a person, especially a person like Rurik, who had treated her and her family with such kindness?

Carl nodded. "Ja, that's the way of it. I don't see any reason to worry until there's something to actually worry about." He reached to take hold of the pew. "Right now I need to rest, so I'll go home."

Rurik kept thinking of Merrill and her contrite words days after the Sunday encounter. He had wanted to accept her apology and tell her that he forgave her, but then his uncle and Merrill's father had included him in their conversation.

When Uncle Carl had needed to get home, there simply hadn't been an adequate opportunity.

"You got a letter from Aron," Carl announced, coming into the kitchen. "I picked up the mail, and this was waiting for you." He handed the envelope to Rurik.

Rurik opened it quickly. "I hope he sheds some light on what's going on with Nils and Svea." He quickly scanned the two pages. "He sends his love and hopes that your health is improving."

"You tell him I'll write soon." Carl went to the stove and put in several pieces of wood. "I'm going to make another pot of coffee. You want me to heat up that stew for supper?"

"Sounds good," Rurik said, trying to concentrate on his brother's words.

From what I've been able to learn, it appears Nils got himself into some kind of financial trouble due to gambling debts. His father learned of the matter and demanded Nils tell him the truth. Nils apparently had been going into Salina for some back-room games of poker. It appears he wasn't very skilled at cards and lost far more than he ever made. In fact, it's rumored that he lost a great deal.

Rurik paused and glanced to where Carl worked to build up the fire in the stove. If Nils had been gambling, it made complete sense as to why he would have argued with his father. The Olssons were leaders in the church, and they would never condone such actions with any family member.

In fact, Mr. Olsson might even find himself dismissed from leadership for being unable to control his family. Frowning to himself, Rurik continued to read.

> *I wasn't able to learn much more than this. Mr. Olsson, in fact, wasn't the one to tell me about the matter. I learned this from a completely unexpected source—Michael. He had gone to collect milk and overheard Mr. Olsson discussing the matter with the sheriff. Apparently Nils owes money to some men in Salina, and they aren't exactly waiting patiently. Michael said something was mentioned about the men coming after Mr. Olsson for payment. I admonished Michael to keep the matter to himself, yet here I am sharing the news with you. However, I wouldn't want to see Uncle Carl hurt in all of this. If Nils is given over to gambling in Kansas, it might well be that he will pick it up again in Minnesota. You should be aware of the problem.*

"So what else does Aron have to say?" Carl asked.

Rurik looked at his uncle, uncertain as to what he should share. For now, it seemed best to say nothing. "Not a whole lot." Rurik quickly scanned the last lines of the letter. "They had a little snow, but otherwise have enjoyed good weather. The family is doing well. Oh, I don't think I told you this, but Michael, too, has an interest in furniture making."

"Michael is Aron's oldest, ja?"

"Ja. He told me just before I came here that he would like to learn the trade. I said perhaps he could join us here sometime in the summer months. That is, if Aron can spare the boy and you agree to have him."

"You betcha. Michael is more than welcome. You just bring him here, and we'll teach him how to make all sorts of things."

Rurik smiled. "I'll let Aron know and see what he has to say about it."

"Have you told your brother about Svea's situation?"

He saw his uncle's concerned look and shook his head. "I didn't want to shame her. I figure it's her news to tell. I did mention that she was trying to get me to marry her quickly, but not why. I think it's best that kind of thing come from her."

"I think you're right." Carl lifted the pot of stew from the back of the stove and put it on the burner. "It's a terrible burden for a young woman."

Rurik nodded. "I know. Yet I cannot make this right for her. It would be different if I loved her." He shook his head. "I care for her and Nils very much. I wish there were an easier way to handle it—for everyone concerned."

"It's never easy to face our consequences." Carl stirred the stew. "But you're doing right by praying for them and being a friend."

Rurik frowned. "I don't guess I feel like I'm being much of a friend. I was kind of harsh with Svea a while back. Nils too. I suppose I need to work on my own heart." He refolded the letter and tucked it back into the envelope. His thoughts went to Merrill, and he knew that more than anything, he really wanted to talk to her.

"I was thinking about riding out to the Krause farm."

Carl looked at him, lips pursed. "It's near to dark, ja?"

Rurik nodded. "I suppose it's not the best idea, eh?"

"Probably not." Carl smiled. "But since when do you vorry about the best idea when your heart tells you to do something? You go on. I can eat stew without you. Besides, maybe you'll get invited to take supper with them. Merrill's cooking is better than this old stew that I threw together."

Rurik laughed. "Miss Krause's cooking beats anything I've ever had."

"Then, maybe you should marry that gal," Carl said with a grin.

Shrugging, Rurik nodded. "Maybe I should."

Chapter 18

Merrill heard a knock, wiped her floury hands on her apron, and moved to the back door. Who could be calling this late? She found herself face-to-face with Rurik. He doffed his hat in greeting and gave a quick nod.

"Mr. Jorgenson . . . This is . . . a surprise." She motioned him inside the kitchen. "I need to check on something in the oven, but please make yourself at home." She hurried to pull out a tray of golden brown *bierocks*. The aroma of the fresh bread dough, cabbage, and meat filled the air.

"My father and brothers should be back anytime, so you're free to wait."

"Actually, Miss Krause, I came to see you." He gripped his hat in front of him, like he was feeling a bit uncertain.

She pulled a second pan from the oven and placed it on the counter before taking a deep breath and turning to face her visitor. Had he come to accept her apology, or was he here to chide her for her behavior? Merrill wiped her hands on the apron and nodded, encouraging him to continue. She'd just as soon get this over with, whatever it was.

Rurik smiled crookedly. "I appreciated your words on Sunday. I know it wasn't easy to come to me like that, and your spirit humbled me."

She released the breath she'd been holding. "I'm truly sorry for the way I acted at the shop."

"I know. I wanted to say as much on Sunday, but . . . well . . . you remember how it was."

She nodded. Turning back to her tasks she placed the baked bierocks on a platter and prepared another dozen to go into the oven. She waited for Rurik to say more.

"I really can't blame you for what you said," he continued quietly. "I knew Svea and Nils coming here was going to open a big crate of problems. I just didn't know exactly how big that problem was going to become—or how I should deal with it. . . ."

Putting the pan in the oven, Merrill checked the fire below. "These things do have a way of taking on a life of their own." She stirred the gravy, finally determining she had done all she could to keep her hands busy to cover her own discomfort. She must now give Rurik her full attention. She pulled out a chair and sat across from him. "Nevertheless, I was wrong, and I realize that. It wasn't just the eavesdropping, either. It was my rush to judgment. I'm afraid I've always been rather inclined toward that. I've been working on it, however." She gave a little shrug. "Apparently not hard enough. But this whole thing has been a good reminder of the consequences."

Rurik shook his head. "I appreciate you being honest with me, Merrill." He paused. "I hope you don't mind me addressing you that way." She nodded her permission, and he said, "Other folks have been talking behind my back or making their own judgments without saying a word to me. I didn't want to cause Svea further shame or pain when I learned about—well, about her condition. I never figured she'd say we were still engaged, however. I don't think too many folks know about the baby, but I'm sure they will soon enough."

"Can't she go back to Kansas?" Merrill asked. "Surely she doesn't expect you to take on the responsibility for another man's child."

Rurik twisted his hat in his hands. Merrill immediately realized she hadn't taken his things. "Oh, do let me hang up your hat and coat. You will stay for supper, won't you, Mr. Jorgenson?"

"I'd like that, but I was wondering if you would do something for me. Would you call me Rurik?" He handed her his hat.

She nodded, feeling strangely shy. He grinned and began to unfasten his coat. "Good, we've got names settled. And yes, I'd like very much to join you for supper. It smells absolutely wonderful in here."

"Why don't you make yourself comfortable here at the kitchen table?" she invited, hanging his things by the door. "Like I said, my father and brothers will be back here soon enough, and then we'll take our meal in the dining room. Meanwhile, would you like a cup of coffee?"

"I would," he said, pulling out a chair. "As for your earlier question, Svea apparently did expect me to take on another man's child. She came here to try to coerce me into marriage. She even told Nils that the baby was mine. I've tried to set him straight on the matter, but he seems reluctant to believe me."

Merrill poured the coffee and brought it to Rurik. "I'm sure they're both quite frightened," she said, though she wasn't feeling all that charitable toward the two right then. "I'm sorry to say I didn't extend much in the way of Christian charity—to you or to her. It was Granny Lassiter who suggested that perhaps Svea had been wronged—attacked, even."

"I'd thought of that, too," Rurik admitted. "However, I know she was acting quite forward with other men around town after our engagement was broken. My brother wrote to say as much. But it's possible that as she got involved romantically, someone took advantage of her."

"It's a very difficult situation for a young woman whatever the circumstances." Merrill met his gaze and lost her train of thought momentarily. Granny's comments about Rurik possibly having feelings for her came back to her. How she longed to know the truth!

But that might mean I'd have to share my feelings for him. And what if I do that and Granny is wrong? He might be completely put out that I've been so forward.

She looked away. Was she ready to face a possible rebuff?

"I know she's most likely afraid," Rurik said after a long pause. "I care about her—just as I do Nils. Our families have been friends forever, and I feel very much like a brother to both of them."

"How did the two of you come to be engaged?" Merrill asked without thinking.

"That was our fathers' doing," he said, not sounding like he was put off by her question. "My father came from a tradition of arranged marriages. In most cases, those unions went well.

However, when it came to me . . . well . . . I don't think my father really understood much about me. He wanted me to be a farmer, and I wanted to make furniture. We got along well enough, but I think I was rather puzzling to him. Especially when it comes to what I want in a wife."

"And what is that?" She bit her tongue. *How could I have been so bold?* she wailed to herself.

He smiled and, as if reading her thoughts, said without a pause, "I need a strong woman. A woman who isn't afraid of hard work and hard times. I need a woman who is knowledgeable about many things, one who is kind and gentle, generous with those in need. I prefer someone who is creative, and above all, she must love the Lord."

Merrill swallowed hard and stared at her work-hardened hands. He'd not once said a word about looking for one who was delicate and pretty or one who liked to fuss with her hair and wear beautiful clothes. Merrill felt a little weak in the knees when she lifted her gaze and found Rurik studying her. She stood to check on the food again, fighting to control her nerves. "I think loving God is the most important thing for anyone," she said as she pulled the pan out of the oven to cool.

"I do, too," he replied as she returned to the table. "My parents taught me that God must always be put first. One of the very first things I remember memorizing was the Lord's Prayer—in Swedish."

Merrill cast a glance over her shoulder and chuckled. "I'd love to hear that."

He nodded. "*Fader Vår som är i Himmelen. Helgat varde Ditt namn. Tillkomme Ditt Rike. Ske Din vilja, såsom i Him-*

melen så ock på Jorden. Vårt dagliga bröd giv oss idag Och förlåt oss våra skulder såsom ock vi förlåta dem oss skyldiga äro och inled oss icke i frestelse utan fräls oss ifrån ondo. Ty Riket är Ditt och Makten och Härligheten i Evighet. Amen."

The words flowed quickly in the singsong manner Merrill had come to expect from Swedes. "That's really beautiful."

"How about letting me hear it in German?"

"I don't really know much German. My family is several generations American. My father could say it for you, but I'm afraid you'd only get bits and pieces of the prayer from me."

He smiled. "I liked the little prayer you translated for me at dinner that first meal I shared with your family."

"German is a harsher-sounding language," Merrill said thoughtfully. "I often tease my father about how angry it can sound. There were times he has spoken in rapid German to friends, and I've wondered if they were having a disagreement."

"I grew up with my parents and grandparents speaking Swedish at home. However, in public we were admonished to speak only English. My family wanted to be seen as American in every way possible."

"Mine too. Perhaps with exception of the food. My father still prefers German dishes over just about anything else." Merrill heard the sound of a wagon outside. "That will be my family. They've been loading ice all day onto train cars."

"Before they come storming in here, I just want to say that . . . well . . . I've enjoyed this time with you, Merrill. I also enjoy our time together at the shop."

She smiled and nodded. "As do I."

"I want to explain something. I feel I owe it to you."

Merrill shook her head. "I'm sure I don't need any explanations. . . ." She didn't know how to finish, but the truth was she really did want to know what he was thinking and feeling.

Rurik looked down at the table. "When your brother Tobe asked me about Nils, I have to admit I had no desire to be complimentary. I didn't want Tobe to take back a good report to your father and possibly complicate your life with someone who really isn't worthy. . . ."

"I see," she said when he didn't continue, mostly to invite him to tell her more about the incident.

"I don't think you do," he said, glancing up. "The real reason, though, is that I didn't want your father to give Nils permission to court you . . . because . . . well, I'd like to have that honor myself."

Merrill felt her breath catch and the words stick in her throat. *He wants to court me!*

"I suppose this comes as a shock, and maybe you have no interest, given all that has happened with Svea and Nils, but I can't help speaking the truth of how I feel. Of course, I really need to resolve everything with Svea before I ask your father for permission to see you, but I'm hoping you approve."

Just then Flynn burst through the door. "I'm half frozen to death—oh, it's you, Rurik! Good to see you. Are you staying for supper?" He didn't wait for a response. "Hmmm, bierocks. My favorite."

Rurik threw a glance Merrill's way, then nodded at her brother. "Your sister invited me to do just that, and from the aroma of her cooking, I knew it would be impossible to refuse."

Flynn walked to the platter of bierocks and pinched a piece of bread from the end. "You won't be sorry," he said around the bite.

Merrill listened as her brothers entered and began their own conversations with Rurik. They led him away from the kitchen, talking about the day and all that had happened.

When she was alone, Merrill stood in wonder of all that had happened. Had Rurik really just declared his interest in her?

"And after I was so harsh with him . . ." she murmured.

"What was that?"

She turned to see her father standing at the door.

"Just mumbling to myself, Father. Rurik Jorgenson is here. I invited him to stay for supper." She wondered if she should mention his desire to court her, but she decided she wanted to keep that wonderful possibility all to herself for a while. And as Rurik said, he needed to resolve matters with Svea once and for all before he'd truly be free.

Father hung his coat next to Rurik's. "I saw his horse out there and put it in the barn. Where's Rurik?"

"In the front room with the boys." She turned to put the gravy in its serving bowl with a ladle. "I'll have supper on the table in a few minutes. Oh, and would you do me a favor tonight?" She glanced at him with a little smile.

Her father returned the smile, rubbing his whiskery chin. "I'm almost afraid to ask what the favor is, but let's hear it."

"Would you say the Lord's Prayer . . . in German this time?"

"That's all?"

Merrill laughed and turned her attention back to the food. "That's all."

Her father laughed, too. "Sometimes I don't know what you're thinking, Merrill Jean, but I have a feeling there's a plan even in this."

"Could be," she said, smiling to herself. *Could be.*

Chapter 19

Early March remained cold, allowing for additional ice harvesting, much to Bogart Krause's pleasure. Merrill had heard her father say that he was trying to put aside as much money as possible, just in case this was the last winter he'd have customers for their ice.

Merrill bustled around the kitchen, packing snacks the men could eat during breaks from their work. She would drive out to the lake with hot coffee a few hours after they began, and then the men would return to the house later for lunch. It was a routine she'd come to know quite well, and today she had the help of Margaret Niedermeyer, making the work go much more smoothly.

"How's George feeling?" Merrill's father asked as Margaret tied on an apron.

"Not good. The doctor fears my husband has grown much too weak. He's had some trouble with his lungs this winter." Margaret looked concerned. "I don't know if he'll make it, to be quite honest."

"We've been praying for him," Father said.

"I was almost afraid to leave him this morning, but he assured me he was feeling better. I suppose only time will tell," the middle-aged woman declared. She picked up a basket. "I'll go and start the laundry now."

Merrill nodded and handed her father a large mug of coffee. "I figured you'd want to drink this on the way to the lake."

He kissed her cheek and took the mug. "You know me pretty well." He took a sip, then paused. "You know, Mr. Olsson has asked to court you."

Merrill shook her head firmly. "I have no interest in him."

"And why is that?" Her father gave her a quizzical look. "Is there something I should know?"

She shrugged. "I do not find him appealing or interesting. Mother always told me that a man should be both in order to have good husband potential. And since he offers neither to me, I see no reason to go out with him again."

"That seems reasonable. I thought maybe you were going to tell me that your heart lay elsewhere."

She looked at her father for a moment. "Well, perhaps. But for now, I'm content merely to continue on as I have. In time, God will show me what I'm to do, I'm sure."

"Do you still enjoy painting the furniture?"

"I do. And . . . and Mr. Jorgenson has a few new projects for me, in fact. He wants me to try my hand at painting a few music stands and tea carts. I think both will prove to be a great deal of fun," she finished in a rush.

"I'm glad you're happy, Merrill Jean. I've seen a change in you since you took on this project for the Jorgensons. I was a little worried about what people might say at first; not too many would approve my single daughter working with a bunch of men. But God helped me to see that it's best to put my trust in Him and not what other folks think."

Merrill leaned over to kiss his cheek, careful not to bump the coffee mug. "I agree. It isn't always easy, but it is always best. I love you, Papa." She turned back to her bread making. "I'll be down in a few hours with coffee."

"Maybe some cookies, too?"

"I've already packed those in the baskets you see on the table," she told him with a little grin.

"Then I suppose I should get on my way. I can't say I'm too anxious to get out there on the lake. It's awful windy today, and the cold is starting to get to me in my old age."

Merrill shook her head. "You certainly aren't old, Father. But you've earned a day off. You could always stay here by the stove and help me."

Her father laughed as she knew he would. "No, I think I'll just keep on with the ice. Your work is much harder."

She chuckled as her father took up the baskets, balancing his coffee mug in his other hand. Merrill went back to forming loaves for the bread pans.

Pausing only to deliver hot coffee and rolls to the men, Merrill busied herself with preparations for lunch. By the time the men came in for the noon meal, Merrill had fresh bread and a large pot of stew ready. The men were cold and famished, and the contents of the pot quickly disappeared, as did the bread and butter. Merrill had anticipated this, however, and brought out several large apple strudels and cream.

"I don't suppose this will fill you up, but at least you won't waste away until supper," she quipped.

Flynn and Tobe took one strudel between them and began to slice away at the dessert. Leo and Zadoc shared another with Father, while the other workmen divvied up the remaining strudel. It didn't take long before the meal was concluded and the men were out the back door.

Hands on her hips, Merrill surveyed the table of empty dishes. It looked like a hoard of locusts had descended. With a shake of her head, she gathered the platters first and then the plates. Once the dishes were washed, she would turn her attention to preparing supper. Margaret was already busy ironing. Merrill checked in with the woman to make sure she didn't need anything. Glancing around the front room, where Margaret had strung rope and hung clothes to dry, Merrill could see she had things well under control. A nice fire in the hearth was warming the room, and she had a second iron heating on a hook over the flames.

"Is there anything I can do to help you?" Merrill asked.

"No, thanks. Things are coming along just fine. I ought to have the sheets all ironed in a few minutes, and then I'll finish up the shirts. I brushed out your father's suit and hung it in the wardrobe."

"Thank you so much, Margaret. I can't tell you how much I appreciate all you are doing, particularly on another ice harvest day."

Margaret offered a hint of a smile and nodded over the ironing board. "I'm the one who's thankful," she said, her voice low.

"I have your pay and some goodies for you waiting in the kitchen."

Margaret nodded again. "George sure likes your treats. He always asks if I'll be bringing any home."

"Well, he'll be happy today. I packed a nice large apple strudel for you. Fortunately our lunch crew didn't find it," Merrill finished with a laugh.

"He'll be glad for that. Maybe it will even help him feel a little better." Margaret touched her finger to her tongue, then to the surface of the iron to check its heat. Hearing the sizzle, she set to ironing again. "I have yet to see him turn down any of your treats."

Merrill returned to the kitchen and began working on pies. She thought she heard the sound of someone coming up the drive and glanced at the clock. Too early for the men to be returning. She went to the back door and found the doctor's sleigh being driven by Granny Lassiter.

"Goodness, Granny, what in the world are you doing out on a day like this?"

"I'm afraid it's not good, Merrill," she said quickly but quietly. "I've come for Margaret. George has taken a turn for the worse. The doctor is with him now, but it doesn't look good."

"Oh no, Granny!" Merrill's hand was at her throat. "I'll go get her right now."

Margaret was busy making beds when Merrill found her. The woman looked up with a smile, but immediately sobered when she saw Merrill's face.

"George needs you, Margaret. The doctor is with him, and Granny Lassiter has come to take you back to town."

"I knew I shouldn't have left him," she whispered, her voice shaky. She looked at the half-made bed. "I'm not quite—"

"Don't you worry about that," Merrill hurried to assure her, drawing her toward the stairs. "Just get back to your husband. Let me know if there's anything I can do. Oh, and here . . ." Merrill went quickly to the basket she'd prepared. "Maybe this will rally him. Your pay is also in here."

Two days later, word came that George had passed on. Though his death had been expected, it was a sorrow shared by the whole community. Merrill hadn't known the man all that well, but Margaret had become a good friend. Now, more than ever, the woman would need work to keep a roof over her head, and Merrill was determined to see to it that she had what she needed.

Merrill loaded up several plates of food to deliver to the new widow and to Carl Jorgenson, as well. She couldn't help but hope she might have a chance to see Rurik. It had been nearly a week since she'd last spoken to him. Margaret, clad in black, greeted Merrill at the front door. She was pale but seemed less grief stricken than Merrill had anticipated.

"Come in," the new widow encouraged.

"I've brought you some food. I knew you probably wouldn't have time for cooking, what with the funeral and all."

"Folks have been so good to me," Margaret said, pointing

to a table already filled with various dishes and baked goods. "I don't guess I'll ever get around to eating it all."

"Is there something else I might do for you?" Merrill asked, pushing aside a couple of plates in order to make room for her own gifts.

"The truth is, I need to get back to work," Margaret said. "I need to keep busy, and I definitely need the pay. Funerals aren't without their costs."

Merrill went to where Margaret stood. "You are welcome to come back to work as soon as you are able, Margaret. You may need the work, but remember, I am blessed to have your help."

"I'll be there Monday. With the weather warming up, though, are you certain you'll need me?"

Smiling, Merrill took hold of Margaret's hands. "I've been hoping you could come even more often. I have additional orders to complete for the furniture shop, and it would be very useful if you could come to the house most every day." Merrill wasn't exactly sure what all she would have the woman do or how she would afford to pay her, but it was clear that this was the most helpful thing she could offer Margaret Neidermeyer at the moment. "I'll probably need you to start cooking more."

The woman looked relieved. "I'll see you on Monday, then. I can work as much as you need." She glanced around the room momentarily, and her eyes filled. "I'm afraid . . . well, this place seems mighty empty without George. . . ."

"I doubt our place could ever feel empty," Merrill said with a little smile. "I'll tell my father that you'll be coming."

Merrill made her way to the furniture shop, her thoughts now focused on speaking to Carl and Rurik about taking on more work. Maybe she could even learn to stain the furniture when she wasn't busy applying the designs. If she could work nearly daily, she might have enough money to pay Margaret on her own, though she knew her father would cheerfully pitch in his support.

"I thought I might never see you again," Nils remarked as she came in from the side door near the office. He started toward her. "I thought maybe you were still mad at me."

Merrill put down the hood on her wool cloak and turned to hang the garment on a peg near the door. "I'm looking for Carl. Is he here?" she asked, looking over her shoulder.

Nils shook his head. "He went with Rurik to handle some business at the bank."

Merrill stopped, uncertain about what she should do.

"Are you going to paint today?"

She decided quickly and shook her head. "No, not today. I have far too many other things that need my attention at home right now. At least the weather is starting to warm a little. Of course, that will mean thaw and then mud and muck to deal with. I suppose each season has its blessings and sorrows." She didn't know why she was babbling on, and turned toward the door.

Nils reached for the basket she held firmly between them. Merrill rather liked having the bit of a barrier in place, however. "I will deliver this to the house and be on my way."

"Why go so quickly, Merrill? You know I enjoy time with—"

"Mr. Olsson," she said quickly, "I know you asked my

father for permission to court me, but I must tell you that I will not allow that."

"I don't understand." He looked hurt and bewildered.

"I thought my actions at the end of the winter party would have made my feelings for you quite clear. I think you are kind to seek me out, but truly our differences are too great."

"But you only think the differences are great," he argued. "You don't yet know me. Isn't it possible you need to get to know me better before——"

"Perhaps," she interrupted again, hoping to stop this increasingly uncomfortable conversation, "but at this place and time, I cannot. Now, if you'll excuse me, I need to deliver this basket and do some shopping." She hurried back out the door without bothering to secure her hood. The breeze on her hot cheeks and in her loosely knotted hair felt good.

I do hope that's the last I hear of courtship with Nils Olsson.

Merrill quickly put away the contents of the basket at the house, then returned to the sleigh and made her way to the mercantile.

When she entered the store, the man behind the counter smiled. "Miss Krause, what can I do for you today?"

"I need flour, salt, sugar, coffee, potatoes, beans, cornmeal." She paused and looked up from the list. "I have the sleigh out front and hope you might be willing to load those larger items while I continued to shop."

He nodded. "Just tell me the amount you want of each, and I'll get right to it."

Merrill handed him her list. "This should help."

She smiled and thanked him before turning back to collect

a variety of other needed articles. She had just rounded the corner of the fabrics and notions when she spied Svea Olsson fingering some white satin. She wanted to say something to the young woman—something kind, possibly helpful—but for the life of her, Merrill couldn't find the words.

Svea glanced up and smiled in her pretty way. "Oh, Miss Krause. Good morning."

"Yes, and good morning to you. How are you today?"

The younger woman returned her gaze to the material. "I'm shopping for some wedding satin. I'm hoping Rurik and I will soon be wed."

Merrill looked at the woman and shook her head. "Rurik has told me that you two are no longer engaged." Svea's head snapped around as if she'd been struck. "I'm sorry," Merrill continued. "I'm sure this whole matter is difficult to discuss. And please know that it isn't my desire to cause you additional pain. Rurik explained how things were between you, and . . . well . . . I also know about your more pressing matter."

"What did you say?" Svea stared angrily into Merrill's face.

Merrill frowned. "I believe you heard me." She took a step closer to ensure their privacy. "I don't wish to make you feel bad, Miss Olsson. I only wanted to offer my friendship. Maybe even some help. Rurik has confided in me about your . . . condition. I know you must feel quite frightened."

"He had no right to discuss it with you," Svea shot back. "This is something that is between the two of us." She whirled back to the material. "I'll trust you to keep your mouth closed on the matter. Rurik and I will soon be married, and then no one need be the wiser."

"Rurik told me he has no intention of marrying you," Merrill said quietly. "He said he has made that clear to you, as well."

"He has a responsibility," Svea said, her tone low but unmistakable in its passion.

"Rurik told me he had nothing to do with your condition."

Svea's mouth dropped open, but she said nothing. The silence didn't last, however. Her face red, Svea began to speak quite loudly. "You have no right to speak to me in such a way. Rurik and I will marry. We must. He has a responsibility to me, whether he admits it or not."

Merrill's good intentions seemed to be fading quickly toward an unavoidable public argument. "He said the betrothal was broken by you prior to him coming to Minnesota," she told Svea. "Why should you try to force marriage upon a man who clearly has no interest in marrying you? Especially when you were the one to end the engagement?"

"I was angry and hurt that he was leaving," Svea countered. "However, I came here to make amends, and given my condition—well—he must marry me."

Merrill lowered her voice. "But your baby isn't his."

"The baby is Rurik's!" Svea almost shouted.

Heads lifted and a half-dozen gazes fixed on the two women. Merrill wanted to crawl in a hole. She heard the hushed whispers of the others and knew without a doubt that gossip would spread around town almost before she got out the door. She looked at Svea, but she was smiling again in a satisfied manner. "Now, if you'll excuse me," she said, "I think I'll go look at one of the other stores for wedding satin." Heart pounding, Merrill watched Svea sway gracefully toward the door, nodding as she passed the other customers.

Merrill's heart plummeted. This would not bode well for any of them.

❧

Rurik and Carl had barely finished supper when a knock sounded on the front door. Rurik found the pastor waiting on the porch.

"Come on in," he encouraged. "We just finished supper, but there are cookies and coffee if you're of a mind to eat."

The man looked a bit sheepish. "No. I mean . . . that is to say . . . well, there's a matter I need to discuss with you. May we talk in private?"

Rurik looked at the man's serious expression and nodded. "Have a seat here in the living room. Just let me tell Uncle Carl of your arrival."

When Rurik returned, he couldn't help but wonder at the man's obvious nervousness. Apparently, whatever he had to discuss had made the poor pastor most uncomfortable.

"I've had it brought to my attention that you were once betrothed to Miss Svea Olsson," he began.

Rurik had a sinking feeling in the pit of his stomach. He nodded. "I was. Our fathers arranged it when we were very young."

"And this engagement was recently broken?"

"Yes, prior to my coming here to Waseca," Rurik said evenly. "Miss Olsson ended it, in fact."

"She tells me that she made a mistake, however," the pastor countered.

"Perhaps she thinks that now," Rurik said, "but I don't believe that to be the case. We were never well suited to each other." He looked at the pastor for a moment, then asked, "Did Svea send you here?"

"No. Not at all." The pastor looked at his hands. "I was made aware of . . . of something else, and . . . well . . . I went to speak to Miss Olsson about the matter. You understand it was done in the strictest confidence."

"And she told you that she's with child?"

"Yes." The pastor let out a long breath.

"The child is not mine," Rurik said, trying his best not to let his anger show.

"But Miss Olsson says otherwise. Since you were engaged to marry, it seems to me . . ." His words trailed off.

Rurik stood and shook his head. "Pastor, I am not the father. I have never been intimate with any woman—and certainly not Svea. She has been like a sister to me since we were youngsters. I have never loved her in any other manner."

The pastor stood also. He was some inches shorter than Rurik but seemed more at ease on his feet. "You said your fathers arranged your betrothal. Perhaps . . . well, since the young woman is willing, you should honor both your fathers' wishes and marry."

"I cannot marry a woman I do not love. And I will not be railroaded into it, particularly when it would be based on a lie."

The reverend must have bought Svea's story hook, line,

and sinker. He said, "Even so, mistakes can be made and temptations can overcome us. What's important is that we repent of sin and make restitution before God." His tone was almost pleading.

"And does God expect me to lie?" Rurik asked.

"Of course not," the pastor assured Rurik. "He hates lies."

"Besides her lies about me, marrying Svea Olsson would be a lie all by itself. You are asking me to pledge my life and love to a woman for whom I do not feel that kind of devotion. You would have me swear before God to love her and honor her, when I cannot." He was sure this was not the time to tell the man his heart had been captured by another.

"But she will suffer great dishonor if you do not. Would you put that upon her?"

"I am not putting anything upon her," Rurik said, his anger and frustration getting the better of him. "I will not marry her." He took a deep breath and continued more calmly. "I have offered to help her return to Kansas and hopefully to the father of her child. I have offered her nothing but my care and understanding, but I will not be coerced into a marriage under these circumstances. I'm sorry for this waste of your time, Pastor, but this is my final word on the matter."

The man looked up at Rurik for a moment, then nodded. He walked to the front door and paused. "I will, of course, have to take up the matter with the elders of the church."

"To what purpose?" Rurik asked, stunned by the idea.

The pastor shrugged. "To decide if you should be put out of our fellowship."

Chapter 20

"Rurik! This is a pleasant surprise." Merrill opened the door wider to admit him into the kitchen. "Come on in." But then she noted his expression. "What's wrong?"

"I had a visit from the pastor," Rurik began slowly. "Apparently I'm the talk of the town." He shook his head in disgust. "It would seem folks have heard about Svea's condition."

Merrill bit her lower lip and nodded. "I can well imagine. I was in the mercantile, and . . . and Svea declared loudly to me that her baby was yours. I'm . . . I'm sorry I didn't have a chance to warn you." Should she tell him the whole thing probably was her fault? If only she had left well enough alone. . . .

"It's all right," Rurik was saying. "Anyway, the pastor is convinced I should marry Svea. He intends to discuss the matter with the church leaders and determine if I can even continue to attend services if I refuse to marry her."

Merrill stared at him in disbelief. "You told him the situation was not of your doing, didn't you?"

"I did. But Svea had assured him otherwise. I spoke to Nils

about it, and he told me he agreed with the pastor and that I better do the right thing."

Merrill wiped trembling hands on her apron and tried to get her whirling thoughts around the matter. "I suppose they both are afraid of what the future holds. To tell you the truth, Rurik, I tried to reach out to Svea in friendship, maybe even help, but all she wanted to do was lie about you two getting married soon. I'm afraid my good intentions quickly got tangled up in my emotions, and I . . . well, I wanted to take her by the shoulders and shake her—make her face the truth."

"Maybe you should have," Rurik said with a crooked grin. He shook his head, and the smile faded. "I don't know what to do about this, Merrill. I don't want Uncle Carl's health threatened by a scandal. And I sure don't want you to be tarnished in any way. . . ." He put his hand to his forehead and massaged the space over his eyes. "This is quickly getting out of control."

"Why don't you sit down and have some coffee? Maybe if we talk this through, something will come to mind." She moved to get Rurik a mug, but he caught her shoulders and turned her back to face him.

"Merrill, I can't marry her. I don't want her to be shamed, but I cannot—will not—pledge my love to Svea." He looked straight into her eyes. "I wish I could tell you this at a more appropriate time than during this difficult conversation. But I have to say this now. I love you."

Merrill's heart leaped like it would come right out of her chest. She stared back at Rurik and tried to speak, but the words wouldn't form.

Rurik seemed not to notice and continued. "I lost my heart to you almost from the start, Merrill. I need you to know that I never once felt that way about Svea." He continued to keep a firm hold on her shoulders. "You may not feel the same depth of emotion for me, Merrill Jean Krause, but I will wait until you do. You are the woman I want to spend my life with."

Merrill felt her heart skip a beat and then race madly. She reached up to touch Rurik's cheek and shook her head. "I may appear calm, Rurik, but don't let that be a judge of my emotions right now."

"Are you saying what I think I'm hearing?"

"Only that I have cared about you for some time now. In fact, I . . . I love you, too."

He pulled Merrill into his arms and kissed her with a passion she'd never experienced. She lost herself in the moment. Rurik's embrace was a confirmation of all she had longed for. She held him tight, as if she'd never let go.

And then Rurik was ripped away from her arms. To Merrill's shock and horror, her brother Tobe had knocked her beloved backward.

"Get out of here and leave my sister alone!" he shouted, imprisoning Rurik against the wall. "We know all about you, you scum, and we won't have you dallying with Merrill."

Leo now stepped forward as if from thin air. "You heard him." Leo looked at Merrill. "He's a womanizer of the worst sort. You'll be glad we did this when you hear the truth."

"I know the truth!" Merrill was nearly beside herself. "You're wrong—very wrong."

Rurik straightened and held up his hands. "I'll go, but I've done nothing to merit this. In time, the truth will come out."

Tobe had dropped his hold, but he shoved Rurik toward the door. "I don't want to hear anything more from you. You'd best leave before our father gets in here and finishes you off once and for all."

Rurik looked to Merrill. "I'm sorry."

"You don't need to be," she assured, stepping toward him. "I promise you I will make certain they know the full story."

Rurik left the house, and Merrill narrowed her gaze at Tobe and Leo. "Find the others," she said through gritted teeth. "Find them now. I want to talk to you all."

ॐ

Merrill had never felt so angry in her life. Especially not at her own family. Sitting across from them at the dining room table, Merrill listened to what they had heard. Her father was on the church board and had already been notified by the pastor about the problem brewing in their little community.

"First of all, you may think you know the truth, but you don't," she began when they had reported the rumors concerning statements made by Svea and Nils.

"Isn't it possible that you're the one who doesn't know the truth?" Father asked, sounding rather stern. "I know you care a great deal about this young man, so it's easy to believe him instead of—"

"I didn't believe him at first," Merrill put in. "I overheard things and jumped to the same conclusion you did. But I misjudged the matter completely."

Leo shook his head. "I think you're just hoping you did."

"The pastor wouldn't lie," Tobe added.

Merrill looked at the five men across from her, and she knew she would have a difficult time convincing them. They cared so much about her, they were nearly as stubborn as goats. "When I first heard the rumors," she said with a sigh, "I went to Granny, and her first words to me really made me think. Why was I so eager to believe what a stranger had to say, over listening to a man I'd come to know? Rurik has done nothing but be generous and kind to this family, and yet you are more than willing to take someone else's viewpoint over his."

"These things are . . . well . . ." Her father appeared to be searching for the right words. "They are delicate. It's never easy when young people fall into this kind of situation, but we can't deny that it happens and must be dealt with as quickly and calmly as possible."

"Shouldn't it be dealt with in truth?" she asked.

Her father nodded. His expression took on a look of compassion. "I know you care for him, Merrill Jean. But it is clouding your judgment. A young woman's life and reputation hangs in the balance, as well as that of an unborn child."

"But Rurik told me that he was never intimate with her, and I believe him." Merrill tried to keep the quiver from her voice. "I don't know what happened to Svea Olsson. I don't know if she brought it on herself or someone took advantage of her, but it was not Rurik, I'm absolutely sure. He doesn't love her. He loves me." She hadn't meant to just blurt it out like that, but now that the words were said, Merrill couldn't take them back.

"That's exactly why you aren't able to judge this matter," Zadoc interjected. "You women get your feelings all stirred up, and that's all you can think about."

Merrill clenched her hands into fists and tried her best to stay calm. "This isn't about my feelings."

"I think Zadoc is right," Flynn said, looking to their father. "That's just the way women get."

"What would you all know about women?" Merrill demanded of her brothers. She turned to her father. "You always taught me to believe the best about a person. You taught that to all of us. Now, without even speaking to Rurik, you are judging him because of something someone else has said. How is that right? That can't be of the Lord. Shouldn't you sit down with Rurik and listen to what he has to say?"

"I intend to do that," her father agreed. "It's true that I can't judge the situation without hearing both sides of the story. The pastor intends for us to hear Rurik out, as well as Miss Olsson. Our intent is to get to the truth and see it resolved in the best way for everyone. However, you forget that while we are perhaps poor judges of a woman's emotions and feelings, you, daughter, are maybe less knowledgeable of a man's thoughts and heart."

Merrill's burst of laughter was sharp. She looked around the table. "I have been raised in a houseful of men," she said. "I've known little but your thoughts and feelings—yes, your hearts—over the last ten years. Even when Mother was still alive it was difficult to hear any kind of discussion besides that of men. More times than I can count, I've been accused of being unable to think or feel as a normal woman because of such an upbringing. Father, you said yourself that you felt you had wronged me in allowing me to work like my brothers."

"True, but that doesn't mean your heart isn't that of a woman," her father replied mildly.

"Given what's going on," Leo interjected, "I think you ought to stay away from Rurik Jorgenson until this can be settled. You don't want to risk your own reputation by getting in the middle of this."

Her father nodded his agreement. "It would probably be best if you were to forego working at the shop for the time being," he added.

Merrill had taken just about all she was going to stand for. Getting to her feet, she planted her hands on her hips and looked at each of her brothers and then at her father. "I can hardly believe my ears," she said, forcing herself to remain calm. "Father, you and Mr. Jorgenson have been friends for a very long time. Before judging his nephew, why not speak to him on the matter?"

"How I plan to handle this is my business, Merrill Jean. I will be talking to Rurik himself, if you want to know the truth, and most likely I will speak to Carl, as well. For now, however, I want you to stay out of it. I don't want you caught in the middle."

"Maybe the time has come for me to get out of this situation," she said, waving her arm over her brothers and father. "I've given you all my love, my devotion . . . my strength and time." She paused to get her emotions under control. "Maybe it's time for me to strike out on my own. It's nearly the nineteen hundreds, and young women are doing more and more for themselves. I have a good job, and Granny has offered for me to stay with them. I hadn't really considered it until now, but maybe that's exactly what I should do."

She turned to leave, but her father said, "Merrill, stay here. Please. Boys, I'd like you to give me some privacy with your sister."

Without a word, her brothers scuffed their chairs back and got to their feet, looking almost embarrassed. Merrill didn't know for sure, however, if it was embarrassment for her outburst or for her calling them on their own judgmental attitudes.

"Please sit down."

Merrill did so and folded her hands together. She said nothing, refusing to look her father in the eye. She didn't want to dishonor him, and she didn't like dealing with him in anger. But that feeling raced through her like a wildfire.

"I know you're angry, and you think me unfair."

She bit her lip, keeping her gaze on her hands. It hit her like a blast of winter air that her concern for Rurik outweighed a lifetime of devotion to her family. How could that have happened in such a short time? Merrill couldn't help but feel a bit guilty. Her family had always been the most important thing in her life.

"Merrill, I am only trying to guard your reputation. The entire town is talking about this matter. I know you were the one talking with Miss Olsson when she declared Rurik to be the father of her child. I heard all about the encounter."

"No doubt. People love to gossip." She finally looked at him and could see the worry in his eyes. "Which, of course, is also a sin."

"There are those who do indeed gossip, and you are right—it is a sin. But that really isn't the point right now. We need to handle this situation in a fair manner. I'm seeking God's direction on this, Merrill Jean—as are the rest of the church leaders."

"Rurik is being falsely accused, Father. It's not just my emotions that are stating this—it's my belief after many prayers and contemplation. I sought wise counsel as you have always taught me to do."

"You didn't seek my counsel," Father replied. His tone betrayed his hurt. "I thought you knew you could come to me on any matter."

"Doesn't your reaction here prove otherwise?"

"Not at all. If anything, your unwillingness to speak to me about this concerns me greatly. It isn't like you to act in this way, and that, more than anything else, gives me cause to wonder."

Merrill knew he was right, but she didn't want to admit it. She had purposely kept this from her father, knowing he wouldn't want her to be involved. Her German ancestors were strong advocates for keeping to themselves and not sharing their business around. They worried about what other people thought, reasoning that it was best to guard the details of their lives from prying eyes.

"I know you care for this man," her father said. "I believe him to be a good man, and I've never said otherwise," he continued. "However, as a man, I know the temptations we face and the mistakes that are easily made in giving in to those temptations. I'm not saying I believe that to be the case, but you must allow me time to seek the truth."

"I hope that you'll be open to the truth and not swayed by rumor or gossip."

He looked at her with a frown. "Have you ever known me to be such a man?"

Merrill immediately felt bad about her comment and shook her head. "No. I'm sorry. That was uncalled for. It's just that . . . well . . ."

"It's just that you care for him. You love him, and you want to believe the best about him."

"Yes."

He smiled just a bit. "Do you still love me?"

"You know I do," Merrill said, mortified that he should even feel he needed to ask.

"Then believe the best about me, Merrill Jean. I will not go into this with any preconceived notions. I will put it all before the Lord to help sort it through and give me wisdom. I ask you to do the same. Will you do that for me?"

Merrill nodded, knowing that it was the right thing to do. "I will, Father."

"And, Merrill," her father added, "please don't leave your home here in anger."

She heard the tenderness in his voice. "I won't. I'm sorry I said such things. It's just that I feel I know Rurik's character, and I don't want to see him misjudged. Not only that, but I love working for Mr. Jorgenson and painting the furniture. I don't want to lose that opportunity."

"I promise you, I'll speak to Carl on your behalf. I'll do everything in my power to see that you can continue to paint.

Perhaps there will be a delay for a time, but hopefully it won't be long. All I ask is that you trust me."

Merrill drew a deep breath. "I do trust you, Father."

Rurik was with his uncle when Bogart Krause came to speak to him, and he immediately knew what Merrill's father wanted to discuss. "I hope you can both give me a moment of your time—in private."

Rurik exchanged a glance with his uncle and nodded. "We could go to the house and have some coffee."

Carl quickly agreed. "There's a pot on from this morning. Ought to be good and strong by now."

The three men headed to the door and were met by Nils Olsson as he came from the office. He looked at the men as if awaiting an explanation. Rurik said nothing, leaving the matter to his uncle.

"Nils, we have some private business," Carl declared.

"Anything I can help with?" Nils asked, sounding hopeful.

"No. We'll be back when we can," Carl said, offering no further explanation.

Rurik could see that Nils wasn't pleased to be left out, but he said nothing more. The trio made their way to the Jorgenson house and once inside, Carl led the way to the kitchen and went immediately to the stove. He jiggled the pot and smiled. "Should be enough for us each to have a swallow." He retrieved three mugs and brought them with the pot to the table.

"Now, why don't you tell us what you need to discuss, Bogart?" Carl invited as he poured the coffee.

Merrill's father nodded. "The church elders have been called together regarding Rurik and Miss Olsson on the matter of her . . . their . . . situation."

"Ja, I thought as much," Carl replied.

"I wanted to talk to the two of you first. You see, I made a promise to Merrill that I would seek the complete truth. It's not that I wouldn't have done so anyway, but knowing how she feels about you, Rurik, I felt more than simple obligation."

"I appreciate that," Rurik said, staring down at his cup. "I assure you, the facts are not as they've been circulating around."

Bogart nodded. "Then I'd like to hear exactly what the facts are."

Rurik looked up to find complete sincerity in the man's expression. He said a silent prayer and pushed back the coffee. "I suppose it would be best to start at the beginning."

Chapter 21

Rurik didn't know what he'd expected once the news got out about Svea being with child, but it certainly wasn't the standoffish manner of the ones who had once greeted him warmly and with open smiles. Now as he passed folks on the street, they were more apt to look away or pretend to be occupied with other matters. At his uncle's business, Rurik could see the uneasiness and confusion on the faces of those who worked with him.

He picked up the mail, barely hearing a grunt from the usually talkative postmaster. When someone called out his name as he left the post office, Rurik halted, surprised to see the pastor.

"Mr. Jorgenson, I was making my way to your house, but it looks like I can save myself a trip," the pastor said. "I wanted to let you know there will be a meeting at the church tomorrow morning at nine. We'd like to speak to both you and Miss Olsson at that time."

"Am I allowed to have character witnesses present?" Rurik asked.

The pastor's eyebrows rose. "This isn't a court of law." He

smiled. "We merely wish to discuss the matter at hand with the both of you and see if there isn't a resolution to be had."

"I suppose that makes sense. I've already been judged guilty by most in this community." He glanced around and could see that those nearby were trying hard not to openly watch his interaction with the pastor.

"Now then, I assure you that isn't the case." The pastor looked about as if to reassure himself. "I hope we can resolve everything in the morning in a manner that is agreeable and fair."

Rurik wanted to say more but figured it would do more harm than good. He'd wait until morning and then speak his mind. He could only pray that the voice of reason would be heard, that God would let the truth be known. Of course, that would also depend on what Svea said.

He looked down the road to the hotel where Svea and Nils were staying. Would it do any good to speak to her one more time? If he appealed to her on the basis of Christian honesty, would that cause her to take back her lies?

Heaving a long sigh, Rurik finally decided it best to speak with his uncle first. He wanted to let the man know what the pastor had said and get his advice. Sadly, Rurik knew that if the matter was pushed and the church declared it necessary for him to marry Svea, he would have to leave the community altogether. That would be a huge blow to his uncle, and the timing couldn't be worse. Even though Uncle Carl was feeling stronger and better than he had a few weeks back, he would not again be able to handle the shop on his own.

And then there was Merrill. . . . He felt as if a knife were twisting in his heart.

Rurik looked around as he walked to the house. He liked Waseca more than he'd figured he would. He acknowledged it had a lot to do with Merrill, but he also found the town suited his needs. At least it had. Would the community be willing to forget this matter and put it behind them if Svea finally told the truth? Would Rurik be able to court Merrill without worrying about how people would react, how they would treat her?

He found Carl in the kitchen, as he usually did. The older man was reading the newspaper and looked up with a smile. "I see you got the mail. Any word from home?"

Rurik shook his head. "The pastor stopped me. There's a meeting planned for tomorrow morning at nine. Svea and I will be questioned about our relationship and her condition. I thought you should know."

Carl nodded. "I'm glad you told me. I'll go with you."

"Thank you," he managed as he sank into an empty chair. A sense of defeat washed over him. "I don't know what to do, Uncle Carl. I've told the truth, and I've put my trust in God. But I feel as if the walls are closing in on me. Is God still listening to my prayers?"

"Sometimes it doesn't feel like He is," his uncle replied. "I sometimes think of the agony Jesus suffered in the Garden of Gethsemane. When you read about Him laboring in prayer for himself, the disciples, and even for us, you have to wonder if Jesus didn't feel like He was all alone in the world. Of course, He knew the Father was listening. He knew God would never forsake Him, and yet Jesus still struggled and suffered. If He has to go through those things . . . well, I guess it's only natural that we would, as well."

Rurik nodded slowly and took a long breath. "God didn't spare His own Son, so why would He spare me?"

"But He has spared you," Carl replied. "Jesus paid the price for all our sins. By taking Him as Savior, we are spared from eternal death and separation from God. God didn't spare His own Son, but willingly gave Him up for us all. There was a reason and a purpose for the suffering our Lord endured. There's a reason for the problems and pain we endure here on earth. We can't always see them. In fact, we might very well go to the grave not knowing why things turned out the way they did. Why did my sweet wife have to suffer and die so young?" He shrugged. "Rurik, I wouldn't worry about this. They can't make you do what you don't feel right about doing. If you aren't supposed to marry Svea Olsson, then God will make provision for that."

"But they can make life very unpleasant for several of us if I don't. In fact, if they decide I must marry Svea, I don't see how I can stay in Waseca. I will have to leave town."

Carl considered this for a moment. "I know it would be hard for you to stay, but I wouldn't want you to run from this."

"I can't let it destroy what you've spent a lifetime building. Jorgenson Furniture has a good reputation. At least it did before I got here."

"Its reputation is still intact. You know, however, that I cannot carry on with the business. Without your help, I would have to sell the business or dissolve it. The men I have working for me are good, but they aren't able to design and implement new patterns like you can. They are just learning this trade, while you have done this since you were a boy. Losing you would mean the end of the business, I'm afraid."

Rurik felt the added burden of his uncle's words. "You could probably find someone else talented enough to help you. I'm sure there are others in the area who've built furniture or designed it. Maybe we could put an ad in the Minneapolis and St. Paul papers."

Carl let go a heavy sigh. "I'm old and tired, Rurik. I don't want to sound like I'm giving up easily, but having you here was an answer to prayers long prayed. If you go, I'd rather just quit the business for good."

Rurik knew the older man didn't realize how this was making him feel. Surely Uncle Carl wouldn't say these things if he understood the added stress they caused Rurik.

"Well, perhaps everything will come around right tomorrow," Rurik finally said. "I think I should go and speak one final time to Svea. She's the only one who can set everyone straight. They will listen to her."

"There's another matter that you need to be aware of," Carl said, looking quite grim.

Rurik knew he wasn't going to like whatever Carl told him. He leaned forward. "Go on."

"There are problems with the books."

"What books?" Rurik knew almost as soon as he asked the question that his uncle was talking about the business ledgers.

"The accounts are not adding up correctly. I've gone over the tallies, and something is off."

"Have you said anything to Nils?"

"No. I don't want to just yet. I thought at first it was an honest mistake or some oversight. But now I'm not so sure—it amounts to several hundred dollars."

"Hundreds?" Rurik asked in disbelief. "How could that be?"

"If I knew that, I'd know why the numbers are off. Like I said, it could be a simple mistake. I need to see all the receipts, however, and compare the figures. That will take me some time, and I want to do it when Nils isn't around. If he is dipping into the company's accounts, I'd prefer to catch him in the act."

"I'm so sorry, Uncle Carl. It seems I've done nothing but bring you trouble."

"I don't see it that way, and you shouldn't either. Nils Olsson is accountable for his own deeds. You are accountable for yours. Now is not the time to go feeling sorry for yourself. We'll get this sorted out and figure what's to be done next. Nils won't be in tomorrow, since it's Saturday. In fact, I believe he plans to go to Mankato tonight, so I should have plenty of time to review everything."

Rurik couldn't help but wonder if tomorrow wouldn't change everything for all of them. "You'll let me know what you find out?"

"Ja, and we'll deal with it together. Just like we'll deal with the church and the town."

Granny Lassiter sat knitting while Merrill tried to explain everything. "Father says there's to be a meeting at the church in the morning. The elders and pastor plan to speak to Rurik and Svea. I'm afraid they mean to force Rurik to marry her."

"That doesn't sound like Pastor John. I can't see him trying to force something like that on someone. He's a fair, even-tempered man, Merrill Jean. I think he'll listen to the truth."

"But it's a matter of Svea saying one thing and Rurik another." She twisted her hands together in her lap. "No one can prove the truth one way or another."

"Goodness, child. Just listen to yourself. 'No one can prove the truth?' Bah! God won't be mocked. His truth will always be revealed. It may not come about the way we think it should or in our timing, but the truth will stand."

Merrill bit her lips to keep from crying. "I'm afraid, Granny. I love him, and he loves me."

The old woman looked up and smiled. "I knew it all along. I've waited so long to hear those words from you. Thank you, Jesus!"

"But don't you see how hopeless this is?"

Granny put down her knitting and raised a gnarled finger toward Merrill's. "Get thee behind me, Satan."

Merrill pulled back in shock. "What?"

"Satan is the spirit of discord here. He's the one who wants to sow doubt and despair, and I won't have it. You are a daughter of God Almighty, and Rurik is also a child of God. Do you suppose He would forget His children? How dare you claim to know God and yet use the word hopeless in the same breath?"

"I didn't mean it that way, Granny."

Granny eyed her with a raised brow. "Then what other way do you mean it? If you think this matter hopeless, then I can only surmise that you believe God has no control of it."

"Of course God has control. It's just . . . well . . . what if this doesn't work out the way it should?" Merrill asked.

"You mean the way you think it should?"

Merrill felt rather embarrassed. "I suppose I do. But I do want the truth to come out. I want Rurik to be found innocent so that we can have a life together."

"God knows the desires of your heart, Merrill Jean. He put them there. He brought Rurik into your life, and He has always watched over you. Don't doubt Him now, just because things are difficult and seem bleak. Remember what you told me that your mama said just before she died?"

Merrill thought back to that tragic time. "She told me not to judge God's love for me in her death. She said that God's love for us came in the form of a baby in a manger . . . but also in the bloodied body of Jesus on the cross." Merrill drew a deep breath and nodded. "She told me to trust God no matter what the circumstances or how things looked." Merrill could nearly hear her mother's words being spoken aloud. "Mama knew my heart. Sometimes I think things need to be a certain way in order to come from God. I guess I need to remember her words more often."

The front door crashed open just then, and Corabeth came flying into the house, tracking mud across the foyer and into the living room. "Oh, Merrill! Merrill . . . you're here. I've . . . I've looked for you . . . everywhere. Come . . . quick! It's . . . horrible!"

Merrill jumped to her feet. "What's horrible? What's wrong?"

Corabeth held her hand against her side and panted out, "It's . . . it's Miss Olsson. She's . . . she's injured."

"What happened?" Merrill and Granny asked in unison. "Rurik," she said, getting her breath. "Rurik pushed her down the stairs at the hotel. At least . . . that's what they're saying."

Chapter 22

"I'm telling you I didn't push her," Rurik told the police chief, shaking his head for emphasis. "I had gone upstairs to see if she and her brother Nils Olsson would join me for a discussion in the dining room. Nils wasn't there, so I told Svea I'd like to speak to her. She agreed, and as we walked down the hall toward the stairs she started yelling at me and accusing me of . . ." He fell silent.

The officer's brows rose and other onlookers seemed to lean in. "Accused you of what?"

Rurik could see that everyone waited anxiously for his response. "She accused me of trying to get rid of her."

"And were you?" the lawman asked. "Were you trying to get rid of her? Trying to kill her?"

"Absolutely not." Rurik looked to where the doctor was tending to Svea. She was still lying near the foot of the stairs, moaning and sobbing as the doctor arranged for a litter to carry her back to his examination room.

Rurik noted that Uncle Carl had arrived. He saw his uncle's concerned expression as their glances connected. Carl pressed through the crowd to reach Rurik. "What happened? They said you were in trouble."

"Svea lost her balance and fell down the stairs, but they think I pushed her."

"She was mighty upset with you," the hotel clerk declared. "I heard it all. Saw some of it, too."

"Did you see me push her?" Rurik demanded, his frustration getting the better of him. "Of course not, because I didn't. She was upset with me, I'll give you that much. But in her frustration, she lost her balance and fell."

"I saw your hands stretched out," the clerk declared. "Looked like you were pushing her."

"I tried to reach out to save her, but it was too late."

"Seems kind of convenient to say she just lost her balance," the police chief said, fixing Rurik with a stern expression.

"This makes no sense, Zed, and you know it," Carl said, turning to the police chief. "My nephew would never hurt anyone—much less this young lady. He's known her from childhood. And even if he were so inclined, why on earth would he do it in sight of others?"

"They are supposed to marry, as I understand it," the lawman said, obviously avoiding the question.

"They were," Carl countered. This drew distinct murmurings in the crowd. "Miss Olsson ended the engagement prior to my nephew joining me here in Waseca," Carl added, his voice raised.

"She's lost consciousness," someone called out. Everyone turned to look to where Svea lay completely still.

"Is she dead?" another voice questioned.

Rurik felt sick to his stomach. She couldn't possibly be . . . dead. He groaned, and his legs barely could hold him upright.

He'd only wanted to speak to Svea and urge her to tell the truth. How had this happened? He rubbed his head, unable to make sense of anything.

"She's not dead," the doctor announced, "but we need to get her to my office right away."

There was a bustling of activity as several helped to get Svea secured on the litter.

Carl stepped closer to Rurik and asked in a low voice, "What happened?"

"Like I was telling the police chief, I came here to talk to Svea and Nils about tomorrow. I went to their hotel suite, and Svea came to the door. She said Nils was gone. I told her we needed to talk about telling the church leaders the truth. I said I'd meet her downstairs in the restaurant."

"And then . . . ?"

Carl's tone seemed almost urgent, and Rurik hurried on, "I didn't want to be the cause of any further harm to her reputation nor add more questions about my own, so I immediately headed down the hall. She flew out the door after me. She grabbed my arm and begged me to just make things right. I told her I'd done nothing wrong and that I had nothing to make right where she was concerned. I continued toward the stairs, and she kept trying to stop me. She wanted me to come back to the hotel room to talk, but I told her that wouldn't be appropriate. She continued to pull at my arm and when I tried to disengage from her it only caused her to become more vocal."

"Is that when you pushed her?" the police chief asked over Carl's shoulder.

Rurik wanted to punch the man square in the nose, but he knew that wouldn't help his case. Besides, the man was only trying to do his duty. "I did not push her," he said once more, each word distinct. "She was ranting and saying something about how I had to marry her—that I had to save her reputation. I stopped long enough to tell her that her behavior was causing a scene—that she needed to calm down before we went to the restaurant."

"But she wouldn't be quiet, is that it?" The man watched him with a trained eye.

"That's true, she wouldn't. She only got louder. I don't even remember what all she was yelling, but I decided to get downstairs and, if necessary, leave the hotel altogether. I started down the stairs, and Svea rushed past me and turned on the step in front of me."

The lawman nodded. "And then?"

"And then she lost her balance. I tried to pull her back, but she fell away too quickly."

Rurik looked at his uncle, who was frowning. When Carl put his hand to his chest, Rurik feared the shock of the matter might be too much.

"Are you all right, Uncle Carl?"

The older man looked at him and nodded. "I'll be fine."

The police chief turned to the hotel clerk, seemingly unaware of Carl's condition. Rurik heard him ask the clerk if this was what he'd seen.

"It looked to me like he was pushing her," the man told the

official. "I heard her screaming, like I said. It was an awful thing to witness."

"I didn't push her," Rurik reiterated. "I couldn't do something like that."

The doctor had instructed the litter bearers to carry Svea away. He came over to where the police chief stood. "I'm taking her to my examination room. She's fainted, but it's probably for the best. She may have a broken leg. She said her head hurt, too, so there might be additional damage."

The man nodded and glanced toward Rurik. "Will she live?"

Another jolt of fear and shock went through Rurik, but he fought to stand still and straight.

"I don't know. I'll have to examine her first. She could have all sorts of internal injuries, especially if she fell from the top of the stairs."

Rurik didn't know when Merrill arrived, but when he looked again at his uncle, he found her there. Her presence, although comforting, was not what Rurik wanted. He hated for her to be in the middle of this madness—to hear the accusations and wonder at his actions. He bowed his head.

"I'm afraid I'll have to take you in," the chief told Rurik. "Until we can determine what really happened, whether Miss Olsson is going to live or die, you'll have to be locked up."

Carl grabbed his chest and began to stagger. Rurik and Merrill reached out to catch him at the same moment.

"His heart," Merrill exclaimed.

The doctor hurried forward. "Put him on the ground, flat out." He knelt beside the older man. "Carl, is it like before?"

"More painful," Carl gasped out through the labored breathing. Rurik had never seen anyone with such a white face.

Rurik looked at Merrill as the officer took hold of his arm. "Merrill, will you stay with him?"

"I will." Her gaze met his. "I'm so sorry," she whispered.

Rurik could see in her expression that she knew he was innocent of any wrongdoing. However, when he glanced around at the others, he found accusation and condemnation. He felt like he had fallen into a nightmare from which he might never awaken.

Heartsick, Merrill watched the police chief lead Rurik away. But her more immediate concern was for Carl Jorgenson. Kneeling, she put her hand on his arm.

"Uncle Carl," she said, hoping the familiarity would console him, "I'll be with you, and I'm praying for you."

He opened his eyes for just a moment. "Ja. You need to pray," he said through stiff lips.

The doctor directed a couple of men to take Carl by the shoulders and legs. "Carry him to my place."

"I'm coming with him," Merrill said, her tone leaving no room for argument. The doctor merely nodded.

The short walk to the doctor's place gave Merrill little time to think. She had to admit the sight of the unconscious Svea Olsson had been disturbing.

Oh, God, she prayed, *please don't let her die. Please let the truth be known, and please, I beg you, may Rurik's good name be cleared.*

The doctor's examination room was small, and because Svea was already in there, the doctor directed the men to carry Carl into another room. "I'll be with him soon," the doctor told Merrill. "I'm going to find something for his heart and check on Miss Olsson."

Carl's pain had intensified, and Merrill could see that his pale skin had taken on a grayish-blue hue. His eyes remained closed, and she wasn't certain if he was still conscious or not. As soon as he was positioned on the bed, she went to his side and took hold of his hand. Praying for the older man, Merrill felt a sudden sense of peace wash over her. She could feel God's presence at the bedside.

After some time, Merrill felt Carl stir. "Merrill?" he said in a weak voice. She quickly bent over him. "What is it, Uncle Carl?"

"Rurik . . . he . . . he wouldn't hurt her."

Merrill nodded. "I know. I know he wouldn't. Soon the truth will come out and everyone will realize that."

"I don't . . . I don't think . . . I'll be here to . . . see it."

She frowned. "Please don't say that. Rurik needs you. We all need you, Uncle Carl."

Carl gave just one shake of his head and closed his eyes. "He has . . . you."

The doctor came in with a small glass of dark liquid. "Get him to drink this. It should help."

Merrill took the glass and slipped her other arm under Carl's neck. "What is it?"

"A foxglove tea. I've made it strong, so hopefully it will

help settle his heart. Have him drink it all. It may cause some stomach discomfort, but that's normal."

"I'll see that he drinks it."

"I'm glad you're here, Miss Krause. You tend to him while I see what I need to do for Miss Olsson."

"You should know . . ." Merrill stopped, uncertain of whether she should say something about Svea's condition or not. No doubt he had heard the rumors along with everybody else. Still, if it helped Svea to survive, Merrill didn't want to hold back. "Miss Olsson is with child."

The doctor raised a brow. "Are you certain?"

"That's what she's told us," Merrill said.

They both looked at Carl when he murmured, "She . . . did."

The doctor grimaced. "Well, a fall like she's had probably will put an end to that." He shook his head. "Let me know if Carl's pain gets worse, Miss Krause."

Merrill watched him go, feeling a sense of utter helplessness. She helped Carl to raise his head and take a drink of the medicine. She could see even that small movement caused him pain. "I'm sorry to be hurting you more, Uncle Carl, but it's necessary for you to drink all of this."

He did as she instructed, never once complaining. Merrill eased him back onto the pillow and watched for any sign of relief. Carl remained ashen, his hand still clutched to his chest. He probably was more worried about Rurik than himself. Merrill wished she could say something to ease his concerns.

What would become of them all? It seemed their world had suddenly gone crazy.

Time dragged by as Merrill waited for Carl to feel better or for the doctor to return. She supposed that since she was with the older man, the doctor was putting his time and efforts into the ministrations of Miss Olsson. Even so, Merrill would have felt a whole lot better had the doctor been there to watch over Rurik's uncle.

Carl's breathing did seem a little less strained, but Merrill couldn't be certain. His face was still a ghastly gray, making her wonder if perhaps this was the end for him. She remembered her mother's pale face. Granny had called it a death pallor.

Merrill struggled to gather her thoughts to pray for Svea. It wasn't that she didn't want the young woman to live—she truly did.

"If Svea dies, they will accuse Rurik of murder." Putting it into words nearly did her in. She covered her face with her hands and began to sob. *God, I'm afraid I don't feel too kindly toward that woman*, she finally began. *I want to care about her, but it's so wrong what she's done. She's hurt so many people with her lies.*

Merrill lifted her head to look at Carl. He had opened his eyes, but didn't seem to be focused on anything in particular. "Is the pain any better?" she asked.

"A little," he said. "But not much. I don't expect it to be. My heart has been giving out for some time now." His voice was barely audible.

Merrill patted his hand. "I'm sorry you're in pain. I'm sorry that all of this has happened."

"You'll . . . be . . . good to him . . . won't you?"

It wasn't really a question. She knew exactly what Carl Jorgenson was saying. "I certainly hope to be."

"He's not guilty."

"I know that, Uncle Carl. Rurik wouldn't hurt anyone— and especially her."

Carl gave the briefest nod and closed his eyes. "Would you read a Scripture to me?"

Merrill glanced around the room. "I don't have a Bible, but I know some passages by heart."

"The Twenty-third Psalm?"

"Yes," she said, tightening her hold on his hand. "I know that one well."

His lips moved along with hers as she began to say the familiar words.

"How is he doing?" the doctor asked, coming at last to check on Carl.

Merrill straightened in her chair. "He's been sleeping for the most part. I think the pain has eased. Is there anything more you can do for him?"

"No. Nothing. His heart is too weak. I'm sorry to say that eventually it will take his life. He knows that." The doctor looked past Carl to Merrill. "I wonder if I could ask you something."

"Of course."

The doctor looked uncomfortable, then motioned her toward the hall. Merrill followed him.

Reaching the hall, Merrill asked quickly, "Is something wrong, Doctor?"

"I realize this is a delicate issue, but I have to ask why you believed Miss Olsson to be with child."

"Because she told me she was. She told Rurik the same. She said he was the father, but Rurik insists he's never been . . . with her . . . that way." Merrill flushed and looked at her hands. "I believe him."

"Actually, I do also."

Merrill's head snapped up. "You do?"

"I do. I gave Miss Olsson a complete exam. She's a little banged up, but no broken bones, no internal bleeding that I can tell, and . . . no pregnancy."

"She lost the baby?"

"There never was a baby. She isn't pregnant, never has been. At least in my professional opinion."

Merrill felt her heart beat faster. "Why would she say she was?"

"That's a good question."

The doctor moved toward the door, but Merrill stopped him. "Is she conscious?"

"Oh yes. She pretends to be otherwise from time to time, but I wave some smelling salts under her nose. I'm afraid she's playing a game with me. When I rally her, she begins to moan and complain about all manner of pain. Even so, I see no evidence for it." He rubbed his chin. "I suppose I am going to have to present her with the truth and try to figure out what this is all about."

"I wish you would. It would most likely help Rurik. Doctor,

I know he would never push her down the stairs. He would never hurt anyone. I think maybe Miss Olsson has only pretended to be with child in order to force Rurik to marry her. I don't know why that is so important to her, but apparently her reasons make it worth lying about."

The doctor nodded. "Given Miss Olsson's performance in my exam room, I'm beginning to think you may be right."

Chapter 23

After writing a short note to be delivered to her father, Merrill made sure Carl was resting comfortably and hurried to the city jail. The skies had turned cloudy and the air cold, but the weather was not on her mind as she rushed through the police station door. "I wish to see Mr. Jorgenson," she told the officer, a man named Clarence Obermeyer. "And, also, Dr. Hickum wishes to speak to the police chief as soon as possible."

"He's out right now," the man replied. "I guess if it's important, I can go find him."

"Please, I wish you would. I believe the doctor has news on Miss Olsson's condition."

The man looked at her for a moment and nodded. "It doesn't seem fitting to have you here. Rurik Jorgenson isn't your kin."

"I assure you that I intend to marry Mr. Jorgenson," she said forthrightly. "That makes us kin, does it not?"

"Well . . . I guess in that case . . . I could let you see him. I'll take you back to where Mr. Jorgenson is." He seemed rather hesitant, though.

To encourage the officer, Merrill began moving toward the cells. "Thank you."

The man led Merrill to a cell where Rurik sat on a narrow bed reading a Bible. She smiled at the sight. "Don't forget to fetch the police chief for Dr. Hickum."

The man nodded. "I'll be right back." He stopped and looked at her. "You didn't bring him any weapons, did you?"

Merrill rolled her eyes. "Clarence Obermeyer, you know me better than that."

The man looked sheepish. "Sorry, Miss Krause. I didn't mean nothing by it." He turned and left.

When Merrill turned back to the cell she found Rurik standing very near the bars separating them. She smiled again. "I have good news."

"Svea?"

She nodded. "She's going to be fine. No broken bones, no concussion. And best of all, no pregnancy."

Rurik frowned. "She lost . . . lost the baby?"

"No," Merrill said, reaching out to touch his hand clutched tightly about the bars. "There never was a baby. She wasn't with child. In fact, Dr. Hickum told me that after examining her quite thoroughly, he doesn't believe she's ever . . . well . . ." She felt her cheeks grow warm. "He doesn't think that Svea has ever . . ."

"I understand," Rurik said, breathing out a long sigh. "I'm so glad. Glad for both her . . . and for me." But he was frowning. "Why would she risk her reputation by saying otherwise, though? She has the whole town believing her to have been intimate with a man."

"I think it was all a part of trying to force you to marry her," Merrill said, letting her touch linger on his hand.

"But why? Why was I so important to her future? She could have attracted any number of Lindsborg fellows. . . ." He pulled away and began to pace the small area. Then he stopped. "I forgot to ask about Uncle Carl. How is he?"

"Resting. He isn't too well, though." Merrill's voice dropped. "Dr. Hickum told me he really doesn't think your uncle will last very long."

"I know," Rurik said. "I've been afraid of that even before . . . and now this." He looked so dejected. Merrill didn't know what she could say to help him.

"Well, we both know how stubborn Swedes are," she finally said with a little smile. "Your uncle isn't going to die one minute sooner than he wants to."

Rurik stopped pacing to face her and responded with a hint of his own smile. "So, now you're telling me you think Svedes are stubborn, ja?"

She had to laugh at the accent he added to his words. "You know they are." She chuckled. "But I have to say, so, too, are Germans. But that's not the point."

"No, I suppose it's not. So what happens now?" he asked, sobering. He reached through the bars for her hand.

"The doctor has sent for the police chief. Doc wants to explain the situation, and perhaps Svea herself will tell the truth when faced with the evidence of her deceit."

"I pray that she will. And honestly, for her sake as well as mine. I can't believe the scene she created at the hotel. It was so out of character for her." Rurik shook his head. "I've just never known her to act so . . . frantic. It almost seems like she's afraid of something . . . someone."

"Maybe her brother has been behind all of this," Merrill offered. "It's a possibility at least."

"A big possibility. I found out Nils is in some kind of trouble at home, and it may have to do with money." Rurik began to walk around the cell again. "And my uncle just learned that some money is unaccounted for in the company books here. He didn't know if it was just a mistake, or if Nils has taken it."

"Do you think he would do such a thing?"

Rurik shook his head. "I don't know. My brother confided in a letter that Nils has had some gambling issues. I sure hope it's not true, but he has asked me for loans several times, telling me he can't afford to take care of Svea properly on the small salary he's paid.

"My brother Aron wrote that Nils and his father argued over something—presumably the gambling debts. Nils and Svea slipped out of Lindsborg in the dead of night without telling anyone that they were leaving. The family was worried sick, but then I wrote to Aron, letting him know they were here."

"Do you suppose Nils is in trouble with the law?" Merrill asked.

"I don't know. I just don't understand any of this. Nils has been like a brother to me. I really thought I knew him, and now I feel as though we're talking about a stranger. The man I used to know would never have gambled or hurt his family by leaving unannounced." Rurik paused a moment, then asked, "Has he come to see Svea?"

"No. Apparently he's not in town. No one has seen him, and Svea told the doctor she didn't know where he'd gone, only that he intended to be away overnight."

"Uncle Carl mentioned him making a trip to Mankato, but I can't imagine why he would. There's nothing there for him."

Merrill held her hand out through the bars of the cell, and Rurik took it in his. "Rurik, no matter what happens, you need to know how I feel. I want you to know that I believe in you. I know God will see us through this." She paused, wondering if she should continue. After a moment she went on, "I meant what I said when I told you that I love you."

Rurik gripped her hand tightly and covered it with his other one. "Merrill, I can't tell you what it means to hear you say that—especially in this place. I'm so sorry that you are involved in all this. A woman of your character and up-bringing should never have to see the inside of a jail. I hate that you have to see me this way. But that makes your telling me of your love all the more of a treasure. You know I love you, dear one."

She nodded, and her eyes filled with tears. She shook her head. "There's a purpose, even in this. I won't continue to question God about it." She smiled as Rurik kissed her fingers. "I've been questioning Him far too much. I know He doesn't mind those questions, but now comes the time to have faith and trust, something I can't do on my own. But I know He will help me even with that."

Rurik stepped closer to the bars. "I've been praying for just such faith."

"As have I," she whispered, pressing her face toward his. Through the bars, their lips met in a kiss.

When they finally drew apart, Rurik's gaze bore into hers. "No matter what happens . . . no matter what they do to me, always remember that I love you, and I always will."

⁂

Merrill discovered the police chief had left by the time she made her way back to the doctor's office. Carl was still resting and seemed to be comfortable. This left Merrill free to seek out the doctor. "Dr. Hickum?" she called. She looked into Svea's room.

The young woman was curled up on her side and seemed to be crying. Merrill's first thought was to leave her alone, but she didn't want to turn her back on Svea's suffering.

"Are you all right? Are you in pain? Should I fetch the doctor?"

Svea looked up and shook her head briefly. "I'm all right," she said over a hiccough.

"You don't sound fine, Svea. Can I do—?"

"I don't want you here," Svea said, cutting her off. She rolled to face the wall. "Go away."

Merrill shrugged helplessly and left. She found Dr. Hickum down the hall in the examination room. "I wanted you to know that I've returned. How was your talk with the police chief?"

The doctor looked at her and shook his head. "Miss Olsson insists that she's with child and refuses to clear Rurik of pushing her down the stairs. She says she'll forgive him and press no charges if he will marry her."

Merrill couldn't believe what she was hearing. "What woman would marry a man who threw her down a flight of stairs? Especially if he believed her to be in such a delicate condition? With his own child?"

"I know, I know. The chief and I have the same questions. Miss Olsson says she loves him and knows it's just a misunderstanding. When we pointed out that she was accusing him of attempted murder in one breath, and telling us it was nothing more than a misunderstanding in the next, she clammed up and refused to say anything more."

Merrill felt a new sense of frustration creep over her. "So Rurik has to sit in jail while Svea Olsson continues to tell her lies. It hardly seems fair, does it?"

The doctor nodded. "I agree, but there's nothing more I can do at this time. However, I am going to allow Carl to return to his home. I wonder if you would be able to stay with him. He shouldn't be alone, and he must remain in bed, no exceptions. He'll need around-the-clock care."

"I can do that," Merrill agreed, thinking quickly. "I'll get word to Mrs. Niedermeyer. She can go take care of my father and brothers and let them know I'm staying on in town."

"I'll get some men to move Carl back to his house later today. Will you be there?"

"I will. It'll only take a few minutes to get a message to Margaret. Then I'll go right over to Uncle Carl's house and make certain everything is ready for him."

"Thank you, Miss Krause. You've a good heart."

Merrill said nothing more, but went quickly to work on the arrangements. She reported briefly to Granny Lassiter and Corabeth and arranged for them to get word to Margaret Niedermeyer. With a million plans racing through her mind, Merrill then made a quick stop by the livery to let them know she wouldn't be coming back for her team that day. She considered having the man take the animals home to the farm, then changed her mind. If her father wanted the team, he would understand the situation and would come and fetch them.

Merrill made her way back to the Jorgenson house, trying to decide what she should do first. The house probably needed to be warmed up, and she'd need to put together a little supper for her patient. She wasn't there but ten minutes, however, when a knock sounded on the front door.

She hadn't expected Carl to arrive so soon, but she hurried to pull down the bedcovers before opening the door. To her surprise, however, two men she'd never seen before stared back at her.

"We're looking for Carl and Rurik Jorgenson," the younger of the two men stated.

"And who might you be?" she asked matter-of-factly.

"I'm Aron Jorgenson, his older brother."

"Oh, I'm so glad to see you, Mr. Jorgenson. There's been a great deal of trouble."

"What kind of trouble?" Aron asked, casting a quick glance at his companion.

"I hardly know where to start." She motioned the two men into the house while she continued. "The worst of it is probably the most pressing. You are familiar with Svea Olsson?" Rurik's brother nodded, and the man beside him opened his mouth, but closed it without saying anything. "Well, she's had a fall down the hotel stairs—only she's telling everyone that Rurik pushed her."

"My Svea? Is she hurt?"

Merrill looked at the other man. Only then did she see the distinct features that clearly confirmed his relationship. "You must be Svea's father."

"I am. Where is she? Is she going to be all right?"

Merrill drew a long breath. "Let me get my wrap. I'll take you both to . . . to her."

Explaining the situation in as much detail as she felt she could, Merrill walked with them to the doctor's office. Mr. Olsson went immediately to his daughter's side while Aron was taken to see his uncle. Within a few minutes, he reemerged. "Take me to see Rurik. Please."

She nodded, and asked him to wait a moment. She told the doctor to delay a bit before moving Carl home.

The two made the short walk to the jail. "I'll wait for you if you'd like me to," Merrill said, stopping in the entryway.

"I'd appreciate that. I shouldn't be too long. I want to assure Rurik that I'll secure a lawyer and get him out of here as soon as possible." He checked in with the officer and was led toward the cells without another word.

Merrill took a seat on a bench and silently thanked God for what seemed to be an answer to prayer. She didn't know Rurik's brother or Mr. Olsson, but both seemed like upstanding men.

"Please, God," she murmured, "show Rurik's brother the truth. Show him how to help Rurik and see this matter put to rest. Let the truth be known. Help Svea to be honest with her father. . . ."

No more than fifteen minutes had passed when Aron reappeared. Merrill gave him a hopeful look and watched his face for any sign that he had been successful in changing his brother's situation.

Aron only smiled and said, "Thank you for waiting."

Merrill got to her feet. "I'm happy to help Rurik in any way."

"I can see that." He held out his arm for her as they walked out of the jail. "I wonder something, however."

"What? I'll tell you anything I know."

He laughed. "Do you love my brother as much as he clearly loves you?"

Merrill couldn't help but chuckle. All at once she felt like a giggly little girl again. "I don't know for sure how much he loves me, but if it's even a tenth of what I feel for him, then I am greatly loved."

Aron nodded. "I'm glad to hear that. You seem a perfect fit for each other, and I don't even know you."

"Can you help us?"

"I can and am. I've asked the police chief to get word to the best lawyer in town. He'll come to see me at Uncle Carl's place. But maybe you could explain a bit more about what all led up to this, what's happened."

"I really don't know what to say. A few weeks ago, Svea and Nils Olsson showed up here acting as though Rurik and Svea were still engaged, and the next thing I knew she was telling Rurik that she was carrying his child."

Aron didn't seem surprised by this, and Merrill figured Rurik had already explained. "Rurik insisted to me that he had never . . . well, had never been intimate with her." Merrill paused. "Excuse me if I seem too forward and bold. I'm given to speaking my mind—especially when I believe the truth can help."

"I agree, and you have nothing to apologize for. In fact, you remind me of my mother. She was also given to speaking her mind."

Merrill smiled at that. "Well, then you might as well know everything. The doctor says that Miss Olson is not expecting. Could not have been. Apparently she made up the entire thing."

"That's what my brother told me."

"Furthermore, I believe Rurik when he says he did nothing to harm her. I wasn't there, of course, but I don't believe he pushed her down the stairs. That isn't in his nature."

"No, it isn't," Aron agreed. "It might have been in mine at one time. And I sure might have wanted to, given what she was saying and doing to Rurik." He paused and rubbed his chin. "So it seems we must figure out how to get Miss Olsson to recant her story. Makes me glad I brought her father along. I doubt she'll be able to continue the lie with him."

"I pray not." They stopped outside the doctor's place, and Merrill realized she needed to tell Aron about his uncle. "The doctor wants to bring Uncle Carl home today. There's really little he can do for him."

"I know."

"I've offered to stay and attend to him, but since you'll be there, I wonder how I might best assist you?"

"I'd like very much if you could remain to oversee his care. That will free me to work on Rurik's behalf."

"I would be happy to," Merrill replied. "I want to do whatever I can to help Rurik and Uncle Carl. As you know, they're both quite precious to me. I can stay with friends nearby at night, but I will see to the meals and housekeeping as well as Uncle Carl's care."

Aron smiled. "And I have a feeling that you are going to be quite precious to all of us."

Chapter 24

"Uncle Carl, the doctor tells me you can return to the house, but on one condition. You must stay in bed for at least two weeks," Aron told the older man. "Miss Krause has agreed to be your nurse." He winked at his uncle. "Kind of makes me want to be sick."

Carl smiled weakly. "Oh sure. I betcha heard about her great cooking."

"I hadn't, but that, added to the fact she's pretty, makes me jealous that you'll be getting all her attention."

"And what would your lovely wife say if she heard you talking like that?" Carl shook his finger at his nephew.

Aron laughed. "She'd elbow me in the ribs and tell me to mind my manners, so let's not tell her anything about this."

Merrill was amazed Aron could be so lighthearted at the same time his brother was in jail. She wanted to trust that God was in control of the whole situation, but her nature was to fret over the details.

"Miss Krause tells me she can stay with you during the day and care for you. She's also agreed to clean and cook for us while I help to get Rurik cleared of these charges."

"Merrill Jean," Carl said, "that's asking too much of you—unless of course you let me pay you."

She shook her head. "Uncle Carl, you're like family to me now. I won't hear of it."

Carl gave a weak grin. "She will be family if Rurik has anything to say about it."

"Of that I'm certain," Aron agreed. "If it meets with your approval, I'd like to stay at the house with you. I can sleep in Rurik's room. Miss Krause has friends in town and told me she would arrange to stay with them at night. That way you'll have someone close by at all times."

"Of course it meets with my approval." Carl closed his eyes. "I'm learning that the Good Lord sometimes works through our weakness." His accent thickened in his obvious exhaustion.

"Yes, He does," Merrill admitted. "You rest now, Uncle Carl, and we'll get things ready for you at home. The doctor said he'll have some men come to carry you to the house."

"I can walk," he protested, but his voice was weak.

Merrill said gently, "You'll do what the doctor says or like a strict mother, I shall discipline you. You'll get none of my strudel."

Carl opened his eyes wide. "I promise I'll be good." Aron and Merrill laughed.

"I will take my leave then and begin to work on your supper."

"I'll escort you," Aron told her. He looked back to his uncle. "Then I'll return to help bring you home."

They'd no sooner stepped into the hall, however, than Svea's wailing cries caught their attention. Merrill slipped into the girl's room. Her father and the doctor were there with her.

"Miss Olsson," the doctor was saying, "it is my professional opinion that you are not now, nor ever have been, with child. Why do you insist on this lie?"

"But I am. I'm going to have a baby. Rurik's baby!" She wiped tears away with the edge of the white sheet. "We must marry." Her voice trembled.

"Svea, what you must do is stop this lying," her father said, shaking his head. "I know that you aren't speaking the truth. I don't understand why you think you must say these things, but I won't let this continue."

"But . . . you don't realize that . . ." Her voice started to sound more desperate. "I have to marry Rurik."

"What you have to do is tell the truth," her father insisted. "If you don't stop lying to me right this minute, I will disown you."

Svea's reddened eyes grew wide. "Papa, you don't mean that." She choked on a sob. "You can't mean that."

Mr. Olsson straightened and gave her a most severe look. "I do mean that, Svea. I will turn my back on you if you continue to lie. You know the Lord hates lies, and so do I."

"But I promised. I promised Nils that I would marry Rurik. I promised." She began to cry fresh tears.

Merrill exchanged a look with Aron Jorgenson. What in the world was this all about?

"Why did you promise your brother?" Mr. Olsson asked. "Why would Nils care who you married as long as you were happy?"

Svea seemed to think she'd said too much and shook her head, saying nothing more. Her father took a seat in the chair beside her bed while the doctor remained by the window. Merrill knew she should give them all privacy and leave, but she couldn't. She had to hear the truth.

When Mr. Olsson spoke again, his voice was that of a broken man. "I've tried to teach you right from wrong. I've raised you in the way of the Lord, but apparently I have failed in that upbringing."

Svea looked at her father, and something in her expression suggested her father's words had touched her deeply. Still, she didn't speak.

"Your mother and I have loved each of you children more than life itself. It was our heart's desire to see all of you grow to adulthood, find love, and have families of your own. But, even more than that, we prayed you would walk with the Lord God all of your days. Now this . . ." He fell silent and sat shaking his head.

"Please, Papa, don't be angry with me." Svea sounded very sober, almost contrite.

He looked at her in disbelief. "I'm not angry, daughter. I'm filled with sorrow."

For several minutes neither said anything. Merrill was just about to turn away when Svea murmured, "The doctor is right. I've never been with a man. I've not dishonored you and Mama that way."

"Then why did you say otherwise? Why dishonor us with lies of this kind?"

"I promised Nils that I would help him. He's in trouble,

Papa. He owes money to some very bad men. They have threatened his life. He told me that if I would marry Rurik, I could get the money he needed."

"How is that?"

"Rurik gets an inheritance when he marries. Nils was certain I could convince Rurik to loan him part of it in order to pay back his debts."

Mr. Olsson shook his head again. "He's been gambling again . . . hasn't he?"

Svea nodded. "He didn't want you to know. He didn't want there to be more trouble between you. He really does love you, Papa. He hates that he's disappointed you, but it's like a sickness with him. He tries . . . really he does."

Her father looked straight into her face. "I want the truth, daughter. Did Rurik Jorgenson push you down the stairs?"

Svea looked away and shook her head. "No." Her voice was barely audible. "I lost my balance. I was so upset, and I felt like Rurik wasn't listening to me. I . . . well . . . I turned to confront him and lost my balance. When Rurik realized what was happening, he tried to grab me. That's what the hotel clerk saw. When I landed I realized I wasn't that hurt. Then the clerk started saying how Rurik pushed me down the stairs and . . . well . . . I thought I could use the situation to get Rurik to marry me."

"Did you not think of the consequences to Rurik, daughter? He sits in a jail cell even now. How could you be so heartless toward him?"

It was only then Svea seemed to notice Merrill and Aron standing at the door. She looked at Merrill for a moment, then turned back to her father. "I love my brother. I wanted to help him. I knew Rurik would understand in time and . . . forgive me."

Her father let go a heavy sigh. "You and your brother have caused a great deal of trouble. Where is he?"

"I don't know, Papa. Truly. He told me he had to go out of town, but I don't know where he went. I think he meant to take the train. He told me to get Rurik to marry me immediately or those men would . . . hurt him. I did what I thought I had to do. I'm so sorry." The tears came again, but this time Merrill could see they were from regret, not fear.

"Since you have no real injuries, Miss Olsson," the doctor interjected, "you are free to return to the hotel with your father. I'll send for the police chief first, however, so you can tell him what you've told us."

"I'll go for him," Merrill declared. Their gazes turned toward the door where she and Aron stood. She didn't wait for their approval. "I'll get him now."

She hurried from the doctor's office and all but ran down the street to the jail. She was panting when she burst through the door.

The police chief looked up from his desk in surprise. "Miss Krause, what's wrong? Is it Miss Olsson?"

"Yes, but it's good news. You are needed immediately at the doctor's place. Please hurry."

He got to his feet and pulled on his coat. "She's all right?"

Merrill smiled and nodded, all the while trying to catch her breath. "She's confessed the truth. Rurik isn't to blame for the accident. She lost her balance and fell. Rurik actually tried to stop her fall."

"I'm glad to hear it," the lawman said and smiled. "I've always liked that young man."

"Me too," Merrill declared. "And, if you don't mind, I'd like to go back to his cell and tell him the news."

The man nodded. "I suppose that would be all right. I'm not used to having women around here, but I guess this time won't hurt."

Merrill hurried to find Rurik. She saw him lying on his cot, Bible open. "Svea's told the truth," she called.

Rurik jumped to his feet. Crossing the cell in two strides, he came to the bars of his jail door. "She did? When? What did she say?"

Laughing and crying at the same time, Merrill related the turn of events. "She seems quite contrite, Rurik," she concluded. "Apparently Nils's gambling has gotten him into trouble with the wrong men. He convinced her that she had to help him, so they came up with the idea of her being with child. Nils thought if you two married, Svea could convince you to give him some of your inheritance. When you showed up at the hotel to talk about meeting with the pastor, Svea realized how little time she had left. She was desperate and not at all mindful of the stairs. She lost her balance and said you actually were trying to stop her fall. The police chief has gone now to hear her official confession." She reached through the bars to take hold of his hand. "Oh, Rurik, I've been so worried and full of grief for you—for us. I was so afraid . . ." She squeezed his hand as tears streamed down her face.

"Wait a minute here," he said, brushing at her wet cheeks with his hand. "You just brought me wonderful news, and now you've gone all weepy on me. I'm looking for a smile."

Merrill sniffed and managed a little smile. "All right, that's over with. Now you'll see how happy I am—" Both hands went to her mouth, and she gasped.

"What's wrong now, Merrill?"

She laughed shakily. "I just remembered. I promised Uncle Carl strudel for supper. I need to get to work."

Rurik and Merrill laughed together. What a relief and a joy it was. Reaching through the bars once more, Merrill took hold of his hand. "God heard our prayers, Rurik."

"Indeed He did." He kissed her hand and looked into her eyes. "In so many ways."

Merrill still felt her heart leap at the memory of Rurik's gaze and kiss. She hurried to put together a welcome-home supper complete with Carl's cherry strudel. Granny was happy to help and offered a jar of garlic dilled pickles, canned cherries, and flour when Merrill found the Jorgenson house to be short on food supplies. She and Corabeth followed Merrill back to the house to assist with the preparations.

"So she finally admitted it was all just lies?" Granny said, tasting the gravy that would soon cover the beef rouladen Merrill had made and adding a pinch of salt.

"She did. She said it was all because of Nils." Merrill sidestepped Granny to check the strudel in the oven. The kitchen was hardly big enough for all three women, but they were managing. Merrill shut the oven door. "I can't say too much more about the details." Granny nodded, and Merrill knew she understood.

"But why would she risk so much, including her reputation?" Corabeth asked. "I would never do something like that. To lie like that in order to help someone else seems doubly wrong."

"She and Nils have been close all of their lives," she explained. "She wanted to help her brother. I know how much I love my own brothers. There isn't much I wouldn't do for them. Of course, I wouldn't go so far as Svea Olsson did, but I think now I can at least understand some of her thinking and actions." She inspected the various pots on the stove. "Would you set the table, Corabeth? Supper is nearly ready."

Merrill went into the front room and smiled at the men seated there, the scene warming her heart. Uncle Carl had his family around him and looked content. And with Rurik safely back . . . she couldn't express how happy she felt.

She invited them to the table, and Aron immediately helped Carl to his feet. "You and Rurik have done nothing but praise this young woman's ability to cook, so I'm anxious to sample whatever she has prepared."

Rurik laughed and went to where Merrill stood. "You won't be sorry, and if I have anything to say about it—this won't be the only time you get the opportunity."

Aron assisted Carl to the kitchen while Rurik remained behind. "Thank you, my Merrill," he said, putting his arm around Merrill's waist. "I think I shall reward you with a kiss."

She felt a shiver of delight flow through her and her cheeks grew warm. She looked up at him and shivered again at the intensity of his gaze. "I think I shall let you reward me."

He kissed her gently, his hands holding her face with great tenderness. Merrill wanted the moment to go on forever, but knew the others were waiting. She pulled away reluctantly. "Come, your supper will get cold."

"I hope you won't mind if my first order of business tomorrow is to speak to your father. I'd like to get his permission to call on you, Miss Krause. That is . . . if you are willing."

Merrill smiled and quipped, "I'll need to give that some thought." They both chuckled, but she quickly turned serious. "You already know I'm most willing, Rurik. I just hope you also know what you're getting yourself into. I'm not—well, I'll never be dainty and frilly. It's best you know that right now."

He laughed and pulled her with him toward the kitchen. "I'm willing to take my chances on you, Merrill Jean. I'm willing to take my chances."

Chapter 25

Merrill lost no time in getting word to her father and brothers regarding Rurik's innocence. She prayed that the truth might circulate as quickly as the lies had so that Rurik's name and reputation would be set to rights. Granny and Corabeth had both assured her that they would discreetly help to set the record straight.

"People love to spread gossip," Granny had told her, "but they're usually in less of a rush to tell the truth."

Merrill supposed it was the nature of the human race to focus on the bad and believe the worst of a person. The negative, it seemed, was far more enticing than the good, positive, noble things of life. Maybe that was why people needed the Bible's reminder to dwell on the latter things.

As soon as she had the breakfast dishes cleaned up and put away, Merrill made a list of items she would need for future meals. She surveyed the cupboards and wrote down the things that were standards in her kitchen. She was nearly finished when Rurik joined her there.

"Merrill, I'm heading out to your house and wondered if

you wanted to accompany me. Aron said he'd stay here with Uncle Carl until our return."

Merrill could see that Rurik had prepared himself as if he were to attend church. His blond-brown hair was washed and neatly combed into place, and his face was freshly shaved. She could see by his expression that Rurik was quite pleased with himself. "You look like a man who's up to something," she said with a little smile.

"I am. I'm up to speaking to your father."

She cocked her head to one side. "And I suppose I am the topic of that discussion?"

One side of his mouth rose. "Shouldn't that be between your father and me?"

"Maybe." She put her hands on her hips. "But if it does involve me, perhaps I'd better come along and make certain I'm properly represented. There's no telling where things might lead otherwise."

"Why do you suppose I invited you? I wouldn't have it any other way." Rurik moved toward the door. "If you don't mind, I'll bring your wagon around in ten minutes. Will that give you enough time?"

"Certainly." She grabbed her list and tucked it in her pocket. "Let me just make certain your brother knows what he needs to tend to while I'm gone. Oh, and we'll need to pick up some supplies if you want me to keep cooking here."

"Of course we want you to keep cooking. I told Uncle Carl that he should just pretend to need a nurse for a good long while so that we could have you with us all the time."

Merrill laughed as Rurik gave her a wink and disappeared

down the hall. She sought out Aron and explained what he needed to do for lunch and then gathered her things. As a last thought she went back to the kitchen and took up a rather sad-looking apple and cut it into pieces for the horses. She stood waiting and ready for Rurik when he brought the wagon around. The Belgian team seemed happy to be out again.

"There you are," she said to the horses. "Did you think I'd forgotten you?" She gave Jack some apple first and then turned to Jill. "I brought you gifts so you won't be slighted by my absence." She rubbed Jill's soft muzzle and laughed when Jack nudged her for another piece of fruit. She fed him quickly before moving to climb into the wagon.

"I hope Jack and Jill behaved for you," she said as Rurik helped her onto the seat beside him.

"They were perfect. We have a good understanding between us," he said, grinning.

The roads, though deeply rutted, appeared dry. The cloudless blue skies overhead indicated they would remain so at least for the day. Everything in creation seemed perfectly arranged for this day. Merrill couldn't help but feel a sense of excitement.

They arrived at the farm shortly before nine thirty, and Merrill was surprised to find her father and brothers busy at work on the roof of the house.

"What in the world are you doing up there?" she called. Her father gave a wave, but her brothers were busy pounding nails and didn't seem to notice her for the moment.

"Figured we'd best take advantage of the weather and get the roof patched up before it rains again," her father called down. "Got your message, but sure wasn't expecting to see you yet." He went to the ladder and started down. "Is Carl doing all right?"

"He's resting at the house," Rurik replied. "My brother Aron is seeing to him until we can get back."

Merrill's father reached the ground and turned with a nod. "I'm glad things worked out for you, Rurik." He extended his hand.

Rurik shook hands with her father and got right to business. "I was hoping we could talk."

"What about?"

Merrill couldn't help but smile. Her father no doubt knew exactly what Rurik wanted to talk about. Bogart Krause had never been known as a slow-witted man.

"I thought we might talk in private . . . about . . . Merrill and me." The pounding had stopped, and Merrill's brothers seemed to be all ears.

"What's going on down there?" Tobe asked, stretching toward the sky. "Rurik, did you come to help us with the roof?"

Her father chuckled. "Boys, you get that patching done. I'm going to go inside and have some coffee with Rurik and your sister."

"Oh sure. Take yourself a good, long break," Leo called down in a jesting tone. "Merrill Jean, did you bring us any of your pastries?"

"No, I've been far too busy to worry about you," she said, giving her brothers a wave. "Besides, I'm sure Margaret has taken good care of you all." She followed her father and Rurik into the house.

Merrill went to the stove for the morning's leftover coffee and poured some for each of the men. Father leaned against the kitchen counter while Rurik twisted his cap in his hands, looking surprisingly ill at ease.

"I'll just go and get a few of my things," she said, handing them their mugs.

"No, Merrill Jean, I want you to stay," her father declared. "I figure this has to do with you, so you should be here, as well." He looked at Rurik and smiled. "Let's sit at the table," he suggested. The three pulled out chairs and sat.

"So what have you got to say for yourself, son?" He looked at Rurik over the rim of his mug.

Rurik cast a quick glance at Merrill and seemed to regain his confidence. "Sir, I would like your permission to court Merrill."

"I see. And she's in agreement to this?" He looked at Merrill and raised a brow.

Merrill met her father's searching gaze. "I am."

He nodded and rubbed his jaw. "And what is your intention in courting my daughter?"

Rurik, who hadn't taken his gaze from Merrill, now gave her a look that revealed all that was within his heart. She couldn't help but smile and lean toward him. He finally turned to her father. "Well, I haven't actually said the words to her yet, but I'd like to marry her."

Merrill wanted to shout in her excitement, but she held herself in check. Her father gave a serious nod and seemed to consider the statement. His silence started to make Merrill uncomfortable, but she knew better than to interrupt his contemplation.

Finally he looked to Rurik.

"You know, there's been many a fella who showed interest in my daughter. Her brothers have been good to keep most of the less reliable at bay." He smiled and winked at Merrill. "Unfortunately, the thought of dealing with them has also caused some of the better men to keep their distance, as well."

"I'm sure her brothers only wanted to keep her safe," Rurik said, adding, "Just like I want to do. I promise you, Mr. Krause, I will guard her and love her for all my life."

"I know you will. You've proven yourself to me on more than one occasion. I sure am sorry for all the troubles you've been through, but you have handled yourself in an honorable way. I never once heard it said that you'd spoken ill of Miss Olsson. In fact, it seems you attempted to guard her reputation, saying very little. That took a great deal of integrity and strength of character, especially since your own good name was at stake. I'd be proud to have you court my daughter and join this family."

Rurik let out a long sigh. "Thank you."

Merrill hugged her father, though she knew such displays usually made him uncomfortable. This time, however, he held on to her for just a moment. "Thank you, Father," she whispered against his ear. "I love you."

She turned to Rurik and held out her hands, palms upward. He quickly placed his hands over hers.

"Well," said Mr. Krause, clearing his throat with a grin, "better get myself back to the roof."

"It was kind of you to invite us for supper," Mr. Olsson said, taking off his hat.

Granny Lassiter took the hat and led him and Svea into the front room. Merrill joined them. "Mr. Olsson, Miss Olsson, we're so glad you could join us." She turned and waved toward Rurik, who was talking to Aron and Corabeth. "We were just waiting for you to arrive. Supper is ready."

"Thank you for having us," Mr. Olsson reiterated.

Merrill was determined to show Svea kindness. She smiled at her in welcome, but Svea remained sober-faced, looking apprehensive and nervous.

"Granny was kind enough to open her house up for this gathering since Uncle Carl's house would have been too cramped," Merrill explained. "The Lassiter house can definitely accommodate us all. Of course, Uncle Carl was less than pleased to be wheeled over, certain he could make it on his own. The doctor lent us a wheeled chair, however, and told Uncle Carl he couldn't attend unless he remained seated and refrained from exerting himself."

Svea gave a slight nod and fussed with her shawl. Merrill was sure the young woman was very uncomfortable after all that had happened. "Would you like to help me in the kitchen?"

"I . . . I'm not sure I would be of much use—"

"Nonsense," Merrill assured her. "It'll give us a chance to talk." Merrill reached out a hand. "May I take your wrap?"

Svea nodded, seeming rather resigned to the situation, but

Merrill hoped they might actually have a pleasant conversation. She hung up the shawl, then led the way to the kitchen.

Svea glanced around at Granny's kitchen. "It . . . the supper smells delicious."

Merrill said, "I hope it will be. By the way, may I call you Svea?"

"Yes. Please."

"Then I hope you'll call me Merrill." She leaned on the counter, carefully considering her next words. "Svea, I want you to know that I'm sorry I've been less than friendly. I'm afraid I didn't act with much Christian charity. I was wrong, and I hope you'll forgive me."

Svea looked at her strangely for a moment. She didn't seem to know what to say. Merrill frowned, wondering if she might have just made things worse. Not knowing what else to do, Merrill took a platter to the stove and carefully lifted the ham from its baking dish and placed it on the large plate.

"I'm so . . . ashamed. I never meant to cause such . . . such harm."

Merrill turned back to the young woman with an understanding smile. "I'm sure you didn't. Sometimes things have a way of getting out of hand. Even so, I've always known God to help us set things right."

Svea looked at the floor. "Papa and I are planning to go back to Kansas as soon as Nils returns."

"Have you had any word from him?"

"No. I'm really worried about him. I thought he'd be back by now." Svea ran her hand down the front of her skirt, smoothing nonexistent wrinkles. "Papa spoke to the police, but they've heard nothing."

"There you are," Corabeth said, coming through the door. "What can I do to help?" She crossed the kitchen and took up the bread basket. "Shall I put this on the table? Is the butter already out there?"

"Yes," Merrill said, sorry she wouldn't be able to speak more with Svea. She gave Svea an apologetic shrug. "Why don't you take the ham out, and I'll get the rest."

Svea started to do as Merrill suggested, but stopped. "Look, I want to say something." She bit her lower lip for a moment. "I know that Rurik loves you."

It was Merrill's turn to feel awkward. "Yes."

"And you love him."

Merrill nodded. "Yes."

For a moment Svea said nothing, but then she added, "I'm glad."

"You are?" Merrill asked, unable to keep the surprise from her voice.

"I am. Our parents had arranged our betrothal, but it was never right." Svea shrugged. "I do love Rurik, but not like you. He's like a brother to me. When he said he felt that way about me . . . I was . . . well, at first upset and then relieved. Rurik is a good man, much better than I knew, in fact."

Corabeth came back to see how she could help. Merrill quickly handed her two bowls. Thankfully, Corabeth seemed to understand and hurried from the room.

"I'm really sorry, Merrill," Svea said, picking up the ham. "I want you to know that I think you and Rurik are perfect for each other. You're the woman he has always wanted and needed . . . someone who wants to stay in one place and raise a family."

"But that's not for you?" Merrill asked.

Svea shrugged again. "Maybe one day, but for now I think I'd like to see more of the world or at least this country. There's so much out there I've only read about . . . places I want to see and experience. Rurik never wanted to travel or go far from home. Yet here he is in Minnesota." She shrugged with a little smile.

"I suppose his love for Uncle Carl was stronger than his desire to remain in Kansas," Merrill replied.

"And I suppose his love of you will be strong enough to keep him here for the rest of his life," Svea countered with another smile.

"I hope so," Merrill said, knowing that nothing would please her more.

Corabeth popped her head around the kitchen door. "Zadoc just got here." Her excitement was fully evident, and Merrill couldn't help but chuckle.

"He said to tell you he's half starved and his stomach is rubbing up against his backbone," Cora said merrily.

"Is that all?" Merrill took up another bowl mounded high with whipped potatoes.

"No. He said if you didn't get a move on, he would get Grandpa to say grace and eat without you."

Merrill looked to Svea and motioned her to the door. "By all means, we'd best hurry. Once Grandpa Lassiter prays, it'll be every man and woman for themselves."

Rurik stood in the lobby with his brother and Mr. Olsson. He and Aron had escorted the Olssons back to the hotel, and with Svea already upstairs, Mr. Olsson wanted a word with the Jorgenson brothers.

"I have no idea where Nils might be or when he might return. I wonder if you have any thoughts on the matter." He looked with unspoken hope to Rurik.

"I don't, Mr. Olsson. Not really. Uncle Carl mentioned that Nils talked about wanting to go to Mankato. It's not that far away—especially by train. Svea said he had only planned to be gone overnight, so unless he really had designs to go elsewhere or has gotten himself . . ." Rurik let the words trail off momentarily. "Have you asked the authorities?"

"I did. They're trying to check it out. They said they'd send out word and check with the depot master. I was hoping maybe you would have another idea."

"I'm afraid not."

The older man nodded. "I was angry at him, but I never thought he or Svea would leave Lindsborg. And I never expected he'd sink so low as to force his sister to lie in order to marry you. I wanted him to be a man and admit to his wrongdoing, make things right. Now I might never see him again."

"I'm sure he'll be back," Aron interjected.

"I told him to get out and stay out until he was ready to make amends." Mr. Olsson didn't seem to even hear the comforting words. He looked at the hat in his hands. "He stole from me, and when I found out about it . . . well . . . I was rather rash."

Rurik exchanged a look with his brother, then put his hand on Mr. Olsson's shoulder. "Gambling does strange things to folks. It's not unlike what happens with those that drink. A little seems to do no harm, but then it turns into just a little more, and soon there are all kinds of problems. Maybe when Nils returns we can talk with him and offer to help."

Mr. Olsson looked to Rurik and for a moment his eyes filled with tears. "You've always been a good friend to my boy. I would have liked to have had you for a son-in-law." Rurik started to say something, but Olsson held up his hand. "I know that it wasn't right to try to force you to marry my Svea. I can see that you are in love with Miss Krause. I'm not trying to make trouble for you, Rurik. I just wanted you to know that I would have been proud to have you in the family."

"Thank you, sir."

Olsson glanced toward the stairs. "As much as I'm worried about Nils, I need to get home."

"I promise you that I'll continue to keep an eye out for Nils. He's still my friend, and I will do what I can to help him."

"We'll stay around another day or two, but then Svea and I must return to Kansas. I can't leave the others to tend the dairy without me." Mr. Olsson looked to Aron. "What about you?"

"I'll need to return, as well. The fields need to be prepared and crops planted," Aron added. "Let's plan to go together as we originally thought to do."

"That would suit me," the man replied, sounding as if his strength was giving out. "I only hope Nils will return before we go. I hate to leave things as they are between us."

Chapter 26

After making sure Carl was fed and settled in the front room with the paper, Merrill made her way to the furniture shop the next morning to do a bit of painting. Carl had promised her he'd do nothing more strenuous than read and doze, and Aron promised he'd watch out for the older man while she was out.

Rurik looked very happy to find her painting. He pretended to closely inspect what she was doing. "You are quite skilled, Miss Krause. I'm glad to see you have finally returned to your duties here." He moved to within inches of where she was working.

She held up a brush dripping red with paint. "I wouldn't come too close if I were you. I might accidentally stain your clothes." She grinned and hoped he might try to steal a kiss.

"This shirt and pants are old," he said with a shrug. "Work clothes. They're meant to get dirty or stained." He studied her face for a moment, and Merrill lowered the paintbrush. He started to reach out to touch her cheek, then stopped. "Still, you're probably right."

She was disappointed as Rurik chuckled and moved away.

"We've a good many pie safes ready for you to paint. I'll have the boys bring them in here today."

Merrill turned her attention back to the job at hand and painted rosy apples on a small kitchen box. She'd barely been working ten minutes when the police chief came into the room from the far door.

Eyeing the lawman, Merrill smiled. "What brings you here?"

"Not good news, I'm afraid. Where's Mr. Jorgenson?"

"Rurik or Carl?"

"Rurik. I wouldn't want to burden his uncle with this news."

Dread washed over her, and Merrill quickly put her brush on the workbench. "I'll get him. Wait here."

She found Rurik hard at work on a dining room table. "The police chief is here," she told him, keeping her voice low. "He needs to talk to you, and it doesn't sound good. He's in the painting room."

Rurik left his work and Merrill followed him, her heart beating her fear.

"Morning," Rurik said in greeting. "Merrill said there's a problem."

"Nils Olsson has been found. I'm afraid he was badly beaten."

"Is he alive?" Rurik asked quickly.

"Barely," the police chief replied. "Some folks traveling into Waseca found him alongside the road. They brought him here to the doctor, but his outlook is grim."

Merrill put her hand to her mouth to keep herself quiet.

The thought of Nils dying had never entered her mind. She began to pray for his recovery.

Rurik was unfastening his apron. "Do Mr. Olsson and Svea know?"

"I thought to get you first. I hoped you'd come with me to break the news."

Rurik nodded. "I want to be there for them." He looked back to Merrill. "Will you tell Aron and Uncle Carl what's happened?"

"I will. Please tell Svea and Mr. Olsson that we'll be praying."

"Ja."

Merrill hurried to put away her things, then made her way to the house to share the news.

Aron immediately put on his coat. "I'll go see if there's anything I can do to help."

Merrill looked to Uncle Carl, who hadn't said a word. "Can I get you anything?"

He shook his head. "No. Just sit with me awhile. Did they say who did this terrible thing to Nils?"

Merrill took the chair beside his bed. "No. Only that some folks passing by found him alongside the road."

Carl leaned back against his pillow and closed his eyes. "We should pray for Nils."

"I promised Rurik we would." She took hold of the older man's hand and closed her eyes.

The days passed slowly, and Rurik did what he could to relieve Mr. Olsson and Svea from their bedside vigil. He'd

never seen a man so badly beaten. The doctor said that whoever had done this had obviously meant to kill him. Still,
Nils clung to life.

Sending Mr. Olsson and Svea to get some lunch, Rurik took
his customary seat beside Nils's bed and opened his Bible to
read aloud. "'This I recall to my mind, therefore have I hope. It
is of the Lord's mercies that we are not consumed, because his
compassions fail not. They are new every morning: great is thy
faithfulness. The Lord is my portion, saith my soul; therefore
will I hope in him. The Lord is good unto them that wait for
him, to the soul that seeketh him. It is good that a man should
both hope and quietly wait for the salvation of the Lord.'"

Rurik looked at his longtime friend a moment, then continued to read from Lamentations three. "'It is good for a
man that he bear the yoke in his youth. He sitteth alone
and keepeth silence, because he hath borne it upon him. He
putteth his mouth in the dust; if so be there may be hope. He
giveth his cheek to him that smiteth him: he is filled full with
reproach. For the Lord will not cast off for ever: But though
he cause grief, yet will he have compassion according to the
multitude of his mercies.'"

"Mer . . . cies."

Nils's voice was barely audible, but Rurik clearly understood the single word. "Nils?" Rurik leaned over as the beaten
man tried to open his swollen eyes.

He looked at Rurik for several moments, then closed his
eyes again. "Water."

Rurik went for the pitcher and called to the doctor at the
same time. "Dr. Hickum, Nils is waking up!"

The doctor quickly entered the room. Rurik held up a glass of water. "He wanted a drink. Is that all right?"

"Just take a cloth and dampen his lips for now. I need to evaluate the situation."

Rurik did as the doctor instructed and touched the wet cloth to Nils's lips. He rewet it and repeated the action while Dr. Hickum examined Nils.

"What . . . happened?" Nils asked between battered lips and missing teeth.

"Do you not remember anything?" the doctor asked.

"No," Nils said, trying to shake his head. The pain was clearly too great.

Rurik frowned. "Someone beat you, Nils. They nearly killed you. They beat you and left you for dead alongside the road."

"Where . . . where . . ." Nils fought to speak, but it was clearly taking its toll. His eyes closed.

"You need to be quiet," the doctor instructed. "Your injuries are great, Mr. Olsson."

"Hurt . . . I hurt."

"Yes, I'm sure you do," the doctor replied. "I'll give you something to help with the pain."

He left the room and Rurik leaned forward. "Nils, don't you dare die on me."

Nils opened his eyes and fixed them upon Rurik before closing them again. "Always . . . tellin' me," he said with a gasp, "what . . . to do."

Rurik smiled. "And this time you'd better listen."

The doctor returned and managed to get two spoonsful of

medicine down Nils's throat. "This will help with the pain. I'll let the authorities know you've regained consciousness, but it will be a while before you'll have the strength to tell them much." He looked at Rurik. "Will you remain with him?"

"Yes."

The doctor placed the spoon on a table by the door. "I won't be long."

Rurik looked again to Nils's swollen face. "I wish I knew what happened and why someone would do this terrible thing." He wasn't really talking to Nils, but his friend re-opened his eyes.

"Don't know."

"I know. You said as much." Rurik gave Nils's hand a pat. "Don't worry about it. Your father is doing everything he can to learn the truth."

"My . . . father?" Nils stared at Rurik. "He hates me."

"Hardly. He's barely left your side since they brought you in. The only reason he isn't here right now is that I sent him and Svea to get something to eat."

"He's . . . here?"

"Yes. He came to see you and Svea. He was worried about you."

"No. I . . . I . . ." Nils blinked his eyes several times and finally closed them. "I . . . hurt him."

"I know. But he loves you, Nils."

"My boy is awake?" Mr. Olsson was hurrying into the room. "He is conscious?"

Rurik nodded. "But very weak."

Svea cried softly, leaning against the door of the room. Rurik moved aside for Mr. Olsson to take his chair.

Tears rolled down the weathered cheeks of the older man. "Oh, Nils. Oh, my boy. God be praised."

The April days warmed considerably, and Carl was able to get up for short walks each day. Rurik was grateful for the additional time with his uncle, but knew it wouldn't last long. Carl no longer even pretended to have the strength for his previous duties. Dr. Hickum told Rurik that he doubted Carl had more than a few months to live. Still, it was precious time to Rurik.

With Nils on the mend, Svea and her father had returned home, along with Rurik's brother. The Olssons had wanted to stay longer, but Rurik had assured them Nils would have good care and promised to send word letting them know of Nils's progress. His recovery would take some time. His injuries included several broken ribs, a broken leg, and multiple bruises—the worst being the blows he'd taken to his head. He still had no memory of the attack.

Mr. Olsson and Nils made their peace, and the moment had touched Rurik deeply. It was as if the story of the prodigal son had come to life. Nils confessed his wrongdoings and begged his father's forgiveness, while Mr. Olsson wept and declared his undying love. It gave Rurik hope for Nils's future.

"You're looking much better," Rurik said, entering Nils's sickroom. Nils was nearly sitting up in the bed, leaning against a pillow.

"Dr. Hickum says I'll be able to leave in another few days. Not sure where I'm going to go, however."

"You're going to stay with us," Rurik said, taking a seat beside the bed. "With that broken leg, you won't be able to climb the stairs at our place, but Uncle Carl suggested I put a bed for you in the front room. We'll be crowded, but well fed. Merrill is still helping out with the meals."

Nils smiled. "You ought to marry her."

"I plan to," Rurik said with a nod. "So have you remembered anything more?"

"No. I wish I could."

Rurik considered all that his friend had endured. "Maybe it's for the best that you don't."

"I want to know who did this to me. I do remember going to Mankato to play cards. I'd heard about a game." He shook his head. "Can't remember who told me. I just knew I needed to play."

"Needed or wanted?"

Nils looked at Rurik with a grave expression. "Needed. It drives me, Rurik. It's like something in my blood." He gave a harsh laugh. "I'm no good at it, so you wouldn't think I'd keep going back."

"I want to help you," Rurik told him.

"I don't think you can. I don't think anyone can."

"God can. The Bible says nothing is impossible for Him."

Nils was quiet for a moment. "I dishonored my father. I

stole from him and from your uncle. Can God really forgive that?"

"Of course He can," Rurik replied. "The question is, do you want Him to? Are you willing to repent and sin no more?"

"I want to, but I just don't know if I can." His face darkened. "I don't know how to fight this, Rurik. Even now I keep thinking about cards and when I might play again. How can God forgive me when I can't even stop thinking about it?" He sat forward, intensity filling his expression and his body.

Rurik thought for a moment. "I don't suppose it will be easy," he finally said. "I do know that you'll destroy yourself and all those around you, however, if you don't stop. I don't want to lose you as a friend, Nils. I don't want this all to end in your death. It nearly did this time."

Nils leaned back in the bed. For a long while he said nothing, and Rurik thought it might be best to leave and let Nils contemplate the matter on his own.

He got up to go, and Nils reached out his hand. "Rurik, do you forgive me for what I did?"

"Are you asking me to?"

Nils nodded. "I am."

Rurik smiled. "That's good, because I already did. Still, a fellow likes to know forgiveness is desired."

"And we're still friends?"

This made Rurik laugh aloud. "I wouldn't be here if we weren't, Nils. I hate sickrooms. I'd much rather be spending my time elsewhere."

"With Merrill." Nils grinned awkwardly around his still-injured mouth and broken teeth.

"That's right. I'd much rather be courting and wooing than listening to you complain about your broken leg and ribs or your headache."

Nils laughed out loud this time. "Then you'd best go, because my leg is starting to itch something fierce."

Rurik shook his head and gave his friend a wave. "I'll be back. Oh, and just to give you something to look forward to, Merrill has promised to send you some of her strudel. Men have fought wars over strudel like hers, so you are among the blessed."

"Where are we going?" Merrill asked Rurik. He had shown up at Granny Lassiter's with a small buggy and a grin as big as Clear Lake.

"You'll see. It's a surprise."

Merrill couldn't imagine what he had in mind as he pointed the horse toward the north of town. She tried to recall if Rurik had mentioned anything before about that area, but nothing came to mind.

"So Granny tells me you're moving in with her on a more permanent basis," Rurik remarked.

"I am. Father needs the team, and it seems pointless to stay in town most of the time and go home for short periods. Not only that, but there's no place to keep Jack and Jill there, so I would have to rely on one of my brothers or Father to get me back and forth. Nevertheless, I need to be here in Waseca. I have my work at the furniture shop and helping out with your uncle."

"For which I really want to thank you. I think the only reason Uncle Carl is still with us is because of your good care."

"That's kind of you to say. I've come to love him like my own family." She hoped the comment didn't sound too forward. Since telling her father that he intended to marry her, Rurik had said very little on the subject.

"I know he loves you, too. At least he loves your cooking." Rurik laughed at his own quip and turned the horses onto one of the streets near Loon Lake.

"So what is the surprise you want to show me?"

Rurik pulled the horse to a stop in front of a rather large two-story house. "This."

Merrill looked at it. It was similar in style to Granny's, but much larger. "It looks very nice. Who lives there?"

Rurik just smiled, then said, "Uncle Carl says our place is too small. He asked me to find a bigger house. He wants to use the current house for office purposes and then eventually expand the workshop. He said it would probably do us both some good to have a place away from the work area."

"Well, I must say, this house is definitely bigger than your current one."

"Would you like to see inside?"

"Are you sure it would be all right?" Merrill wondered, looking around at the nearby homes.

Rurik climbed down from the buggy and reached up for her. "Come on. It's just fine. I know the owner."

He led her up the walkway. "The house has just been painted. What do you think?"

Merrill considered the white structure. "It's lovely. The porch is especially inviting."

"I thought so, too. I think Carl and I could be very happy here."

She could tell by the tone of his voice he was playing a little game. Merrill decided he deserved to have her play right back. "Yes, I think Carl would be happy here. The steps might be difficult for him, but once he's up here on this porch, I doubt he'll ever want to leave. I suppose I won't see as much of him if you two are living all the way up here."

Rurik didn't seem to pay any attention to her comment. "There are five large bedrooms. One is downstairs for Uncle Carl." He opened a beautiful glass-and-wood door. "Come inside."

Merrill stepped into the house and looked around in awe. The woodwork and papered walls spoke of an elegance and refinement she'd never known. This was not a house to have men tracking mud into all day.

Rurik led her around the first floor, pointing out the various rooms. When they arrived at the large kitchen, Merrill couldn't help but exclaim, "This is wonderful! Just look at all the space. Why, you could practically cook for an army in here." She caressed the door of a cabinet as though it were silk. "So beautiful."

"It doesn't yet have electricity, but I'm told it won't be long until that's available."

Merrill turned to Rurik, her eyes wide with delight. "I think it's perfect." Then she added with a little grin, "Yes, just right for you and Uncle Carl."

He grinned back. "I'm so glad you think so. Uncle Carl hasn't seen it yet, but I told him all about it, and he seemed pleased. Would you like to see the upstairs?"

"Yes, please."

They made their way through the house and up the beautiful mahogany stairway. Merrill wondered at the care that had gone into the place. She didn't know who had built it, but whoever it was had definitely shown great attention to each detail and its upkeep.

"This is the largest of the four rooms up here. The other three are about equal in size."

Merrill stepped into the room and smiled at all the light. The windows were large and the draperies were pulled back to give a full view of the landscape. "You can see Loon Lake," she said, stepping closer to the window. "Why, it's lovely."

Rurik came to stand behind her. He put his hands on her shoulders. "So do you think that maybe one day you wouldn't mind living here?"

She turned and saw the love in his eyes. "I think a woman would be quite blessed to have this as her home. Why, that kitchen alone would entice anyone to fall in love with this house."

He grinned again. "I was hoping you might feel that way. Especially since I signed the papers yesterday to purchase it."

"No wonder you know the owner." She couldn't help but laugh. "I must say, you do move quickly, Mr. Jorgenson."

He pulled her into his arms. "I've only just gotten started."

Chapter 27

"Surprise!" More than a dozen people shouted their greeting when Rurik led Merrill into the large finishing room at Jorgenson Furniture.

Merrill gasped. "A party? But what—?"

"Happy birthday," Flynn declared. Her other brothers followed suit, and her father came forward to embrace her.

"Merrill Jean, happy twenty-first birthday." He kissed her cheek and smiled. "You surely do look like your mama. She'd be mighty proud of the way you've turned out."

"Thank you, Father," she said, near to tears. "I hope you're proud, too."

"That I am, daughter. A man couldn't be more so."

Granny and Grandpa Lassiter came up. "You're as pretty as a picture, Merrill Jean," Grandpa told her. "Happy birthday."

"We brought you some presents," Granny began, "but you can't have them just yet. You'll have to be patient."

Merrill thought Granny sounded rather secretive but didn't question her. "That's quite all right. It's enough that you're both here. And, Corabeth," she said, looking beyond them to her best friend, "you never so much as hinted at there being a party."

"I know how to keep secrets," her friend said. Zadoc came to stand beside her, and Corabeth cast a shy glance over her shoulder at the tall man. "But I thought for sure your brother might give it away."

"It wasn't easy," Zadoc admitted. "The only thing that saved the day was that Merrill was staying in town with you."

"And it's been wonderful having her. Just like having a sister of my own," Corabeth declared.

"Happy birthday, Miss Krause," Arne, from the furniture shop, said. He handed Merrill a small jar. "My mother sent you some preserves."

"Why, how kind. Please thank her." Merrill looked to Arne and then to his brother Lars. "I'm sure I'll enjoy these."

The other workmen for Jorgenson Furniture were also in attendance. Most had brought their families, and Merrill was delighted to meet them all. In a rush of faces and names, Merrill received their blessings and gifts. Their kindness touched her in a way that moved her to unexpected tears.

"Are you all right?" her brother Tobe asked.

Merrill dabbed at her eyes. "Yes. I'm just happy."

Rurik and Uncle Carl joined them. "It's time for more surprises," Rurik simply said, looking to Merrill's father.

Her father nodded. "Yes, I suppose we should get on with it."

"What in the world are you two talking about?" Rurik grinned, making Merrill all the more suspicious. "You are clearly up to something."

Rurik motioned for her to turn around. "Now close your

eyes." He put his hands over her eyes to ensure she did as he directed. "Now walk forward."

"I'll stumble," she protested.

"And I will catch you."

Merrill shook her head slightly, but stepped out in faith. "How far?"

"Just a few more steps. Okay, boys, you can take down the covering."

Merrill felt Rurik tighten his hold over her eyes and lean closer. His warm breath on her ear gave Merrill a delightful shiver. "Are you ready?"

"I hope so," she said, barely able to speak.

"All right, then, this is from your father and brothers." He pulled his hands away.

Merrill opened her eyes and stared in wonder at the piece of furniture before her. Her father stepped closer. "It's a schrank. I promised your mother I'd have one made for you. I meant to have it done for your eighteenth birthday, but . . . well . . . time got away from me."

"It's absolutely beautiful." Merrill stepped closer to touch the polished wood.

Her father added, "Rurik is the one who built it for you."

"But your father planned it all out. I just followed his directions."

"When did you ever have time to make this?" she asked in wonder. "I would have noticed you working on it."

He laughed. "I did it at night in my spare time. It was a pleasure knowing it would one day be yours."

"Now open it up," Granny declared. "You'll find some presents from Corabeth and me."

Merrill went to the double doors. The grand piece was taller than she was by several inches. Inside were drawers and compartments, hanging rods and shelves. On one of the shelves she found a folded quilt.

"Oh, Granny, it's beautiful!" She reached up to take the piece down. The delicate quilting stitches suggested the hours of work that had gone into it. "I'll cherish it forever."

"There's more," Corabeth said, pointing to the drawers.

"This is more than enough," Merrill said as she replaced the quilt on the shelf. She began opening the first of three large drawers. Inside there were stacks of embroidered dish towels. The next drawer revealed pillowcases and towels, and the third drawer held a variety of doilies, tatted handkerchiefs, and a table runner.

"You've done too much!" she exclaimed.

"Nonsense," Granny said, moving to stand beside her. "A girl doesn't come of age every day. Besides, I know you haven't done a lot to save up for having a home of your own. Been too busy keeping your father's house. So Corabeth and I have been working on pieces for you for some time now. We'd make up one for Corabeth and one for you."

Merrill choked back a sob and hugged the old woman. "Thank you, Granny. Thank you so much."

"I think she likes it." Zadoc chuckled.

Merrill looked up to find him beside Corabeth. "I love it. It's the best birthday I've ever had."

"Well, there's more," Rurik said, taking hold of her arm.

"You see that finished dining room table and chairs?" He led Merrill to a beautiful set crafted from maple wood. "This is Uncle Carl's gift to you."

Merrill shook her head. "I don't know what to say. I . . . I . . . never expected any of this."

She ran her hand along the top of the table, imagining the gatherings she could have. There were eight perfectly crafted chairs, each with a lovely upholstered seat.

"We all had a hand in making them," Rurik told her. "The boys wanted to be a part of it as soon as Uncle Carl explained what he wanted."

Merrill turned and looked at the gathering of people. "You are all too wonderful. I'm so blessed."

She wiped away her tears, certain that the evening couldn't possibly get any better. But when she looked back at Rurik, she found him on one knee beside her. In his hand he held out a ring.

"Merrill Jean Krause, would you do me the great honor and pleasure of marrying me?"

Her breath caught and words failed. Merrill had known in her heart that this day would come, but she'd not expected it like this. Rurik stood and put his arms around her. "I know we haven't courted for long, but I feel as though I've known you forever. You're the woman I've been waiting for all of my life. Please say you'll marry me."

She lost herself for a moment in his gaze. This was everything she'd ever dreamed of. "Yes," she whispered. "I will." A cheer went up as Rurik slipped the ring on her finger, then lowered his head to kiss her. Before his lips touched hers, however, a voice called out.

"You'd better be careful."

Merrill and Rurik parted to see Nils standing not far away, balanced on crutches and wearing a big smile. "The only time I tried that, Miss Krause punched me in the mouth. Hit me harder than most men."

Rurik looked at Merrill, then back at Nils. "I think I'll . . . take my chances." He gave her a tender kiss and looked back at Nils. "See, it's all about one's skill."

Everyone roared in laughter at this, and Merrill couldn't help but laugh herself. Nils gave a slight bow. "I stand corrected." Since he'd recovered enough to be on his feet, Nils had proven himself to be a changed man.

"So when's this wedding going to take place?" Granny asked. "We've got a dress to make."

Rurik looked to Merrill, his brow raised in question. Merrill had already determined the date. She wanted to be married on the same day and month that her parents had chosen years earlier. "May, like any proper German bride."

Rurik nodded, adding, "Or a proper Swedish bride."

Merrill's brow rose in acknowledgment of this fact. "How very appropriate."

"And the date?" Rurik asked.

"I'd like the thirty-first like my parents . . . if you approve."

"You heard the lady. It's May thirty-first. You're all invited."

⸎

"Thanks for inviting me to the party," Nils told Rurik. "I wouldn't have blamed you if you hadn't."

"The past is behind us," Rurik replied.

Nils looked to Uncle Carl. "I know this isn't the right time or place, but I want you to know that I intend to get a job and pay back everything I . . . I stole from you."

"You have a job, young man, and I expect you to be here bright and early on Monday morning to do it," Carl said. "We'll work out a payment plan for you to pay back what you owe, but we're also going to discuss our newest contract and expansion."

"Expansion?" Nils looked at Rurik, who only smiled.

"We just got word today that Sears & Roebuck wants to carry some of our furniture in their mail-order catalogue," Carl said. "I told the boys this morning. It's going to mean doubling the size of this building. We're going to set the office up in the house here and build right across the yard. There will be a small covered walkway to join it to the house."

"That's incredible news." Nils shook his head. "And you . . . you're willing . . . you'll give me another chance?"

Carl reached out and touched Nils's arm. "Everyone deserves a second chance, son. Rurik told me about how you're trying to overcome your desire to gamble. I figure you're going to need our help to fight off those demons. You need to understand that your work will be watched closely. Rurik will be double-checking it for me."

"I do understand. I'm . . . grateful for the chance to prove myself. You won't be sorry." He looked to Rurik and added, "I promise."

Bogart Krause joined them and motioned toward Rurik's friend. "Did you tell him the news?"

"We did," Rurik replied. "I think he's just about as dumb-founded as we were."

"More so at knowing you would give me another chance," Nils said. "The contract with Sears & Roebuck doesn't surprise me at all. The furniture you make is incredible. I've always thought so."

Krause nodded, then put his hand on Carl's back. "Carl, I promised Rurik I wouldn't let you hang around here for too long. How about you let me drive you home in your new carriage and we have a game or two of checkers? The boys can bring Rurik back and pick me up when this party is over."

"The new carriage belongs to Rurik, but if he doesn't mind, I think I'd like that," Carl said. "Just be sure to have Merrill pack us some of that birthday cake to take with us. I heard Granny say she made her special red velvet cake for this occasion, and I'm quite a fan."

Bogart laughed. "I'll get Merrill to take care of that right now. Rurik, if you'll help your uncle, I'll get the cake and be right out."

"Thank you, Mr. Krause." Rurik glanced at Uncle Carl, who appeared quite tired. He wondered if it had been a mistake to let his uncle attend, but Carl had insisted. "Are you ready, then?"

Carl motioned to the door. "My hat is over there."

❧

Sometime later the party finally wound down, and Rurik and Merrill bid good evening to the guests as they departed for their homes.

"We had such a good time," one of the women told Merrill. "I can hardly wait for the wedding."

"Me either," Rurik quipped.

Merrill elbowed him in the ribs while the woman laughed.

"Well, we're going to get this mess cleaned up and head home," Granny Lassiter told them. She looked at Merrill and shook her head. "That hair of yours, Merrill Jean. I tell you, I've never seen the likes."

Merrill put her hand up to tuck in the flyaway curls. Rurik stilled her attempts, however. "I like it that way, Granny. It looks all wild and free—kind of like Merrill herself."

The older woman nodded. "That it does. I guess Merrill will always be that kind of a woman. I tried to tame her for a while, but I can see she's better off this way. Not everyone can carry her kind of strength with such beauty and grace. I guess I'm just starting to realize that. Merrill Jean, I'm sorry I ever tried to change you."

"That's all right, Granny. I know you were just trying to help. Besides," Merrill added, "it got me this lovely gown. I've had quite a few compliments on this blue-and-green plaid."

"It suits your complexion, Merrill, but you would be just as lovely in your brother's cast-off trousers."

The woman's words touched Merrill deeply. Granny had been the only mother she'd had the last ten years, and Merrill was a better woman for her love. "I've always understood your desires to help," she said, giving Granny a kiss on the cheek.

"Well, no more of that kind of help."

Merrill frowned. "Does this mean you won't help make me a lacy wedding dress?"

Granny laughed. "We'll make whatever kind of dress you desire. If you want to wear trousers under it, I'll make you a pair in white satin."

"I just might take you up on it," Merrill laughed. "Especially if the weather is chilly or the biting flies are bad."

They all three chuckled, and Rurik looped his arm through Merrill's. "Why don't I walk you home, Miss Krause."

"Not yet—I need to help clean up."

"Nonsense," Granny told her with a pointed finger. "This is a party in your honor. You go on now. Let that young man of yours walk you home and have a few moments to steal a kiss in the dark." She shuffled away, calling for Corabeth.

Merrill looked at the gifts she'd been given. "But what about these gifts? My schrank and the table and chairs?"

Rurik shrugged. "How about I deliver them up to our house tomorrow? You can visit them there and save us a trip hauling them out to the farm and then back into town after we wed. After all, we'll be married in a little over a month."

"I think that's a wonderful idea." She looked at the schrank. "You know, my mother told me about having one of these. Does this one break apart into smaller sections?"

"It does. I followed your father's carefully drawn instructions. I think, in fact, we might want to design something similar for sale. Maybe not quite so intricate or large."

"I could see that being a popular piece. Especially if you offered it in a variety of sizes and pieces. People could almost design their own that way. Oh, and I had another thought: Lars was talking about burning designs on wood. He can make patterns in wood by carefully burning them in. Don't you think that might be something I could learn to do along with the painting?"

"Merrill Jean, that's a great idea. But no more talk of work tonight. The moon is up and the stars are out, and I think Granny had a wonderful idea."

"A wonderful idea?"

"About stealing kisses in the dark. Now, come along and let me escort you back to the Lassiters. Your brothers are already hard at work helping Granny clean up."

"Since when do they clean anything?" she said in disbelief.

Rurik leaned close to whisper. "Since Granny told them to."

Rurik put his arm around her waist and guided Merrill outside. The night air was heavy with the scent of rain. "Looks like the clouds moved in while we were enjoying ourselves," he said as they walked down the street. "It'll no doubt be raining by morning."

Merrill sighed and leaned closer to his tall, muscular frame. "Nothing could have made this evening less than perfect. I've never had such a grand party in my honor."

"Well, if I have anything to say about it," Rurik replied, kissing her temple, "it will only be the first of many."

Chapter 28

With the new contract signed and supplies ordered for the expansion, Rurik had never seen his uncle happier. It was the culmination of a lifetime's hard, diligent work, and perhaps that was why the older man quietly slipped through heaven's gates two weeks after Merrill's party. Rurik found him in bed with a peaceful look on his face, and he immediately realized his uncle was gone. Merrill came to prepare breakfast shortly after the discovery, and together they had shared tears over the loss.

Carl was buried on the fourth of May with most of Waseca in attendance to remember the man who had been a friend to all. Rurik found the loss created a huge void in his life. It was no longer proper for Merrill to visit the house, although she and Granny stopped by from time to time with items of food. They were also good to invite him for supper each evening.

Evenings were when Rurik missed his uncle the most. They'd often reminisced about the past, sharing stories and recalling childhood events. Rurik valued the old family lore and committed them to memory, determined to one day share them with his children. *Our children*, he thought to himself.

The wedding plans kept him occupied, even though he had very little to actually do. Merrill, in true German fashion, had decided it would make good sense financially to share her wedding day with her brother Leo and his bride-to-be. Although Sally Myers had been married once before, she'd never had a real wedding. Her first union had come about from an elopement, and Merrill wanted this occasion to be special.

Merrill told Rurik that sharing the day with Sally would afford her the wedding she'd never had. Rurik thought her more generous than any woman he'd ever known.

He had asked Merrill if she wanted to take a wedding trip to Minneapolis, like her brother was planning as a surprise for Sally. Merrill had turned down the idea, however, telling Rurik in her practical way that they had much too much work to attend to and couldn't be off gallivanting all over the state. "I'll be wanting to settle things into our new home, Rurik," she told him.

A week after Uncle Carl was buried, the framework for the expansion went up. Rurik had been surprised when his soon-to-be father-in-law showed up with his sons to help in the building. But that was nothing compared to the shock of seeing half the townsfolk arrive with food and drink and additional workers. It was like a barn-raising, and by evening Rurik was delighted to find the walls and roof completed. There was still much to do on the inside, but plenty of time to manage it.

"We thought," the police chief told him as the day concluded, "that we owed you this much. You're an important part of our community now, son."

Rurik had been touched by his comment, along with similar statements from the townsfolk. Merrill had been more than pleased at the communal gift of help, and she assured Rurik that this was affirmation of his acceptance.

"You're truly a part of Waseca now," she said, giving him a kiss on the cheek. "And not just because you're marrying a Krause."

With her wedding day finally here, Merrill couldn't help but feel a sense of nervous excitement. She tried to survey her gown with the small mirror Corabeth had brought, but it was difficult to get the full view.

"Does the back lay properly?" she asked Granny.

"It's perfect." Granny inspected the bodice once more and adjusted the lace that decorated the high neckline. "Just perfect." She went to a small table and took up Merrill's wedding slippers. "Now for your shoes."

Merrill raised the skirt of her gown and stood ready to receive the dainty white slippers. First, however, Granny sprinkled dill and salt into each shoe, then placed a gold coin in one. "Your groom tells me this is a Swedish tradition that assures you will never do without. Gold in one shoe—usually given by the mother." She then produced a silver coin. "And usually the father gives silver. I promised Rurik I would see to the tradition, so I hope you don't mind that I have taken that job."

"Not at all, Granny. I'm blessed to have you here." Merrill slipped into the shoes and felt the cold metal of the coins.

"Are you ready, Merrill Jean?" her father asked, entering the small room. "There's a church full of folks waiting on you."

Merrill nodded. "I'm ready. Granny just put the dill and salt in my shoe for luck." She smiled at the old woman. "And Swedish coins for prosperity."

Granny stepped forward and kissed Merrill's cheek. "Now that you're all proper, I'll go take my seat. You make a mighty pretty bride, Merrill Jean."

"Thanks to you and Corabeth." She touched the ring of flowers and ribbons in her carefully pinned curls. "I think my hair might actually stay in place."

Granny nodded. "It will," she said, then left Merrill and her father to themselves.

Merrill looked up at her father and couldn't help but notice the tears in his eyes. Reaching up with her bridal handkerchief, she touched the drop of moisture, then drew the cloth to her lips.

He looked at her in surprise. "Your mother did that once."

"I know," Merrill said, her own smile a little wobbly. "She said she'd only ever seen you cry once, and that was when Berwyn died. She said she reached up and touched the tear to her handkerchief and then to her lips. She said it was her way of taking a part of your heart into hers."

"She had my whole heart." His voice was husky. "Just as I know Rurik has yours." He took her arm. "Come. It's time."

They walked together to the front of the church where Rurik, Nils, and Corabeth waited with the preacher. On the right side of the church, Rurik's brother Aron sat beside his family. She wished his other brothers and sisters could have attended, but it was far too expensive. Then, too, they were farmers—and June in Kansas was a very busy time.

Glancing to her left, Merrill found her family and friends. Their smiling faces reassured her of her actions. Not that she needed much encouragement. Marrying Rurik was absolutely the best choice she'd ever made and no one would ever convince her otherwise.

The ceremony itself was rather short, and once she and Rurik had said their vows and exchanged rings, they took a seat to allow Leo and Sally to have their moment. Afterward, the two couples joined together with the congregation to celebrate the nuptials.

To Merrill's surprise, her father first led the two couples outside to the back of the church, where two sawhorses stood holding large logs.

"The *Baumstamm Sägen*," she whispered to Rurik. He looked at her oddly, and she explained. "We have to saw the log together to show our ability to work as one."

"Really?" He looked at her in surprise but without hesitation grabbed the saw her father handed him. Gripping one handle, he extended the other to Merrill. Together they stepped forward and began the task. Leo and Sally did likewise. The wedding goers called out words of encouragement, and it only took a moment to turn the sawing into a race. With barely a second to spare, Rurik and Merrill gave a final push and pull and severed the log in two. Leo and Sally finished right on their heels. Cheers went up from the crowd for both couples and laughter filled the air.

Well-wishes and blessings were given to both couples, and

the church was soon filled with a party spirit. It was everything Merrill had dreamed her wedding might be. Simple, personal, and filled with loving family and friends.

Leo and Sally quickly departed for the train to Minneapolis. Merrill had hoped they might share in the reception, but Sally had wanted it this way. Leo assured his sister that he was just as satisfied to miss the revelry. She embraced Sally and kissed her on the cheek.

"I'm so glad to have a sister, and I'm blessed that you shared this day with Rurik and me."

Sally returned the kiss. "It was so kind of you to include me. Your family is truly wonderful, Merrill."

"We're your family now, you know."

Nodding, Sally smiled. "I promise we shall always be close."

Merrill noted Leo's firm hold on his wife and nodded. "It looks like your husband is ready to depart."

"If we don't hurry," he said, "we won't get to the train in time."

Rurik leaned close to Leo. "You'd probably do well to slip out the side door. I overheard your brothers talking of some mischief."

Leo's eyes narrowed. "They wouldn't dare." He glanced over his shoulder, then looked back to Merrill and Rurik. "But just to be safe, I think I'll heed your warning."

With Leo and Sally safely on their way, Merrill and Rurik enjoyed dinner, wedding cake, and games. Merrill's father offered a cider toast and blessing to the couple. A few other German traditions were kept, ending with the *reis werfen*, throwing the rice. As they prepared to walk to their carriage across fir boughs that signified hope, luck, and fertility, Granny couldn't help but tease Merrill.

"You do know that tradition says that however many pieces of rice stay in your hair is how many children you'll have. With that curly mass of yours, you'll probably wind up with more grains than you can count."

Rurik guffawed, causing several heads to turn and Merrill to duck her face in embarrassment. "Ready?" he asked.

"Yes."

The rain of rice came upon them, and Merrill shook her head a bit to avoid too many pieces finding a home in her hair.

"Oh dear," Merrill said, trying to brush the rice from her curls with little success.

Rurik laughed heartily. "Guess we'll need a bigger house," he whispered in her ear.

Without warning, Merrill was pulled from his grasp and swept away in arms and hands that turned her in circles until Merrill's head began to spin. She heard Rurik's roar of protest and turned just in time to see her brother Tobe throw a gunnysack over her groom's head. Flynn and Zadoc wrestled him into the back of the wagon, then climbed in while Tobe jumped into the driver's seat. In a flash they were headed down the road in a flurry of dust and rice.

"Father!" Merrill pushed away from her captors and rushed to his side, holding her wedding skirts up with her hands. "You told me they would behave themselves."

He laughed. "They are behaving. I told them they could take him out for only an hour, but after that they had to deliver him to the house." He gently brushed some rice from her hair. "You mustn't be angry with them, Merrill Jean. They've waited your whole life to do this."

She shook her head in mock disgust, but a grin curved her lips. "Wait until they see what I arrange for their weddings."

Her father put his arm around her. "I'm sure you'll make it all up to them."

Rurik was sore and dust-covered by the time his brothers-in-law brought him to the house. He should have known to expect such horseplay from them. When they dumped him unceremoniously on the front lawn, it was dark, but the house was lit brightly. Apparently Merrill had found her way home without him.

Making his way up to the porch, Rurik attempted to stretch his neck and shoulders. It seemed like he'd spent an eternity bound up in the back of that wagon. Flynn had assured him this was just a little family tradition, and Rurik had promised—well, threatened—to carry it out when he married.

He opened the door to the house and listened for the sound of his bride. "Merrill?"

She appeared at the top of the steps still clad in her wedding finery. He smiled and forgot about his soreness. He barely remembered to close the door behind him before taking the stairs two at a time to reach her.

"I wondered if I'd ever see you again," he said, pulling her into his arms.

Merrill melted against him and wrapped her arms around his neck. "Father promised me that the boys wouldn't keep you long. In turn, I promised Father that I would have my revenge when they married."

"Funny, I've promised your brothers the same thing."

She laughed and kissed him. "Then we're in one accord, just as we're supposed to be."

Rurik lifted her into his arms. "It isn't at all difficult to be in one accord with the woman who has clearly stolen your heart."

Merrill shook her head. "I didn't steal it, Rurik. You gave it to me. I'm just safekeeping it for you."

He nuzzled kisses against her neck. "The icecutter's daughter holds my heart."

"And the furniture maker holds mine." She touched her cheek to his. "And he always will."

An excerpt from the next book in the
LAND *of* SHINING WATERS series

THE
Quarryman's
BRIDE

Available Summer 2013

Chapter 1

Seventeen-year-old Emmalyne Knox tried to suck in air but found it impossible to breathe. Her throat constricted, and air couldn't seem to get past her mouth and into her lungs. Blackness edged her vision.

She reached out and gripped Tavin MacLachlan's hand, not caring if anyone thought it inappropriate. They were, after all, engaged to be married in less than two months. His presence strengthened her, and at last she found she could draw in a shuddering breath.

"Let us pray," Reverend Campbell announced in sober tones. "Father, we commit these bodies to the ground and these spirits to you. May your comfort be upon those who have suffered these losses. Amen."

"Amen," Emmalyne whispered along with the rest. She looked up to meet Tavin's sorrowful expression.

"Are you all right?" he asked softly.

"As well as I can be." She looked to her left where her mother, clad in black, stood pale-faced and rigid. Rowena

Knox's eyes were dry at the moment but swollen from long hours of weeping. Emmalyne's young brother, Alpin, stood on the other side of their mother. Barely twelve years old, he favored his mother in appearance with his dark brown hair and smoky blue eyes. The woman's Scottish and Welsh ancestry made her a handsome, albeit petite woman, while Alpin already stood inches taller than Emmalyne. He would no doubt surpass even his father.

Luthias Knox might have been short of stature, but there was no doubt that he was a man of strength. Even now, Emmalyne's father showed no emotion. His ancestry, beginning with his origins in the Highlands of Scotland, was proven in his red hair and fierce blue eyes. His brogue and hesitancy to spare a coin for anything even remotely frivolous left no doubt.

"I'm so sorry for your loss," Emmalyne heard Tavin's mother say softly, coming up to them with her hand outstretched. Emmalyn nodded, seeing Tavin's younger brother, Gillam, and sister, Fenella, standing just behind their mother. Fenella and Emmalyne were the best of friends.

Emmalyne looked into the warm gaze of the woman she would soon call mother-in-law and nodded. "I can scarcely believe they're gone." She let her glance return to the two open graves where her younger sisters, Doreen and Lorna, had just been laid to rest.

"The tornado took so many lives," Morna MacLachlan said, nodding her sympathy.

It hadn't yet been a week since a massive storm ripped through St. Cloud and Sauk Rapids. The devastation had taken lives in both cities, but Sauk Rapids had borne far more of its destruction. Emmalyne's family was just one of hundreds who had suffered the tornado's wrath. The house they had lived in was now merely a pile of wood.

"God's wrath," her father had said with an angry fist raised to the heavens. The memory made Emmalyne shudder even now.

"Dory was just fourteen," Emmalyne murmured, forcing her thoughts away from her father's near blasphemous anger. "Lorna only ten. How can they be . . . gone forever?" Her eyes welled with new tears.

Morna embraced Emmalyne. "'Tis a hard truth to bear. I dinnae see your older sisters. Were they unable to come?"

Emmalyne nodded returning the embrace. "They live too far away and couldn't afford the trip. They have their own families to worry about now, so Mother didn't really expect they would come."

"Still, they would have offered her comfort," Mornar replied.

Fenella stepped closer to join in the hug. "Oh, Emmy, I'm so very sorry. You know I loved them so." She, too, began to cry.

"I know you loved them," Emmalyne whispered. "They loved you, too." She relaxed in the warmth of the three-way embrace, relishing their comfort and support.

"At least I needn't bear this pain alone," Emmalyne said, finally pulling back. "You have been so good to my family. Mother said she would never have made it through those first few nights without your kind intercession and invitation into your home."

"Letting you stay with us was the least we could do," Morna replied. "You're soon to be family in every way, and there was no need to delay welcoming you into our numbers."

"And I have always wanted a sister," Fenella assured her. "Soon that very wish shall come true." She smiled, but the sorrow of the occasion kept it from lasting very long.

"Yes, but I know that our presence in your home hasn't been easy. My father . . ." Emmalyne let the words trail off as she cast a quick glance to see if he'd overheard. But he was busy scowling at something the pastor was telling him.

"He can be most difficult." Emmalyne let out a long breath as if the truth had been pent up inside her for quite a while.

"He's grieving the loss of his children, Emmalyne. You'll need to be patient with him. Come, Fenella. We must offer our condolences to Mr. and Mrs. Knox."

Morna's excuse for Emmalyne's father was gracious, but Emmalyne knew there was no good reason for her father's unyielding temper and harsh words. She'd never witnessed or received gentleness or kindness from her father, and she seriously doubted he was capable of either. Emmalyne had grown up to fear and venerate him, to never question his decisions or commands. Perhaps that was why she always cherished Tavin's tenderness towards her.

Emmalyne felt a gentle squeeze on her shoulder and turned to find Tavin there, his green eyes showing concern. She felt a rush of comfort from the love she found there. "I'd best speak my condolences, as well," he told her. "I wouldn't want your father to think me rude."

"Father won't think of anything," Emmalyne muttered,

"except how much this is costing him." She was glad Morna had already moved away to speak with her mother.

"Try not to fret, love," Tavis said close to her ear. "'Tis but a few short weeks, and you'll no longer have to worry about what he thinks." He drew her along with him and walked over to her father and mother.

Extending his hand, Tavin met Mr. Knox's hard-fixed stare. "May the peace of God be upon you. I'm heartily sorry for your loss, sir."

Father refused to take Tavin's hand, and Emmalyne's heart sunk at the sight. Her father could at least receive the sympathies of others without being uncivil. Tavin appeared unconcerned, however, and moved to give Emmalyne's mother a hug.

"Mother Knox, you have my deepest sympathy. I was very fond of Doreen and Lorna."

Mother nodded, her expression one of disbelief and shock. She had cried herself out in the previous days and now seemed at a loss as to what she should say or do. She looked down and shook her head. "I . . . I . . ." There were no words.

Tavin patted her arm, then turned to speak to his own mother. "I'm going to walk Emmalyne back to the house."

"Nay." Emmalyne's father suddenly interrupted the conversation. "Ye'll not be doin' that."

Shocked gazes fixed upon Luthias Knox. Emmalyne couldn't imagine what had gotten into him, but from the look on his face, she knew it didn't bode well for any of them.

"If you need us to stay, Father . . ." she began, but her words quickly trailed off.

By now the few attendees of the funeral were making their way back to their carriages, as the grave diggers began shoveling dirt atop the small caskets they'd recently lowered into the ground. Emmalyne hated the sound of the dirt hitting the wooden lids.

"Ye and Rabbie have been most good to us," Father finally said, looking with a grim nod to Robert MacLachlan, Tavin's father. "I'm sorry to say I canna stay and repay ye just now."

"There's nothing to repay," Robert MacLachlan declared. "You would've done the same for me and mine."

Father nodded once, and Emmalyne thought she saw just a hint of softening in his expression. He fixed her with a gaze just then that almost seemed regretful, something she'd never witnessed in her father's countenance before.

"We're movin' to Minneapolis," Father declared in his abrupt manner.

"But surely nae until after the wedding," Morna interjected. "'Tis but a few weeks away—"

"There will be no weddin'."

Emmalyne's heart began to pound, and her jaw dropped open. She held her breath and thought to do the unthinkable and contradict her father.

Tavin spoke up. "What are you saying, sir?"

"I'm sayin' the weddin' is off. Emmalyne has a responsibility to her own family. With her younger sisters dead and her older sisters married, it falls to her to remain and care for her mother and me."

An icy chill settled over Emmalyne. *The tradition!* She'd forgotten all about it. Having been the third oldest and far from the last daughter in the Knox family line, she had seldom given the tradition much thought. Now, however, she was the youngest daughter, and in the Knox family lineage that made her responsible to give up a life of her own to care for her aging parents. It had been done that way for generations.

"You gave your blessing. The wedding has been planned," Tavin protested.

Emmalyne looked at her father. His ire was up, and there was fire in his eyes. "Ye'd do well not to question me, boy. The wedding is nae gonna take place, and that's ma final word."

"But, Luthias—"

Father waved Robert off. "We have our way of doin' things, Rabbie. You know that as well as any man."

"For sure I do, but—"

"There's nothing more to discuss. I've just buried two of ma daughters, and we have a long trip ahead of us."

"Surely you can stay one more day," Morna argued.

"Please, Luthias. I don't feel at all well," Mother inserted, seeming to wilt before their eyes.

Emmalyne watched her father wrestle with the moment. He finally took hold of his wife's arm. "I suppose ye'll just be faintin' on the way if I try to see ma plans through. We'll stay one more night, but on the morrow we take our leave."

Emmalyne fought back a wave of nausea as everything she'd planned for crumbled to dust around her. The tornado had not only taken the lives of her sisters and destroyed their home; it had cost Emmalyne her future.

Sleep refused to come that night. Tavin's sister, Fenella, tossed just as restlessly as Emmalyne, and given the narrow bed, when one moved, they both did.

"I can't sleep," Fenella finally declared, turning over once more, this time onto her back. "I can't believe your father is doing this, Emmalyne. You must not allow it."

Emmalyne stared into the darkness. "What choice do I have, Fenella? I must respect his wishes. The Bible makes clear that I owe him honor and obedience."

"But you love Tavin."

"Aye. I do love him."

Fenella leaned up on one elbow. "And he loves you. You cannot go and leave him like this."

Emmalyne wished with all her heart that there might be another way. "I don't *want* to leave him. You know I don't."

"Then don't. Go to him. Elope tonight." Fenella got up from the bed. "I'll go get him right now. You two can leave before anyone wakes up."

"I know you mean well," Emmalyne whispered through trembling lips. "But, no. I cannot. It would be a dishonor, and my father and mother would never speak to me again."

Fenella was already pulling on her robe. "Just talk to Tavin about it. Maybe he'll have some idea of how to make it all work. Your mother and father won't reject you. You'll see." She hurried to the door, pulled it open, and gave a little shriek.

Emmalyne sat straight up in bed. "What's wrong?"

"It's Tavin," Fenella said, stepping back. "He must've had the same idea."

Tavin stepped into the room and stopped at the foot of the bed. "I won't lose you, Emmalyne. You're to be my wife."

"Tavin, you can't ask me to go against my father and mother," she said, clutching the blankets around her. "It wouldn't be right. I love you, but we must give them time. Perhaps Father will see the pain he's causing and change his mind. I plan to speak with him in the morning."

"Let's just leave tonight and be married," he begged. "Once it's done . . ."

"That's what I suggested," Fenella put in as she lit a candle.

The warm glow barely punctured the darkness of the small room, but it was still enough to see the desperation on Tavin's face. Emmalyne wished she could offer him some comfort, but she needed it herself. She knew her father's mind was set, and she had never known him to back down once he had determined his course of action.

"Once we're married, they won't be able to undo it," Tavin tried again. "We can show them that we still intend to see to their well-being. I want your parents to be assured that they would have care in their old age."

Emmalyne shook her head miserably. "Father says that marriage divides the heart and mind. He doesn't think a woman can be both answerable to her husband and to her parents. He believes the tradition—"

"Curse the tradition," Tavin spat out. "It's ridiculous to put such a demand on someone's offspring. Your parents are being totally unreasonable in their expectations."

"But they're still my parents, Tavin." Tears were filling her eyes, and she blinked them away. "We both believe in the one

God and that the Bible is His Holy Word. The Bible says that I am to honor my mother and father, that my days may be long. Don't ask me to defy the Word of God."

"I'm not asking you to defy God. I just don't want to you to throw away our happiness together. The Bible also talks about a man and woman leaving their parents and cleaving to one another."

"Tavin, don't you see? We could never be happy . . . not with my father's curse upon us, and that's what it would be. He would never forgive me."

Tavin's expression changed from one of loving desperation to an expression Emmalyne had never seen in him before. "And that's your final word? You choose to worry more about your father's forgiveness than my love?" His implied accusation made her stomach clench.

"I choose to honor God, Tavin, as best I know how," she finally said, "and do as He would have me do."

"Right. So that 'your days may be long.' Well, have it your way. Your days will be long . . . and no doubt very lonely." He stormed out without another word.

Emmalyne felt a single tear trickle down her cheek. *So that's the way it is to be*, she mourned, pulling her knees up and leaning her head on them while the new flood of grief escaped.

Her father's anger, God's judgment . . . or her beloved's wrath and deep disappointment.

Somewhere in the midst of it all were the shattered remains of her heart.

Tracie Peterson is the author of more than ninety novels, both historical and contemporary. Her avid research resonates in her stories, as seen in her bestselling HEIRS OF MONTANA and STRIKING A MATCH series. Tracie and her family make their home in Montana.

Visit Tracie's Web site at *www.traciepeterson.com*.

More Adventure and Romance From Tracie Peterson

For more on Tracie and her books, visit traciepeterson.com.

In the years following the Civil War, loyalties in the Lone Star state remain divided. Amidst the bitter prejudices and harsh landscape of the Texan plains, is there any hope that the first blush of love can survive?

LAND OF THE LONE STAR: *Chasing the Sun, Touching the Sky, Taming the Wind*

As the lives of three women are shaped by the untamed Alaskan frontier, they find it's a land of heartbreak and healing—and romance and adventure.

SONG OF ALASKA: *Dawn's Prelude, Morning's Refrain, Twilight's Serenade*

Romance and intrigue abound on beautiful Bridal Veil Island. Amidst times of change and disaster, three couples struggle to find hope. Will their love—and lives—survive the challenges they face?

BRIDAL VEIL ISLAND: *To Have and To Hold, To Love and Cherish, To Honor and Trust* by Tracie Peterson and Judith Miller
judithmccoymiller.com

More From Bestselling Author Tracie Peterson

When dark memories surface of their ill mother and their father's desperate choice, is the silence these sisters keep hurting them more than the truth?

House of Secrets

From her own Big Sky home, Tracie Peterson paints a one-of-a-kind portrait of 1860s Montana and the strong, spirited men and women who dared to call it home. The rich, rugged landscape of the prairie frontier presents a dangerous beauty that only the boldest can tame.

HEIRS OF MONTANA: *Land of My Heart, The Coming Storm, To Dream Anew, The Hope Within*

When Deborah Vandermark meets the new town doctor, conflicting desires awaken within her. Is it the man—or his profession—that has captured her heart?

STRIKING A MATCH: *Embers of Love, Hearts Aglow, Hope Rekindled*